OPERATION
SUPERGOOSE

ALSO BY WILLIAM HART
Never Fade Away

OPERATION SUPERGOOSE

A NOVEL

William Hart

William Hart (signature)

TIMBERLINE PRESS
FULTON, MISSOURI
2007

Copyright © 2007 by William Hart
All rights reserved
Printed in the United States of America

Published by Timberline Press
6281 Red Bud
Fulton, Missouri 65251
www.timberlinepress.com

ISBN 978-0-944048-38-2

Book design & type: Studio E Books, Santa Barbara, CA
www.studio-e-books.com
Set in New Caledonia

Cover design: Jayasri Majumdar

For the peacemakers—
may they inherit the earth

"The nation prompted by ill will and resentment sometimes impels to war the government contrary to the best calculations of policy. The government sometimes participates in the national propensity, and adopts through passion what reason would reject. At other times [the government] makes the animosity of the nation subservient to projects of hostility, instigated by pride, ambition, and other sinister and pernicious motives. The peace often, sometimes perhaps the liberty, of nations has been the victim."

—President George Washington
farewell address to his fellow citizens
September 19, 1796

o

"In the councils of government, we must guard against the acquisition of unwarranted influence, whether sought or unsought, by the military-industrial complex. The potential for the disastrous rise of misplaced power exists and will persist. We must never let the weight of this combination endanger our liberties or democratic processes."

—President Dwight D. Eisenhower
"Farewell Address to the American People"
January 17, 1961

o

"Oil is much too important a commodity to be left in the hands of Arabs."

—Henry Kissinger
former U.S. Secretary of State

o

"The three richest men in America own more personal assets than the combined assets owned by the entire populations of the sixty poorest countries."

—Michael Moore
in Stupid White Men

OPERATION
SUPERGOOSE

PROLOGUE

THE Pentagon office was dark. The only illumination came from a flat panel monitor. It lit the intent face of a man seated in a leather chair with his coat off. He was in his 60s, 70s maybe—hard to tell with someone so fit. The handsome, confident features were lean, the salt and pepper hair oiled and combed close to the head. A knock, loud in the silent room, made him jump. He stood, walked to the door and opened to a plump man with a silver comb-over. The man looked worried. "I'm not getting any picture from the military satellites. How about you?"

"I got picture and it ain't pretty." The owner of the working monitor ushered in his visitor and offered a chair. They sat, eyes glued to the immense blaze onscreen.

"Oh my," said the portly fellow. "Did you see that?"

"Wrong day to wear a skirt to work, baby!"

"Can we zoom in?"

"This magnification is best. When you zoom in, you can't hold them in frame."

The plump man began looking around. "Why so dark in here?"

"Think the bastards behind this wouldn't love to blow me up too?"

"My God, good point! Maybe we'd be safer somewhere else."

"The president needs us on the job."

"True."

Again they watched. The lean man growled. "Lord, I'd love to get my hands on that Moolah. I'd snap his scrawny neck."

"You should be grateful. He's just handed us our dreams on a silver platter."

"What the hell are you talking about?"

"You can't see?"

"Can I see he's kicked us in the nuts worse than the Japs back in 'forty-one? Yes, I can. Can I see he's kicked us like nobody ever kicked us before? Oh, you betcha!"

"Everybody sees—which is why Joe and Betty Boobtube are going to support anything we do right now. We can start wars with impunity."

"Wars?"

"As many as we want."

"It's time for the plan?"

"Behold," said the chubby man, gesturing to the monitor. "From the flames of destruction rises a fiery star to guide the destiny of the fatherland." Silence reigned as the import of this pronouncement hung in the astounded air.

His host began to grin. "Jesus, you're right. Here's our chance to build that pipeline through Ragistan and tap into the Caspian oilfields. To sell our invasion, all we gotta do is say we're going after Moolah."

"We'll pop the hell out of that raghead and his merry crew from the air while our ground forces topple the government. Then we install a democratic system and secure the pipeline rights. Should be wrapped up in a month."

His leaner colleague frowned. "But according to the plan, we take control of the Persian Gulf oil, too, which means war with Qroc. How do we justify that?" He pointed to the monitor. "Madmahn Badassi isn't connected to *this* bullshit."

"We use people's fears to spin a connection. We say, ummm...we say Badassi is giving Moolah al-Razir military support. No, no. We claim Madmahn Badassi is supplying Moolah with *weapons of mass destruction* to attack us with."

The lean man chuckled. "Beautiful. So we invade Qroc, topple Badassi, and grab his oil. At that point we're pretty much holding the world economy by the seed sack."

"Where's your vision?" piped the stout man, jumping up. He flung his arms wide. "Our brazen attacks, laced with shock and awe, will showcase the terror of our weapons for all to see. No nation, friend or foe, will dare question our march as we spread democracy throughout the Middle East and to all mankind—delivering peace and prosperity to the survivors."

His enthusiasm was contagious. "Women in all lands, no matter

OPERATION SUPERGOOSE 13

how backward or poor, will be equally free to serve their men! Workers everywhere will be equally free to obey their masters!"

"Capitalism, long under fire, will at last be safe from its attackers."

"Just imagine. Worldwide utopia at our fingertips." The fit man swaggered to a built-in refrigerator, opened, pulled out a magnum. "This was for a certain in-house hoot, but under the circumstances..." He took two champagne flutes from a cabinet and handed them to his colleague, then expertly launched the cork. Soon bubbly was dispensed and raised on high. "To the future!" offered the lean man.

"To this new millennium and the advent of unleashed Plunderian power!" shouted his companion. He lowered the flute to his mouth. Dramatic irony, however, intervened to nip his celebration in the bud. The flute bounced on the carpet as he grabbed his left bicep.

"You okay?"

"Feels like a sword through my arm." Fear seized the fleshy face. "Oh my God, Clayton. This is how my last coronary started." His knees buckled and he stumbled backward into a chair, holding his arm.

His colleague strode to the phone and punched a button. He barked into the receiver. "This is Secretary Minefield. Get Dr. Dingus and the paramedics up here *pronto*! The vice president is having a heart attack!"

1

THE most lethal weapon in the military arsenal of the world's most powerful nation opened his forthright blue eyes to the morning that would upend his life. First Lieutenant Ernest Candide, sensing the menace not at all, welcomed the malignant day with boyish cheer. What a lucky man am I!, he thought. Only five installments left on my car loan; the doctor says the cancer I self-diagnosed is merely a gumboil; and in a week I shall wed my dearly beloved—the beautiful and nearly chaste Baroness Solange Cunegoody.

In pinstriped boxers he passed through his living room, punched on the TV and continued into the kitchen where he pulled down a box of 12-bran cereal. Before he could dispense the healthful husks, a newscaster's baritone, trembling with horror, drew him back to his entertainment center. Onscreen a huge factory was burning, one he and every other Plunderian knew well. Screaming Eagle Flagworks was the old textile mill in Concord, New Hampshire that manufactured official Plunderland flags for the armed services, for police departments, and for millions of Plunderian patriots who demanded the real deal, as opposed to some shoddy foreign knockoff. Much to the lieutenant's agonized disbelief, the thirty-story brick and wood icon was fast being consumed.

Fireman on ladders shot streams into the inferno as helicopters dumped buckets. Factory workers plunged against the blaze. Only the tall flagpole rising from roof center and the massive rippling patriotic symbol that it bore stood above the conflagration. And as Candide watched, the flag's bottom corner, abandoned by the traitorous wind, dipped into the fire. Shouts were heard as flames scampered upward, consuming horizontal stripes of red and white, then a star-spangled blue eagle and the evil hamster clamped in its beak.

A chiseled face drained of color and credulity replaced the holocaust. Chaff Gentry, the nation's smoothest news jockey, was seated behind his anchor desk at Plunderland Broadcasting Corporation headquarters in New York. "Here's what we know. At eight seventeen A.M. Eastern Daylight Time, an unidentified person drove a three-bedroom blunderbus, apparently fully loaded with fuel, into the west wall of Screaming Eagle Flagworks. The explosion started a fire in the lint vats on the first floor. At eight thirty-eight, a second kamikaze blunderbus hurtled into the plant's east wall, igniting the carding room. Our local news crew was able to tape that vehicle as it struck."

A shaky video opened on a maroon three-bedroom Ferdmobile Guzzler jumping back and forth in frame as it raced by. For a moment the driver's head could be seen clearly—his joyous grin framed by a flowing black beard, a white turban covering his scalp. The blunderbus swerved across some lawn, almost tipping, then struck the plant wall, vanishing in a ball of fire.

Chaff Gentry returned. "As we saw, the driver seemed to be some sort of desert nomad. Witnesses report the first blunderbus was piloted by a person with similar characteristics. I think we have to ask ourselves: could this coordinated assault on a cherished Plunderian institution be linked to other terrorist acts our nation has suffered in recent years?"

Ernie Candide was wishing he could lay his hands on a few flag killers. He'd rip them to pieces, as he was fully capable of doing given his superhuman strength. In frustration he absentmindedly shredded the throw pillow he was holding, littering his vicinity with yellow foam stuffing. He saw the flaming factory shudder. The roof sank suddenly into billowing smoke and the walls buckled outward. Screams and shouts were swallowed by the rumble of debris. A cloud of dust rushed camera and the picture broke up.

The phone rang, informing Candide how starved he was for the voice of a fellow Plunderian, someone to commiserate with. To his annoyance, a recording puked in his ear. "HI, NEIGHBOR! READY TO TRADE IN THAT PESKY HOME EQUITY FOR A MORTGAGE LOAN AT ROCK-BOTTOM INTEREST? YOUR FREE BONUS TRIP TO VEGAS COULD MAKE YOU RICHER THAN YOUR WILDEST DREAMS!"

The lieutenant slammed down the receiver. "The nerve!" he shouted. "And at a time like this!" Then he realized the call was capitalism at work. If everyone took his attitude, what would happen to the nation's banks? The phone rang again and he picked up, resolved to be more fair minded.

"Are you watching?" asked a tremulous feminine voice. A strong Southern lilt almost masked the caller's native Nebraska twang, identifying with considerable certainty the Baroness Solange Cunegoody.

"Oh honey," the lieutenant desponded. "All those flags...Gone!"

"The world we knew is no more, Ernest. Blown away by evil."

"How could anyone hate our flags so much?"

"What did our flags ever do to them?" There was a pregnant silence. Then the baroness queried with a note of pleading. "Ernie—are you still coming for dinner?"

"Darn right. They want us to cower under our beds. I'll be early just to show them!"

"My brave soldier!"

"Bye and out."

The brave soldier was diligently chewing unprocessed fiber at his kitchen table when the phone rang yet again. This time it was the raspy voice of his task group leader, Colonel Phil "Kick Ass" Rutledge. "Lieutenant, you will report to base heliport at 0800 tomorrow. The commander in chief is personally calling on your special services. Plan to be gone at least a year."

Candide was electrified. Now, finally, after all the training and all the tests, he'd been chosen to serve his country in some special way—by the president! Quite likely his life would be placed in jeopardy. "Yes *sir!*" he enthused. "An honor, sir!"

"Try and pull some sleep, soldier. You've got one hell of a job ahead of you."

As Candide hung up he remembered something that popped his balloon. Golly, he chagrined, how is the baroness going to feel about me postponing our wedding for the sixth time? Break it to her gently, whispered his male intuition.

2

LIEUTENANT Candide, dashing in dress uniform, cruised Tennessee State Highway 96 in his one-bedroom blunderbus. Even on this direst of days his vehicle gave him a liberated feeling of command and momentum, being the logical culmination of the sport-utility vehicle. It was a three-ton SUV carriage raised high off the ground on fifty-inch wheels and containing all the accommodations of a luxury RV: kitchen, breakfast nook, bath and bedroom(s). You could almost live in one, and given the new economy many families did.

The lieutenant downed his window, allowing the fragrant air of an early fall afternoon to buffet his clean-shaven face. The leaves hadn't turned yet—unlike those he'd seen on TV in New Hampshire. Only the yellow Tennessee weeds signaled the coming season. Three miles out of Puckerville, just over the crest of a wooded knoll, the soldier turned off the highway onto an asphalt road leading to a three-story antebellum mansion. Behind the main house lay the former slave quarters, and beyond those a large bluegrass pasture studded with shorthorn steers.

Some might have judged the sprawling estate needlessly aristocratic, but Candide knew well why his betrothed had chosen the place. She was trying to recapture the milieu of her early childhood on the great and grand Cunegoody cattle ranch just outside Quotidian, Nebraska. Her father had been the wealthiest cattle baron in the region, her mother a beautiful and stately baroness. Candide's grasp of reverse psychology enabled him to understand how the premature deaths of Solange's parents—in a stampede of recently deballed steers—implanted in the seven-year-old instant baroness a strong attachment to vast acres grazed by horned quadrupeds. The orphan would no doubt always feel most secure in such a habitat. After her parents' passing, ranch servants had raised her, and that helped explain why, at age 24, she still employed a butler, one Webner Conklin, Jr.

It was Webner who answered the door and admitted Candide. He accepted the lieutenant's dress cap and led the way into the main parlor with considerable aplomb given his height of 42 inches. With a snap of the wrist, the servant frisbeed the cap onto a coatrack, then turned and eyed the generous gifts Candide bore in his arms: a bouquet of long-stemmed roses, a fancy box of low-carb chocolates, and a carafe of Depth Charge cologne, Solange's favorite. "Calling off the wedding again?" Webner inquired, grinning.

"Please announce me to the baroness," Candide replied frostily.

Webner formed a megaphone with his hands and shouted. "Yo' white boy's here!"

Moments later Solange swept into the room, stunning in a beige cowgirl outfit festooned with swinging fringe. Noticing the gifts, her blue eyes narrowed below the brim of her western hat. "What's that stuff for?"

Candide, a bit uncertain under her burning gaze, raised his three-part offering. "Tokens of my affection."

With a swipe of her lithe arm, the baroness knocked the gifts from Candide's grasp, spilling them across her lush Ragistani carpet. Chocolates rolled. Roses lost petals. The cologne, on its side and unstoppered, gurgled into the intricate rug. Webner dove, but by the time he righted the carafe more than half its contents had departed.

"*Ernest Lafitte Candide!*" seethed Solange through bared teeth. "Are you calling off our wedding *again*!?"

"Honeybun, please understand. After I talked to you, old Kick Ass called. I've got orders to fly out tomorrow. My country needs me."

The baroness looked like she'd been sledgehammered. She sank to the couch, lowered her pretty face into her hands and wept. "Oh, Ernie. I knew you'd have to go. I just didn't think it would be so soon."

Candide sat down beside her and insinuated an arm around her shoulders. "There, there," he said. "It's nothing to worry about."

"The Pentagon may think you can't be hurt, but I don't believe it for a second. Even Superman has his kryptonite. Someday, Ernie, you're going to find yours, I just know it."

Silence was now appropriate, the lieutenant realized. In fact, both knew their roles. He was a soldier brave and true, ready to perish for the motherland. She was a soldier's girl, prepared to wait and wait and wait. As the shoulder of Candide's uniform absorbed the tears and makeup of his dearly beloved, he noticed the butler, with a rag, pretending to lift scent from the carpet. Irked by the eavesdropper, the lieutenant dreamed up an errand. "I feel thirsty, Webner. Please bring us the usual."

Webner rose, folding the rag. "Coming right up. Two mint juleps, hold the julep." He marched out of the room, mouth twisted in contempt.

Solange sniffed. "I wrote a new song today. Would you like to hear it later?"

"Golly yes!" said the lieutenant with inflated enthusiasm.

They supped on bounty of the ranch: aged sirloin culled from Solange's herd and fresh steamed broccoli and carrots from her truck garden. Afterward, fully sated and as happy as lovers can be who soon must part—perhaps forever—they retired to the parlor and turned on the widescreen. The president of Plunderland was scheduled to reassure a nation shaken to its core. Every channel carried the same scene—an empty podium laden with mikes. Opinion makers chattered.

Webner was serving coffee au television when the recently appointed chief executive of Plunderland, Buzz Twofer II, strode with purpose to the podium. The president's demeanor and voice were grave as he began. "Today's darkest hour will stink up history forever. Cowardly servitors of an evil force attacked our brave and free nation. A treasured national treasure was knocked down in a fiery blow unlike any the earth has ever witnessed. More than 45,000 Plunderian flags were aborted in the womb—never to flutter joyfully above us—and many flagmakers died as well amid their sacred doings.

"My fellow citizens, I swear to you on a pile of Bibles taller than my sainted Grammy (may she rest in peace), *this rapscalient blow will not go unpunified!* Our intelligence operators, ever alert, have pinpointed the evildoers. The proof is overwhelmacious, but top secret. It cannot be revealed for reasons of national security. Therefore, I stand before you tonight able to say with absolute confidence that the cowards who murdered our flags are all members of the terrorist conspiracy known as ASP. The leader of ASP, Moolah al-Razir, is a desert crawler who wants to overthrow our free system and our family values. This viper chose to strike us when we were trusting and our pants were low. But never again! With smart bombs pounding, we will pursue him and his roving band to the ends of the earth. We'll smoke them out of their holes and bring them to justice dead or alive. I swear with every fiber in my mortal bean!"

Twofer smoothed his red tie. "Now I must speak frankly and honorably to our trusted allies overseas, and to all the other little nations of the earth. At two o'clock this afternoon, using the war-making powers invested in me by preemptive executive precedent, I declared our nation officially at war with evil everywhere. As we go forward robustly into the future, any country or group or person that threatens to attack us, or gives aid to terrorists, or opposes our legitimate defense of our values, our flags, or our commercial interests, will be declared an enemy, inviting our fury. For as a great man once said, you're either with us or you're against us, and if you're against us, may the Lord take pity on your carcass. Heh, heh, heh." Jubilant, the president thrust his open hands into the air. "GOD BLESS YOU!" he boomed, "AND GOD BLESS PLUNDERLAND!" Thunderous applause swept the combined houses of Congress.

"Gosh," said Candide, who had voted for Twofer entirely on a party basis. "I didn't know he had it in him. What a speech!"

"Times make the man," opined the baroness sagely.

"Man?" Webner sniffed, standing behind the couch with a coffee pot. "More like a suit full of hot air and whatnot."

Silence greeted this backward observation.

Later, after Webner had retired to his quarters, the lieutenant sat savoring his betrothed's new ditty, "Weep Not, My Loving Soldier Boy." She performed to karaoke support, incorporating stage gestures and eye-catching choreography. Much about the song the lieutenant found to his taste: Solange's striking chord progressions on her rhinestone guitar, the snappy heartfelt lyrics, and certainly her mournful voice, clear as a bell and extremely rhythmic. But as always when she sang, there seemed to be something missing, not much but something. Something the country superstars all seemed to exude.

If Candide could have fingered the missing ingredient, he certainly would have told his sugarplum, to boost her career. Instead he applauded vigorously and offered insincere praise. "Gee, hon, that was terrific. Hopped right inside my heart. I could just sit here for hours watching you sing." He glanced at his watch—and noted the hour was late.

"Are you trying to humor me?" Her eyes were drilling him.

"Heck no. Why would I?"

The proud baroness wilted. Even her guitar seemed to droop. "I've tried so hard to break in, Ernie. Talking this cornpone. Dressing up in these stupid clothes. I even moved here to Nashville to let my star shine bright. But nothing seems to work. Grand Ole Opry still doesn't want me."

"I thought you moved to Nashville to be close to me," said Candide, miffed.

"Of course I moved here to be close to you. But wasn't it lucky Nashville turned out to have a thriving C&W scene?"

Candide realized he was being selfish. His fiancée had a genuine problem. He wrinkled his forehead and applied his mental powers to her dead-in-the-water singing career. An idea bobbed up. "Maybe it's your title. Maybe these country and western folks are prejudiced against royalty."

"Prejudiced against royalty?"

"They seem to come from humble backgrounds. They almost seem proud of it. Maybe a baroness is a little too much for them."

Solange was incredulous. "But I have to be myself. If I stop being me, where will the music come from?"

"Can't you drop the title till you get famous? Once they're all eating out of your hand, tack it back on."

"If you can say that, you don't really love me. Going without my title would be like going without my clothes."

OPERATION SUPERGOOSE 23

The lieutenant's mind did a loop-de-loop on that intriguing concept. He felt an involuntary nudging deep in his brain as his eyes shifted, against his will, into X-ray mode. Under his penetrating vision the baroness' clothing began melting away.

"Are you undressing me, Ernie?" Solange asked in surprise.

The clean-minded soldier was mortified. "I...I..."

"Oh, Ernie, why not do it for real? This is our last night together. Let's make it one to remember."

The stirring in Candide's brain accelerated to an uncontrollable humping and his whole body swelled slightly. To the soldier's bugging eyeballs, Solange's slim yet delightfully rounded physique was now fully revealed. She shone like a vision of loveliness plucked from the center of a men's art magazine. Smiling mischievously, she swung her shoulders, making her assets quiver. Closer to making love with his bonbon than ever before, Candide moaned and threw a forearm over his eyes. "No, Solange, I can't. However much I want to, I can't bring myself to ruin your reputation until we're married."

She looked at him, exasperated. "I guess you want the usual."

He nodded timidly.

She sat down next to her man and unzipped him. From his regulation drawers, she extracted the critical element. With the fringe jumping on her vest and boredom stealing over her lovely features, the baroness pumped the good lieutenant steadily toward poor man's heaven.

3

THE army chopper bearing Lieutenant Candide flew east from the heliport at the Special Weapons Research Center near Murfreesboro. The lieutenant was asleep, his close-cropped blond head fallen forward. He was dreaming of the warm, magical hand of the Baroness Cunegoody when the chopper hit a downdraft that jolted him awake. For a moment he didn't know where he was. Three hundred feet below he saw wooded hill country. A pond flashed in the sun. As always when riding in a helicopter he was struck by the slow speed. Strange to poke along at 100 knots when he could fly under his own power at over 450.

His life was entering a new phase, probably a culmination, and he was very aware of that. It was natural to reflect back over the extraordinary chain of events that had marshaled him front and center at such an explosive cusp of world history. It had all started when he was five. Earlier than that he'd been a normal Nebraska male child, average in every way. Average height, average weight, average intelligence, average amount of affection for his parents, his dog and his chicken. In Nebraska, with so much Germanic DNA loose in the gene pool, even his honey-blond hair hugged the norm.

The first unaverage day of little Ernie's life was the Saturday he accompanied his mother on a visit to his father's workplace. Mr. Candide—mild-mannered and small in stature—was a supervisor at Quotidian's nuclear power plant. He was head honcho of unit cooling controls, which is to say, he more than others bore responsibility for preventing a meltdown. Emboldened by the awesome significance of his job, he dared hope the boy might follow in his footsteps.

On that fateful morning, Ernie climbed the rail around the reactor core, trying to get a better look at the swirling water below as his father performed a coolant flush. Mr. C had raised the core cover, naturally. How else could his son admire his best work? Mrs. Candide was watching mesmerized as her mate selected and depressed buttons on his console. Even after twelve years of marriage she found it fascinating that the bumbling milquetoast she knew at home became, on the job, a nimble-fingered maestro of the coolant keyboard. When she thought to check on her son, he'd managed to climb high on the rail and was leaning out over the core.

"Ernie, get *down* from there!" she screeched. Startled, the boy slipped the foot that was sustaining him and dropped 20 feet headlong into the coolant. He surfaced between radioactive rods and began paddling to stay afloat in water shot through with eerie green light. There was a rescue, an ambulance, and two days in the hospital for a thorough checkup. Other than a pale green skin rash that itched like the dickens, Ernie seemed to be okay, despite the fact he'd dog paddled for half an hour in the core of a nuclear reactor.

The lad probably would have remained normal but for a second accident, more serious, that happened when he was sixteen. A male rite of passage in Quotidian was induction into the Plunderland Rifle Association. At the club range, while practicing with his .22 in sitting position, Candide was struck in the head by a ricochet bullet from his own rifle and knocked comatose. The coma lasted two months, his hospitalization six. There was an operation to remove the bullet, but when the surgeons saw it with their eyes—wedged tightly against a major artery, a crucial nerve, and the pineal gland—they decided not to touch it. They feared any attempt to extract the lead might end Ernie's life. In time the young man made what appeared to be a full recovery, though he lost a year of school.

Recovery did not mean a return to normal, however. Two weeks after Ernie rejoined his classmates he was bullied by a much larger lad. Young Candide, never meek of heart, decided to get in a few licks whatever happened next. Soon he was flat on his back, arms pinned down by two fat knees, eating fists with his face. He heaved hard trying to throw off his opponent and felt something give in his brain. He heaved again and whatever it was began moving back and forth. Lo and behold, with the oscillating motion strength flowed into Ernie's torso and limbs. He could feel it surging. The teenager willed the mysterious oscillation to increase and it wasn't long till he sustained a rapid cerebral humping that pulsed raw might to his every muscle. With an elephantine grunt he threw off his tormentor and leapt to his feet. He grabbed the surprised bully by the belt and slung him across two lawns and into a rose bush. Bleeding, the cad tore free and skedaddled.

Ernest Candide's life was never again even remotely average. He practiced controlling the mysterious motion in his brain as he channeled the energy it generated into various athletic pursuits—running, jumping, slinging cow pies for distance. Long before the scientists came to agree with him, he correctly intuited what was happening when he powered up. He was humping that .22 slug into his pineal, causing the secretion of a strength hormone. His earlier irradiation in the reactor core was, he supposed, in some sense the catalyst, and in that too he was correct.

Soon the novice jock was challenging the most gifted lettermen at his school in pickup games. He went out for track and began to whip some of the top sprinters in Nebraska. By the state meet he could move his legs so fast they blurred—resulting in new national prep marks in the 100 meters and the 200. With the arrival of fall, Candide utilized this blazing speed on the gridiron, leading the nation in rushing from the first game of the season, scoring touchdowns at a clip never before imagined.

Hardly the ladies' man, young Ernest was surprised to note that a number of his female classmates now looked at him in a provocative way. Through sports, it seemed, he'd morphed into a stud. One girl caught his eye far more than the others: the Prairie Dog head cheerleader and wealthy orphan, Baroness Solange Cunegoody. Ernie had always admired this blonde bombshell—but from afar, considering her out of his league. Now she seemed to be giving him the eye. Impossible, he thought, and yet…was he the same Ernie as before? One afternoon following practice he asked the baroness out for a cherry cola and the rest is history: their going steady, their engagement, the six wedding postponements for reasons totally beyond the control of the groom. (Most stemmed from training crashes brought on when he'd exceeded his hormone reserves.)

Candide was offered an appointment to the Plunderian Military Academy at Westport, due more to his athletic feats than his classroom prowess. It was a hard decision for him because his dream was to become an architect and he realized his studies at Westport would focus more on blowing things up than on building them. In the end though he simply couldn't turn down such a valuable free education. There was a bonus, too: after college he'd serve his country, which he loved ever so much.

That fall, the redoubtable cadet with the humping bullet and churning legs was well on his way to establishing an NCAA freshman rushing record that would have lasted centuries when the brass at the Pentagon stepped in. A full-bird colonel from Army Intelligence visited the academy and took Candide for a long drive in his German luxury car. As they rolled along a road overlooking the ocean, the colonel laid out "the opportunity of a lifetime." If Candide would agree to give up sports, the army would train him into a one-man ten-megaton attack.

"What about the team?" Candide fretted. "We're on our way to the BCS."

"Son, we're beginning to have a problem…"

"A problem, sir?"

"How many yards did you gain last Saturday?"

"Seven hundred eighty-six."

"Quite a few, isn't it?"

"Yes sir, but I know I can do better."

"And there's the problem. When you gain seven hundred yards or do a backflip over the crossbar, it catches people's attention. See what I'm getting at?"

"Request further clarification."

"Children all across this great land of ours are pulling on football jerseys with your number. Every time you juke a linebacker millions of Plunderian women get hot panties. As we speak, the top selling male hair dye is blond, after twenty straight years of red leading the pack."

"I still don't get it."

"You think the Rooskies haven't heard of you? The Chinese?"

"They know I'm going to kick their butts in the next Olympics."

"Soldier, that's exactly what you're *not* going to do. If you listen to me."

Candide looked sad.

"Athletic triumphs are wonderful in their place, but you've got a higher calling, soldier. You have the potential to be the greatest goldarned military wonder in the history of organized warfare. Not, however, if you let the enemy know how you tick. Once those screwed-up bastards get a load of your history, they'll set up government programs to dump their children in nuclear vats and shoot them in the head, trying to create equalizers."

"Now I see, sir." An air of dejection settled over Candide. He loved sports. He'd established so many sports-related goals, dreamed so many dreams of athletic conquest. On the other hand, Uncle Sam was picking up the tab for his education and therefore had a claim on him. He felt it wouldn't be cricket to say no.

"You'll continue your studies here at the academy, but on weekends we'll fly you down to Tennessee. There you'll be trained till you're ready for deployment in the field."

Candide said nothing.

"Don't take it so hard, soldier. We all make sacrifices. When I was your age I wanted to design women's hats. Thank god my dad kicked *that* crap out of me."

So it was that Ernest Candide put aside sports and began transforming his athletic skills to martial ones, a process that took five years—and which brought him ultimately to this helicopter ride. As his reverie bumped up against the present, he snapped out of it. He looked down and saw the Smoky Mountains under a blue haze. Now he could guess where he was headed.

4

THE chopper put down at Quantico as Candide had expected. He'd been there many times before on visits to the Pentagon. He assumed he was headed to the Pentagon again. But oh how wrong he was. No sooner did he touch the tarmac than two aides hustled him into a black limousine with deeply tinted windows. The driver, he noticed, had close-cropped hair and wraparound shades—shades as impenetrable as the vehicle's glass. Candide could have called on his X-ray vision, but thought it impolite under the circumstances.

Minutes later the limo was waved through the post checkpoint and the driver turned onto an expressway teeming with civilian traffic. Candide witnessed there a scene that stirred his soul. Nearly every car or blunderbus flew a high-riding flag, whipping and popping in the wind. Some vehicles sported two flags, three, or even more, so freedom loving were their owners. Some flags were enormous, expressing the occupants' supersized pride in their homeland.

Entering downtown Candide saw pedestrians wearing flag hats, flag T-shirts, flag trousers—even a flag bustier! One woman had woven a flag into her long blonde hair to create a stunning tiara, impossible to miss. She, to Candide, was the most flag loving of all. Take that, Moolah! By attacking our flags, you hoped to demolish our national spirit—but instead the opposite happened. Plunderians of all walks were rallying around, under, even inside the flag. Never had the country been more unified.

Later, Candide watched as marines opened gates to admit the limo. Then up a long drive and around a building the lieutenant recognized all too well, though he'd never visited. It was the White House, the home of President Twofer and his first lady. It crossed Ernie's mind he might run into the first daughters. Then he realized they'd probably be out on the town, tying one on. The driver stopped behind the impressive abode and a young man in a gray pinstripe with lavish blow-dried hair hustled toward them. This well-coiffed individual escorted the lieutenant through a rear entrance, up some stairs and down a long hall to a stately door, which he opened for Candide.

On entering, Ernie felt a patriotic tingling climb his spine. It was the Oval Office, the place where the president worked to keep the country safe and free! Candide saw his commander in chief standing with his back to the door, coat off, sleeves rolled. He was sweating over the noisiest pinball machine the lieutenant had ever heard. Twofer did an amazing bugaloo with his lower body, grunted, then smacked the side panel loudly with his palm. "Crap!" yelled his excellency. "Some asshole greased my flippers!" He pulled off his baseball cap and hurled it across the room—turning just enough to see Candide. The president's tiny eyes widened to dime size. He dove for the carpet and rolled behind his desk.

Candide wasn't sure what to make of this unusual greeting. As he waited, curly gray hair, then a wrinkled forehead rose from behind the desk. Two dull, close-set eyes stared at him over polished wood. Finally Twofer rose to his full height, reinflating with cockiness. He hitched his pants. "Heh heh heh heh," he sniggered. "You spooked me, lieutenant."

Ah, thought Candide, the presidential plunge was a counter-terrorist move. "Precautions are in order, sir. Especially for a key target like yourself."

"Darn tootin'," said the president, smirking.

"I fully approve of what your pilot did yesterday. His evasive maneuvers to keep you out of harm's way. I know there's been criticism."

Twofer's face darkened. "I'll have you know the Secret Service ordered those maneuvers. Personally, I wanted to fly straight back here lickety-split. If those A-rab sidewinders come for me, fine and dandy. My dog Barfy could use a good snakeskin collar. Right, Barfy?"

A black Scottie trotted out from under the presidential desk and looked up at Twofer. "Pffweeet!" the insolent pet replied with his nether trumpet.

Candide realized the chief executive was staring at him. It made him a little uncomfortable. He couldn't tell what was on Twofer's mind.

"You're not as big as I expected," the president said, a smile playing on his lips.

"My strength comes from a hormone, sir."

"As I understand it, you're normal without that stuff pumpin' in your blood." The smile had become a smirk.

"True."

The president swung a hard punch into Candide's gut. The officer's breath whooshed out and pain rose all the way to his skull as he buckled.

"Heh heh heh heh," chortled Twofer. "Weren't ready for it, were you?"

Candide's voice was pinched. "No, sir." He started his bullet humping in case Twofer unloaded another sucker punch.

"Hurt, didn't it?"

"Yes, sir."

"Let that be a lesson. Keep your eye on the ball or you'll get your eggs scrambled."

Nodding, Candide decided the sneaky blow was intended to help prepare him for his mission.

Twofer strode with assurance to his blue baseball cap, snatched it up and tugged it down on his scalp. The silver message on the front could now be read: 43RD PRESIDENT. "There's somebody here wants to mee'cha," said the 43rd president as he stepped to a door. He opened and an older man entered—tall and familiar. He too wore a baseball cap, identical to the chief executive's except for its message: 41ST PRESIDENT. Holy smokes, thought Candide, it's Buzz Twofer the First! The young man's internal celebrity meter topped out on "Big Shot" for the second time in minutes. What a day, what a day!

Twofer Sr. crossed to the soldier on long legs and extended his hand. "Welcome. Heard a lot about you, lieutenant."

"Likewise, sir," said Candide smiling, unaware of his own irony.

"Heh heh heh heh heh," sniggered the elder Twofer with deep resentment. The irony was not lost on him in the least, and he noted the soldier's smile.

Candide continued, "I'm darn proud to meet the man who kicked Qroc's butt (pardon my French). That was one heck of a show."

The ex-president brightened immediately. "Ah that. That was nothing. They wouldn't let me use nukes or you'd have seen something really pretty."

"I'll bet," said Candide.

"To my way of thinkin'," said Twofer, Jr. with an air of condescension, "it wasn't much of a victory. Madmahn Badassi remained in power to gas his own people, develop weapons of mass destruction and threaten our oil supply."

"We had no authority from the World Congress to invade Qroc," said the 41st president testily. "All we were authorized to do was rescue little Qtip—which we did with honor and dispatch."

"World Congress!" his son snorted. "Whose ass have they ever kicked? A bunch of fart-lighters and do-nothin's. And you let them lead you around by the nose."

Candide saw fury in the former president's eyes. If looks could kill... Then Twofer Sr. glanced at his watch. "My my, look at the time," he remarked lightly. "I'm late for polo practice." He extended his hand to Candide. "A great pleasure, young man. May we meet again." He raised his eyebrows. "Under less trying circumstances, shall we say? Good luck on your mission."

"Thank you, sir."

Twofer turned to his son. "Your mother and I both regret we didn't change your diaper more often. Now the whole world has to pay, I guess. Well, carry on! Bully, bully." He strode to the door and departed.

"Heh, heh, heh, heh," chortled Twofer, Jr. "Never could take a joke." He shot a fist into the air and grabbed his bicep in the Italian manner.

Candide, learning only now that a son could disrespect his father in such a manner, stood gaping.

Twofer smirked happily. "Got somebody else for you to meet. A man of action like us." The president led the way into the adjoining room, which contained a long conference table. Seated at the table was a lanky, hawk-nosed gentleman in his sixties who appeared dressed for desert safari. The man rose, taller than Candide expected—and somehow familiar. "Lieutenant," said President Twofer, "the greatest desert warrior of modern times, Brigadier General Jack Pangloss!"

"G-G-Gosh," said Candide, "Old N-Nutcracker. What an honor! I've read all your books." He timidly pushed his hand forward where it was swallowed by the general's huge mitt.

"The honor's mine, lieutenant. I've been following your development closely. You never cease to amaze."

Candide blushed. "Really can't take much credit, sir. It was pure accident I fell into that nuclear core then shot myself in the head."

"General," said Twofer, looking peeved, "he gets all his fizz from a chemical in his brain. Without it he's a wimp. I cold cocked him with one punch."

General Pangloss, appalled, turned quickly back to Candide. "Err...lieutenant. Our commander in chief has an assignment I think may interest you."

"That's right," said Twofer. "Why don't we all sit down?" They took chairs at the head of the table, with the president in the middle. The general removed his pith helmet and placed it on the polished mahogany.

"Lieutenant," Twofer began, "I don't need to tell you our country is facing a crisis more direatious and threatsome than any in our history. Terrorists have rampaged our innocent flags, pissing all over our national pride. What these varmints might pull next is anybody's guess."

Candide nodded, face grave. Boy can this guy mince words, he was thinking, but of course that's why he was appointed president.

"As I'm sure you're aware, the Evil One is cowering right now in some dark hole in Ragistan."

"Yes sir."

"Your mission—code name Operation Supergoose—will be to go there, find him, root him out, and bring him to justice. Do you understand me?"

"You want me to arrest him and fly him back here for trial."

The president and General Pangloss looked at one another. The president tried again. "Justice has got to be one hundred percent certain. Remember, if Moolah wriggles though some legal loophole, he'll jump our flags again."

It was true that Moolah couldn't be trusted. And, after all, this was war. "So you want me to kill him."

Again the president and the general exchanged glances. Twofer rubbed his chin. "Ernie, let's just say you should bring him to justice, then come back here with his head in a box."

"His head in a box?"

"You heard me, soldier. Do I need to draw you a picture?"

"No sir."

"Meantime," said the president, "you and the general have a little date in the Mojave for some special trainin'."

Later, in his room at the base, Candide watched the president speak to the nation from his ranch in Crawdad, Texas. Twofer, wearing a blue denim jacket, looked robust as he gripped the podium with rawhide work gloves. Conspicuous in the background was a chainsaw on a stump. Brow furrowed, Texas twang twanging, the cowboy head of state commenced to speechify.

"We have given the Ragistani government twenty-four hours to smoke the Moolah al-Razir out of his hole and turn him over to us—but they have refused. They say we need to prove Moolah is actually on their soil and that he is behind the Screaming Eagle attack. Our proof, on both counts, is watertight, but also top secret—for our eyes only. To expose it needlessly would blow the lid off our loyal agents in the field. The Ragistanis have begged us to be reasonable, but we do not reason with those who suckle terrorists.

"It is therefore with a sad and heavy heart—but also with an angry and righteous heart—that I hereby defend our homeland by declaring total war on Ragistan. Operation Infinite Liberation is about to blow. A contingency of aircraft carriers is even now surrounding Ragistan's landlocked harbors and coastlines. Soon, but at a time known only to us, the sound and fury of a great republic will begin to boom in that dark land.

"To the people of Ragistan, let me say this. I have great respect for you, for your religion, for your charming carpets, for your bounteous dates and figs. I feel a burning commitment to your future, and therefore I've directed our military to bomb you toward democracy. None of your interfructure will be spared. Your hospitals and schools, breeding grounds for young terrorists, will be wiped off the map. Your whole country will be visited by a trial of fire to purify you and your loved ones, making you ready for freedom and the capitalist way. Because, as we like to say here in Plunderland, 'What doesn't kill you makes you stronger.'

"On the home front, Vice President Chain Dickey has been remanded to a secure undisclosed location to preserve continency of office should the president's person be stricken. Naturally, I'm sending a budget request to congress to fund this war. This is a necessary war, a rightful war, a war we cannot fear to flub!" He paused, eyes sparkling with purpose. "And I'll tell you this, too. With our laser-beam weapons and computerized soldiers, we're going to kick serious butt. Heh heh heh. God bless you and God bless Plunderland! Let's roll!" Twofer held aloft triumphant fists.

Candide felt a lump in his throat. His president had defended eloquently the upcoming invasion of an evil land crawling with vermin. His own part in the war had been clearly defined. Ready to roll he was!

5

AS a chapel bell tolled eleven, a long sedan swung into a wooded cemetery in north D.C. The car followed a curving road to a row of crypts and stopped. The headlights went dark. Two men in trench coats got out, one half a head taller than the other. They walked toward a crypt as a cloud eclipsed the moon, deepening the gloom.

"Cold for September," said the tall man.

"More spooky than cold," said his companion. "I hate this detail."

"Not ours to reason why," said the other, producing a key. He slipped it into a large padlock on the crypt door and popped the clasp. The door yielded to his shoulder as he pushed into a burial chamber, empty except for cobwebs and dust. The men stepped to the back wall and the taller felt along it, then pressed with his thumb. A narrow beam of red light shot into his eye. The wall began to rumble as it rolled aside to reveal a modern stainless steel elevator. Above the elevator door a single arrow pointed down.

The stylish, close-cropped gray hair of the taller man glowed under the elevator lights. He pushed B28. The descent was accompanied by an efficient hum. A minute later, the doors opened onto a concrete hallway. Two marine guards armed with M16s stood on either side of what appeared to be a locked commercial bank vault. "CWAP needs Pappy," said the tall man with authority as he stepped from the elevator. The marines saluted. One put down his weapon and began opening the safe. Soon the thick circular door swung wide on massive hinges.

The trench-coated men entered the vault, filled with a vast array of medical apparatus. In room center was a glass casket raised to waist level. Inside lay the supine corpus of the Vice President of Plunderland, Chain Dickey, preserved in liquid methane at minus 122 degrees Fahrenheit. He was dressed in a black business suit, his cheeks blue, nose white with frost. On his balding dome was fitted a stainless steel cap. Steel bands encircled his wrists and ankles.

The two men worked quickly. The shorter switched on a pump

to suction methane as his partner activated the microwave thaw and started warm blood flowing through a tube into the head of the now moving corpse. Chain Dickey was rotating like a porker on a spit, frost melting and dripping into the collectors. In three minutes he was fully thawed. Pressing a button, the taller man halted him face up—ready for his charge.

His partner threw the lever that sent 50,000 volts surging through the VP's convulsing body. Sparks popped from the steel contacts as Dickey shook and shuddered. Then it was over, the electrified flesh quiet again except for the eyes—which snapped open. Dickey sat up in the casket. A hopeful smile lit his face. "Am I president?" he asked, blue electricity traveling his teeth. Strands of his comb-over stood erect.

"CWAP is meeting in emergency session. We've declared war on Ragistan."

"Hot damn!" shouted Dickey, leaping from the casket. "The game is afoot."

6

IN the living room of a Maryland suburban split-level, recessed lighting brought out just the right touch of class in the expensive furnishings. Secretary of Defense Clayton Minefield carried a scotch and water from his wet bar to Parson Rupert Weed, seated on a white leather couch. Weed was the president's national security adviser *and* the president's personal chaplain. He also happened to be Plunderland's leading televangelist. "Well?" Weed asked the secretary.

Minefield seated himself in a black Snoreboy, squinting genially. "The sweetest investment of all, huh? That's a toughie."

"Go back as far as you want."

The secretary shrugged. "I guess I'd have to say the Bermuda Triangle. That one where you bought a Bermuda estate, rechartered it as a bank, incorporated your family in Delaware, then laundered money while writing it off as taxes. I made a killing before they shut that down."

"The triangle was sweet, but not the sweetest. The sweetest is legal even today."

"You got me."

"Shorting employee pension funds."

Minefield frowned. "Don't know it. How's it work?"

"Well, you find a corporate retirement fund that is secretly being sucked dry by management. Then you short it, leveraging to the gills. When the fund goes belly up and the suckers are left holding the bag, you cash in."

"How do I know which funds to short?"

"Clayton, you play golf with the same people I do. Ask around."

Minefield smiled reflectively and took a sip of his drink as the doorbell began chiming the opening bars of "God Bless Plunderland." The secretary of defense got up and left the room. Soon he returned with Chain Dickey in tow. The circle was now complete. The key members of CWAP—the Committee for a World Ascendant Plunderland—were now gathered. These three Mastodons were the most powerful men on earth except for the president, and, if certain whispers were correct, they pulled the strings on Mr. Big.

"Well, we got our war," said Dickey. He and Minefield exchanged a high five. "What next?" The veep plopped down on the couch next to the parson.

Looking thoughtful, Parson Weed swirled an ice cube in his glass. "War offers excellent cover for items of domestic agenda one doesn't want the public examining too closely. But we have to act while the beast is riled. Ideas?"

"A tax cut," said Dickey, eyes sparkling. "A big tax cut."

"Needs to be sexier," said Minefield. "A tax cut with a theme would be better."

Weed held up a finger. "Why don't we call it the trillion dollar tax cut for a free Ragistan. The refunds we'll call war bonds. We'll say Plunderians earned their bonds by backing the invasion."

"That's too much money," objected the vice president. "If we cut taxes by a trillion while funding a new war, we'll drive up interest rates, maybe tank the economy." Silence as the three wise men cogitated. Minefield took Parson Weed's glass, poured new drinks and carried them back.

At last Weed spoke. "How about if we phase in the tax cuts over ten years, so that when the bill comes due, we're long out of office. Let some future Jackass Party president explain to the Plunderian people how their treasury became a big hole all the way to Asia."

Minefield laughed in appreciation but Dickey looked dubious. "With the baby boomers retiring soon, a tax cut that size will bankrupt Medicare and Social Security."

Weed scowled. "Both of those are socialist programs, profoundly un-Plunderian. We're a capitalist nation—and a godly nation I might add. The Bible speaks not of such programs."

"The man's right," said Minefield. "The Jackass Party rammed Social Security and Medicare down our throats when we were weak. But now we're the party with the balls."

"I still see a possible problem," said the vice president.

They looked at him.

"What if Buzz Twofer's like his old man? What if he wants to raise taxes instead of cutting them?"

Weed smiled into his glass. "Little Twofer can be brought around. You two work on his head, such as it is. Leave his soul to me."

Chain Dickey raised his drink. "To the trillion dollar tax cut!"

Two other glasses joined his. "God bless the trillion dollar tax cut!"

7

FALL is a season unknown to the Mojave. From a cloudless sky the morning sun beat down on sand and rock as waves of heat rose from desolation. A lizard sunning on a basalt shelf slowly closed its eyes as the warmth of the day seduced it toward slumber. Without warning, Lieutenant Ernest Candide swept down from the sky at incredible speed and passed over the shelf in a blur as the lizard scrambled into a crevice.

General Pangloss strode out onto the basalt, his pith helmet shading his eyes. He watched Candide rise from his dive, decelerate, and bank against the pale blue sky. As the lieutenant's arms slowed, it became apparent he was swinging them in a motion similar to the Australian crawl—though at tremendous RPM. The supersoldier completed his aerial return and landed in front of Pangloss, heels together, shoulders drawn to attention.

"So, Goose. What went wrong?" asked the general.

"Can't figure. I came from behind, its eyes were shut, and I was gliding. It couldn't have seen me and couldn't have heard me."

"A lizard with ESP, do you think?"

"It felt my presence somehow."

Pangloss turned his head to stare at the horizon where a purple mountain range stood half lost in heat haze. The wary eyes took on an almost reflective look. "Years ago men lived here who knew this land as the animals know it. Do you suppose one of them would've blown his lunch like you just did?"

"Guess not."

"So tap into their ancient wisdom. Expand your mind to the bigger picture—to the whole enchilada of cosmic existence. What have you missed?"

Candide scanned his environment, looking every which way. At last his eyes rested upon a desert weed casting a shadow on the sand. "The lizard sensed my shadow," declared the lieutenant, "because the sun was behind me."

"Precisely. Remember, Goose. Enter the mind of the hawk. Become the hawk. Let the soul of the hawk fill your soul with hawkness."

Candide closed his eyes and concentrated. Soon he could feel his wings stretched wide and wind tickling his tail feathers. Imbued with hawkness, he began whirling his arms and rose into the air.

Later, when the sun was down and the sand cooling, the young soldier and his wizened mentor sat with a campfire between them. Four plump lizards, gutted and scaled, rotated on a spit as Candide cranked. The general was preparing a nutritious salad of tumbleweed sprouts, sage leaves and cactus berries. In the distance coyotes yipped at a rising moon.

"Sir," said Candide. "You mentioned earlier how superbly adapted the Native Plunderians were to their environment."

"Yes, yes."

"So what happened to them? We haven't seen a single one since we came here."

"You touch on a great tragedy in our nation's history. Really want to get into that?"

"I do, sir."

"Well, after the first Thanksgiving—which of course was just fabulous—our forefathers got to know the Indians better and couldn't help noticing grave flaws in their character."

"Flaws, sir?"

"For one, the natives couldn't hold their hooch. No sooner did they lay their hands on alcohol than they began drinking themselves to death. Also, while liquored up, they tended to murder and maim one another."

"How awful."

"Yes, but there's more. Their personal hygiene went against them too. It's hard to wash your hands while you're living off the land, so they picked up deadly diseases such as smallpox. They carried the germs around in their blankets and so forth and didn't think twice about it. Whole tribes were wiped out."

"So sad."

"Saddest of all is that many of the natives died on the swords and bayonets of the Plunderian Army's cavalry divisions."

"I know. We learned about that in fourth grade, sir. It's because those bad Indians were slaughtering the innocent white settlers and stealing their trinkets."

"*So* unnecessary. If the Indians had only been patient, in time they could have acquired civilized ways and had everything the settlers had—trinkets, beads, toothbrushes, even snazzy log cabins. But no, they had to lust after *other* people's things—even their women!"

"Blondes were especially prized," said Candide with ice in his heart. "Because they're prettiest."

"Perfect example. Everybody knows you can bribe a blonde with

OPERATION SUPERGOOSE 41

diamonds to do almost anything you want, yet these savages insisted on stealing them. So *grabby*. But why didn't the cavalry just catch the thieves and put them in jail? Why wipe them out? Did they teach you that?"

"It was because the Indians were evil, sir. They scalped people and shot them with burning arrows. They staked Christians on anthills. Bloodthirsty types like that would be sure to break out of jail and attack more peaceful settlers, who were just tilling their land and building strong fences."

"Right on every point, but not quite the whole story."

"That's what I remember."

"You didn't learn about Indian tribal organization?"

"Oh, yeah," said Candide. "Each tribe was a dictatorship, and the dictator, or chief, ruled with an iron hand."

"And did they share, the Indians?"

"Yes, my gosh, they shared everything. They shared their land, their food, even their wives!"

"What conclusion must we draw?"

"People who share everything are called communists, and so we must conclude that the Indian tribes were communist dictatorships—the very worst form of government. Naturally we had to wipe them out. They would have turned our democratic capitalist system into a barrel of rotten apples."

"Now we're getting at the whole picture. But there's one more factor. One more reason…"

"Resources. The Indians were squatting on Plunderland's natural resources, allowing them to rot unused instead of developing them for the good of mankind. Once the Indians were gone, young Plunderland could push ahead to her manifest destiny, fueled by the resources that had been freed to serve democracy and *all* the citizens, not just the selfish few."

"Damn that's beautiful, Goose!" said the general.

"What is?"

"To me it's beautiful when a young person knows his Plunderian history. It's our duty as patriots of course—but so many neglect it."

"I can't really take credit, sir. I always found the truth about my country fascinating. When I think about all the good things Plunderland has done, it makes me tingle."

The general, choked with emotion, perhaps was doing a little tingling of his own.

8

A MORNING meeting in the Oval Office found the president at his desk, on the edge of his chair, a baseball cap twisted in his hands. Across from him looking relaxed and confident sat Vice President Dickey, Secretary Minefield and Parson Weed.

"I don't care," said the president defiantly. "Us Twofers is fiskile conservatories. We believe in lowerin' the national debit—not raisin' it up with tax cuts."

"What makes you think tax cuts raise the national debt?" Chain Dickey asked mildly.

"If you take money out of the pot and give it back, then there's less in the pot. Who can't see that?"

"Top economists wouldn't agree," countered Dickey.

"Economists," scoffed the president. "Those eggheads are wrong most of the time."

Clayton Minefield took a turn. "Seems I recall a recent Mastodon president failing in his bid for reelection."

This made Twofer sit up. "What of it?"

"Well, do we want that to happen again? Do we want another President Twofer spinning down the toilet just because the economy crapped out?"

The chief executive stood and began pacing. Worry puckered his forehead—in fact his whole face.

Minefield continued. "Some of us warned your dad, 'Don't raise taxes, sir. More taxes will shoot the economy through the heart.' But he wouldn't listen. Three years later the economy was on life support and your dad was out of a job."

"Well," said Twofer, still pacing, "Don't happen to agree—not for one damn second—but just for the sake of argument, how does this tax cut thing work?"

OPERATION SUPERGOOSE

"It's really very simple," said Dickey. "First you cut taxes. Then you send out refund checks signed Buzz Twofer, which makes the voters love you. And when they spend their refunds, that stimulates the economy and lifts all boats."

"Plus there's a wonderful bonus," said Minefield. "Cutting taxes actually increases tax revenues, because once the economy starts humming again, more people make more money and pay more taxes."

"Sounds pretty slick," said Twofer, pursing his mouth forcefully as he paced. He shot a look at Dickey. "How much would a taxpayer get back under this here scheme?"

"Depends on income," said Dickey, whipping out a calculator. "How much did you make last year?"

"Countin' my pension from the Texas Air National Guard?"

"Whole ball of wax."

"One million, two hundred thousand and change."

Dickey's fingers flew. "You'd get back just over a hundred eighteen grand."

"Hmmmm," said the president. "And how much would I get back if I made minimum wage?"

"Okay, let's say a family of four, both parents working for minimum..." The VP's fingers blurred again. "Six hundred bucks."

The president stopped pacing. His arms were behind his back, hands clasped. "How come I get back so much more than them? The voters will shit blue thunder."

Dickey smiled. "You get back more because you paid more, and because Plunderland wants to encourage its entrepreneurs. Also, it costs a lot more to be rich than to be a peon. We eat caviar and filet mignon; peons eat hot dogs. We live on estates with a staff and a stable; they live in trailers with a mortgage. There's no comparison."

"Heh heh heh heh," sniggered the president. "I like that word 'peon.' Sounds like what it is: pee-on."

Minefield chuckled.

Parson Rupert Weed, long fingers templed thoughtfully under his chin, finally spoke. "Isn't there something we're leaving out?"

All eyes turned to him.

"What did the greatest president of the twentieth century do regarding taxes?"

Twofer bit. "What? What did he do?"

"Rod Raygun passed the biggest tax cut in Plunderian history," said Weed, lifting his eyebrows.

"And what happened?" asked Twofer.

"Three things," said the parson. "First, in the middle of a terrible recession the economy stood up on its hind legs and started humping again. Second, a lot of rich guys like us got even richer. Third, Raygun got reelected."

"Boys," said the president, scratching his armpit, "thanks for your good and frank opinions. I got to give this some serious thinkin'."

9

BUZZ Twofer the younger descended deep beneath the White House on an elevator. The leader of the free world was garbed in the manner of a dude ranch cowboy, with a huge silver belt buckle, poodle chaps and heavily tooled western boots. When the elevator stopped, the president exited bowlegged into a carpeted hallway and proceeded to a door that read

PRESIDENTIAL THINK TANK
TOP SECRET

Twofer offered his iris to a red laser beam, pushed open the steel door and entered. The walls of the room were covered with enlarged photos of Rod Raygun in western garb. In one corner stood a hat rack, and upon it hung tooled holsters stuffed with a beefy pair of .44s. Twofer brought down the holster belt and strapped it around his waist. He practiced a fast draw with both hands, dipping his knees in the gunfighter's squat.

He swaggered to a table where rested five wooden boxes labeled "Chaparral," "Sage," "Cow Pie," "Cactus Flower," and "Hot Leather." The presidential drover opened the box marked Sage and

OPERATION SUPERGOOSE 45

selected two sticks of incense. These he inserted in the horn tips of a steer's skull. He struck a match on the sole of his boot and lit the incense.

Stepping to a full-length mirror, he watched himself as he worked the holster belt down his hips just so. He cocked his hat just so, then began to chant:

> "Mirror, mirror on the wall,
> who's the fastest gun of all?"

The mirror darkened, then filled with light as a life-size image of former president Rod Raygun swam into focus. Raygun was decked out in western wear as in the wall photos. He began to speak in the smooth voice of the earlier cowpoke chief exec:

> "You're the fastest, Mr. Bad,
> even faster than your dad."

"Bogies at six o'clock!" shouted Twofer as he drew his .44s. He swirled to confront crash test dummies made up to resemble Moolah al-Razir, Madmahn Badassi, and Satan. Both presidents—one living, one deceased—fired into the rocking dummies until their revolvers were empty and smoke hung heavy in the room. Twofer turned to the mirror, where Raygun was blowing smoke from his barrels. Again Twofer chanted:

> "Mirror, mirror, tell me true.
> Should I cut taxes just like you?"

The mirror responded:

> "Better do it, son of Twofer.
> A tax raiser is a sure loser."

The Raygun image flickered and was gone.

"Couldn't be much clearer," Twofer said with conviction. "Cut taxes."

10

"IS it time?"

"Almost. Better get in here."

"One minute, sir. Maybe you could warm up the TV."

General Pangloss picked up a remote from the lizard-hide couch and snapped on a big screen encased in cactus skin. A telejournalist was interviewing two talking heads on the remarkable IQ of Plunderland's smart bombs. Pangloss punched down the sound.

Candide entered carrying drinks in frosted tumblers. He handed one to the general. "I don't think you'll find a more nutritious cactus smoothie anywhere."

"Only one vitamin I need. It's in here, right?"

"Three shots of Joshua root brandy, just like you said."

The general took a sip. "Ahh, perfect. To your health, Goose."

Candide lifted his smoothie. "To your health, sir."

"We've got a nice lifestyle here, thanks to my desert lore and your physical prowess. Won't be easy returning to civilization. Did you finish the war room?"

"Done. I also planted an orange grove and threw together a lawn mower."

"Lawn mower? Way out here in the desert?"

"While I was waiting for the tennis courts to dry, I buried a drip system around the house. In a few days we'll have a nice bluegrass lawn."

The general looked alarmed. "I'm allergic to bluegrass!"

"Sir," said the lieutenant, "it's the commander in chief."

Twofer was seated behind his desk in the Oval Office as the camera moved in for a close-up. There was no sound. General Pangloss pumped up the volume. "...evening, my fellow Plunderians. I bring you glad tidings of our war in Ragistan. Our flawless victory plans are going forward swiftly and flawlessly, exactly according to plan. In layman's terms this means we are kicking serious butt—rooting out the evildoers with our carpet bombing, our bunker busters, our cave-sniffing ordnance, our cruise missiles, and our depleted uranium shells.

"At this moment brave Plunderian bomber pilots are flying into the teeth of death, risking musket fire from horseback. Our eager ground troops stand ready to assist our Ragistani allies who have charged into the mountains to flush out the enemy. So far, God be praised, only six of our boys have bitten their mortal dust, all when a Patriot missile shot down their helicopter. As to enemy losses, thousands of terrorists have been blown to shish kebabs and thousands more lie bleeding and bawling in the desert night.

"The interfructure of Ragistan, what there was of it, has been pounded to grit. Terrorist hideouts lie in ruins beneath hospitals and Red Cross warehouses. Schools promoting terrorism have been blown off the map. Yet thanks to our careful and courteous smart bombs, the good-guy citizens of Ragistan have been left in peace and good health. Soon, when all the terrorist towns have been levelled, our freedom-hungry Muslim friends will crawl out from under the rubble to forge a true democracy on their native fundament."

"Hope the Ragistanis appreciate our sacrifices," said General Pangloss with marked sarcasm.

"Why wouldn't they?"

The general looked disgusted. "I can't count the times we've been bitten on the ass while trying to liberate an ungrateful people. Look what happened in South Vietland."

This was before Candide's time. He turned his attention back to the president.

"Certain doubting Toms ask how we'll pay for it all. Here's my answer. I propose a trillion dollar tax cut, one of the boldest in history. This daring release of ill-gotten government gains will light a fire under economic growth, spur bidness, whip up jobs, and lockbox Social Security and Medicare. Once our economy is pumping robustly again and profits are shooting sky high, billions in new tax dollars will be germinated to pay for the war. We may even have money left over for another war."

"Just imagine," said Candide. "By cutting taxes we increase tax revenues. What a genius move!"

"The man's a business wizard," replied the general. "While his partners were going bankrupt right and left, he made millions."

The president continued. "Now a word to those in congress who might try and torpedo my stimulatory tax cut package. Better ask yourselves—is it wise to stab your president in the back during a war? Is it smart to defy him at the very moment he's pulling the economy out of a tailspin? Don't be so foolish as to flirt with traitorism. And on my final note I say to all the war-hardened citizens of Plunderland, spend your tax cut wisely. Give our economy a quick and bodacious goose right in the old wallet! God bless you, and God bless our blessed country."

Chaff Gentry appeared on screen behind his anchor desk. Before he could speak, the general killed the TV and turned to Candide. "Notice what he left out?"

After a moment, a light came on in Candide's eyes. "Moolah. We attacked Ragistan to find Moolah and bring him to justice and the president didn't even mention him."

"What do you make of that?"

"He's leaving Moolah to me. On Operation Supergoose I will smoke him out of his hole, bring him to justice, and, uh...kill him, and, well, my orders are..."

"Soldier, you sound weak."

"Does he really want me to cut off Moolah's head and bring it back in a box?"

"That was probably a figure of speech, the box. It could be a beer cooler, a carry-on, maybe a bowling bag. Security will dictate the container."

Lieutenant Candide looked a little green around the gills. "But that's barbaric. Why can't I just photograph the body?"

"Psyops, soldier, psyops. The enemy has to know you'll always go him one better. Listen, the Moolah and his followers are a primitive, bloodthirsty lot, capable of anything. When I was humping a stinger with the Moujahedeen back in 'eighty-six, I came across some poor sucker who'd been tied to a post and his face carved away alive, right down to a staring blue eyeball on a grinning skull. I put him out of his misery to stop the most god-awful screams I've ever heard. I understood then what you'd better understand: these are vicious savages we're dealing with. Show the Moolah and his kind no more mercy than you'd show a nest of cobras in your sleeping bag."

"Why do they hate us so?"

"Envy. They see on TV how high and free we Plunderians live. And they get a load of our world-class toys. It fries them and they go berserk."

"Well, why don't the Moolah and his men create their own capitalist democracy, so they can be free and rich and happy? Then they wouldn't have to hate us."

"There you have the warped thinking of the desert nomad in operation. Crazed by their senseless tribal feuds, they'd rather kill each other off than cooperate to build a new and better tomorrow."

"But if they can't cooperate, how will they ever form a democratic government like we're promising?"

"After we bomb them to their senses, we'll have to teach them what we know. Perhaps, at times, an iron hand will be needed to keep them in line. If all this ends up costing us, they can pay us back with their oil."

"Sometimes I think Moolah and his men are jealous of other things too. Maybe they'd like to get their hands on some of our women."

"Oh yes. If one of our really pretty blondes fell into their clutches, I'd hate to imagine the bestial daisy chain she'd be subjected to. Better death than such dishonor."

"Golly, you're right."

11

TWO weeks later Lieutenant Candide flew at a lazy 175 knots above the snow-capped Hindu Kush of northern Ragistan—peaks nearly as tall as Mt. Everest. His X-ray vision was on full power as he scanned the caves honeycombing the sheer slopes. For the fourth time that day he detected suspicious movement, this time inside a cave halfway down the mountain he was crossing. He fixed his arms in glide position and swooped the mountain face, homing in on the hole with his earth-penetrating peepers. He made out eleven bearded men dressed in Ragistani robes. Along the cave wall were automatic rifles, grenade launchers and a machine gun. The airborne soldier punched the cave coordinates into his GPS belt buckle, ascended to a high peak across the valley and put down in hard-crusted snow. He lifted his wrist radio to his mouth. "Supergoose to Big Buddy. Come in Big Buddy."

A deep, gravelly voice sounded in his earpiece. "Big Buddy here. Got your coordinates. What gives, Goose?"

"Another sewer full of ragrats. Bust 'em up."

"Affirmatory. Stand back and watch the fun."

Candide scooped out a seat in the snow and sat. He was feeling fatigued, not so much from flying as from intense use of his eyes. His vision was slightly blurred and he had a headache. Minutes later plumes of dust and smoke began to blossom soundlessly on the mountain next to the cave mouth, "walking" toward it, then across. The sounds arrived delayed, a series of dull thuds. By the time they stopped, a new series of explosions was following the same line as the first. This pattern repeated several times.

Sensing something behind him, Candide turned to see a cruise missile sail over like a flying silo. It nosed downward and plunged, accelerating, glinting in the sun. The huge projectile disappeared into the cloud of dust hanging over the cave entrance and the cloud quickly doubled in size. A big **KA-BLOOM** came rolling across the valley.

As dust settled, the lieutenant glided down to survey the damage. He landed on the mountain above the rubble and pressed his ear to solid stone. He could barely make out faint cries—and what sounded like an anguished prayer. He was learning to expect these things. This was how evildoers died of suffocation in the belly of a mountain. He did not use his X-ray vision as he'd done the first time. Though Candide knew these men were vicious terrorists, it still wasn't easy to watch them suffocate.

That night, as the trooper lay bundled in his sleeping bag under a cloudy sky, he calculated he'd been instrumental in the deaths of about thirty men during the course of the day. Well, that was what war was all about, wasn't it? This indeed was the real potato.

12

THE afternoon of Candide's fifth day in country he had a close call. He was flying over a high mountain valley when he saw a surface-to-air missile not far below, rising fast. He took evasive action, dropping a fireball from his buttpack, then upped his arm rotation to maximum RPM, accelerating as he banked. But he was no match for the missile, bending its flight path and quickly closing. When it was mere yards from his heels Candide jackknifed into a dive. The SAM clipped his boot and was gone. Over his shoulder he saw it slip into a cloud.

The lieutenant's heart was racing. He guessed he might survive being hit by a SAM, but knew he'd be wounded, perhaps badly. He put down on a snowy peak to collect his wits. A brisk wind blew ice crystals against his shins as he used X-rays to scan the mountain he believed the SAM had come from. His eyes fastened on a cave a thousand meters above the valley floor. Inside he could see people wearing Ragistani traditional dress, five or six of them—hard to be sure because of his blurred vision. He stared for a long time before he decided there were definitely six terrorists. The one he found most interesting had a long face, big almond eyes, and a tapering beard. Candide rubbed his peepers and looked again. Sure enough, atop the old fellow's head sat the familiar pillbox hat of Moolah al-Razir!

With trembling fingers, the excited lieutenant punched in the cave coordinates. "Supergoose to Big Buddy."

"Big Buddy. Over."

"Lock your worst nightmare on that snake hole and you'll squash King Cobra and five of his worms. No more than twenty meters inside the cave entrance."

"Gotcha Goose! Nightmare number nine coming up. You well clear of the mountain?"

"Affirmatory."

"Strap on your nut cup, baby."

Minutes later a tremendous explosion at the cave mouth more than three miles away shook the earth and knocked the lieutenant to his knees. He watched through blowing snow as concussions too fast to count piled into an immense, billowing conflagration that rocked the mountain under him. It went on for a long time. When it was over, airborne debris choked the whole valley. Using X-rays, Candide examined the place where the cave mouth had been. He saw a yawning crater full of rubble. Past the rubble he could detect no movement.

It crossed his mind that Moolah al-Razir might be buried so deep it would be impossible to find him and take the "trophy," per orders. Hopeful of this, he flew down through the dust and landed just above the acres of shattered rock. He pressed his ear to the mountainside, expecting to hear the silence of death but instead the faint, inconsolable wail of a human infant raked his soul. What on earth? A baby? He tried to peer through the many tons of loose stone between him and the little wailer—but failed. Too much rock. There was only one thing to do. With his arms whirling like the blades of an earth tiller, he began to scoop out the tons of broken stone clogging the cave mouth.

It was evening before the lieutenant—totally exhausted—finally broke through and felt warm, stale air pushing against his face. Now the baby's cries were much clearer, but weak and interrupted by hiccups. Candide was clawing the opening wider when he saw something coming his way. He stepped back and drew his sidearm. A woman emerged from the hole and stood up, all five feet of her. She looked to be in her 30s and wore Ragistani peasant dress. Her long black disheveled hair was blown full of sand, and in her arms was a baby, blinking in the light and greedily filling its little chest with air. Both the baby's arms were missing. Crude tourniquets tied off the stumps.

The mother appeared by her movements to be uninjured though her clothes were soaked with blood. With grieving eyes she regarded her torn offspring. At this piteous moment the child gave up the ghost in one rattling final breath that left behind a bloody bubble on its lips. Already the small brown eyes were losing luster. The mother closed them in an act of infinite tenderness. She kissed the pale forehead, then lowered the tiny body to blasted rocks. She turned her attention to Candide and came at him, yelling in her guttural tongue, gesturing. She poked him in the ribs. He finally understood she wanted him to move. He let himself be guided to the hole he'd opened into the cave. When she motioned for him to enter, he did.

The lieutenant crawled on his hands and knees, losing light as he went. He humped his embedded bullet to give him night vision and soon saw in the spooky green illumination things that sickened him. Among the scant provisions of a farm family driven from its home lay the chopped and sliced corpses of an old woman, a man about 40, and two teenage girls. They lay in a wide pool of blood.

Several unexploded bomblets from a cluster bomb explained a lot. Not far from the people lay a dead goat, its rear hooves entangled in its entrails. The old billy's long lean face, baleful eyes, and pointed beard startled Candide, as did the swept-back horns, which resembled a cap. Here was his King Cobra! The lieutenant realized he'd called down the wrath of God on a family of civilians and their four-legged garbage disposal.

The confused and guilty soldier crawled back to the light of day, hardly seeing what he looked at. He stumbled downhill past the keening mother holding her child. He knew he should stop and provide information the woman would need to collect war reparations, but he couldn't face her awful eyes. He careened downward through rubble to the solid granite face of the mountain. There he leapt outward into a dive, intending to fly, but discovered his arms were too weak to sustain him. Apparently all the digging had drained his pineal hormone to the dregs. Helpless, he belly flopped onto the sloping granite, bounced, and began tumbling out of control. His elbows, knees and head smashed into rock again and again as he swiftly descended the mountain.

Halfway to the valley floor he had the good fortune to smash into a boulder with his back. It almost snapped his spine but ended the cruel tumble. He picked himself up, bones aching, skinned like a rabbit—yet alive. As he probed with his tongue for possible missing teeth, a shadow crossed his combat boots. He looked up and saw four men in Ragistani robes training Kalashnikovs on him. Others, he sensed, were behind him. Then his mind exploded with white light.

For him, the world was no more...

13

THE men seated around the White House dining table partook of gourmet food served on the finest china. They lifted centuries-old crystal to their lips with confidence and delighted in confounding the wine steward with their exotic requests. In this magic room a snap of the fingers brought immediate obsequious service. No gastronomic desire went unindulged. But who *were* these elegant men breaking bread with the president? Foreign heads of state?

On closer inspection, probably not. The kings of old wore suits as expensive as these suits—but rarely did modern heads of state. The manicures in this sparkling room were too fine, the hair plugs too skillfully woven for the men to be mere prime ministers. These elite 38 were in fact the potentates of Plunderland's premier corporations, the blue chip CEOs, the mega-kahunas of bidness. Such flat-eyed skinflints bought and sold mere kings and queens on the open market. They were rich beyond comprehension, pumped up with their obese salaries, obscene stock options and insider trading snookeroos.

To what purpose were they now gathered? As though to answer that very question, the president of Plunderland rose, accompanied by an unconcealed belch, and rapped his crystal water glass with a fork. Chocolate milk sloshed onto the tablecloth. "Gentleman, welcome. As you know, I invited you here tonight to commend you for your heroic acts of patriotism in support of our great nation—may she wave forever freely!" There was applause. "When Plunderland called, you and your companies gave willingly and generously to our needs, in amounts beyond those of all others. More than half of the many millions raised for my recent presidential campaign came from you noble knights of my round table—which right now, I realize, is really more rectubular than round, heh heh heh."

OPERATION SUPERGOOSE 55

Embarrassed laughter. "But be that as it may, and as I was saying, you loyal troopers really humped the extra mile for your dear fatherland, and for me. The most generous of you humped many extra miles."

The president picked up his wet notes and began to read, as chocolate milk dripped. "Now we are engaged in a great foreign war, testing whether our nation—or any nation so conceived and so dedicated—can long endure being attacked by terrorists. We are gathered here on behalf of that war, to pray that our brave boys get shot as little as necessary, and to prepare for the democracy soon to be rigged up in Ragistan. War, which is hell, oddly enough confords us opportunities to help our fellow human beans. Just think: at the end of hostilities, Ragistan's entire interfructure will have to be rebuilt. To feed her hungry citizens, oil and gas pipelines will need to be laid. You men and the companies you represent are the very ones with the know-how, and quite frankly the balls, to get the job done. That and your past acts of patriotism have handpicked you to join in bidding for the reconstruction contracts." Vigorous applause.

"The bids will be blind, of course, but it's only fair to advise you that those who commit further patriotic acts—in the very near future let's say—will be justly rewarded." A smattering of applause. "All contracts, big or small, will of course be cost-plus, so that in the national interest your corporations will be guaranteed robust profits while taking zero risk." Big applause. "Lastly, do not ever doubt that your country stands behind those who stand behind it! It is the least your country can do for you, and the most you can do your country for. God bless you and God bless our blessed blessings." Sustained applause as Twofer smirked, repeatedly thrusting his head forward at the neck in a manner likely to remind his detractors of a chicken.

14

CANDIDE awoke with a jackhammer headache, lying on a cot in a cell. He felt the back of his head with his fingers and discovered a two-inch gash caked with dried blood. A guard watching him through the bars turned and spoke to someone out of view. More guards appeared carrying three sets of leg shackles and three sets of manacles. When they tossed these into his cell, obviously expecting Candide to put them on, he realized they knew who he was. They of course couldn't know he'd drained his superpowers.

An armed escort of eight men accompanied the lieutenant along a carpeted hall while he clanked like a chain gang. The earthy odor of the place suggested a cave—as did the absence of windows. Didn't look like a cave, though. More like the basement of an office building. The group, coming to a spiral staircase, descended several floors and exited into another hall. A short walk brought them to an imposing door made of wood beams bound with steel straps. Two guards opened for Candide and motioned him inside.

Our superhero found himself alone in a large room with a mosaic tile floor and ornate tapestries. Plush cushions lay along the walls, fronted by low tables. In room center rested a beautiful multicolored rug with an intricate design. Candide was trying to understand how the decor could strike him as both luxurious and austere at the same time when, at the other end of the room, a door opened. A tall man dressed as a Bedouin warrior entered. The lanky nomad made a beeline for Candide and as he did his familiar looks and effeminate movements set off an alarm in the lieutenant. Holy smokes! It's Moolah al-Razir!!

"Kind of you to drop in," said the world's most fearsome terrorist.

Candide, stunned that the ruffian spoke flawless English (with an Oxbridge accent), knew not how to respond. He opted to harden his gaze into a glare.

"My goodness, what frightening eyes, young man. You look like you mean to sever my head and carry it off in a box."

Candide's mouth fell open in surprise.

"How did I know?" Moolah smiled. "Your warmongering president is such a buffoon he hasn't noticed his Puerto Rican maid is really an Arab. She happens to be my seventh wife, adept with flatulence potions."

"How sneaky! But I'm not worried. Good always triumphs over evil in the end."

"Of course good triumphs. But whose good—yours or mine?"

"What would you know about good? You murdered thousands of innocent flags and people. You're EVIL!"

"Say I am evil if you wish. But to me those murders, as you call them, were collateral damage. What's important is the message to your people, written in blood so they pay attention: Stop killing us or we'll kill you."

"We're not killing you. Liar!"

"You were going to cut off my head without killing me?"

Candide, unable to retort, manifested another tough stare.

"But leave me out of it," said Moolah with a shrug. "What about the bombs your air force is dropping on Ragistan right now—you think those aren't killing people?"

Images of the butchered family in the cave suddenly flooded Candide's mind, making it hard for him to deliver a stinging riposte. He found he wanted to push the painful memories far away, where they belonged. He lashed out, therefore—changing the subject. "What deceitful bull pucky! You don't care a bit about Ragistanis being killed. You're a hater, not a carer. You hate us most of all. You hate our democracy and want to blow it up."

"What democracy?"

"Plunderland is the best democracy ever! The whole world knows that."

"I'm no final authority on democracy, but I thought when a few wealthy persons controlled everything important in a country, it was called 'plutocracy'—rule by the rich. Democracy is rule by the many, isn't it?"

"You've never lived in Plunderland. How would you know about us?"

"I watch CNN."

"Pay better attention, then, because apparently you haven't noticed that everyone in Plunderland can vote, even *women*. Voting is what democracy's all about!"

"Technically, I believe the votes have to count. Your current president was elected by just five Supreme Court justices, all from his own party. Is that the democracy you mean?"

Candide sensed the need to shift ground again. "At least Plunderland has a free press. No democracy can exist without one of those."

"Your media spoon-feed you corporate propaganda, shocking murder cases, and tales about the mating behavior of your celebrities. Free of real news—that's how your press is free."

"Ingrate! Even while we stand here running our mouths, Plunderian soldiers are placing themselves in harm's way to liberate this dark land. And all you can do is knock us."

"Plunderland invaded Ragistan to liberate the Caspian Sea oil. That's the great cause your soldiers are dying for. That and the right to drive blunderbuses."

"I know what you're doing. You're trying to brainwash me, aren't you?"

"Impossible. Your brain is scrubbed so clean of valid content it's running on empty. What's there to wash?" The Moolah yawned in Candide's face. "I thought it might be entertaining to have a little give and take with Plunderland's magnificent superweapon before defusing him, but the clash of wits I'd imagined obviously isn't possible. Like most of your countrymen, you're atrociously educated, barely rational and addicted to fallacious arguments. When it comes to repartee, my poor goose, you thrust about in the dark with a paper foil, more likely to poke yourself than anyone else." The Moolah clapped his hands and called out in his tongue. Guards entered and dragged Candide from the room.

15

LIEUTENANT Candide had heard his death sentence. He knew he had to act. He feigned sleep until the early morning hours, then humped some night vision into his eyes and glanced about, looking for the chink, the weakness that might yield to his reduced physical abilities. The only exit he felt capable of overpowering was the air vent a foot from the ceiling.

Luckily, his guards had fallen asleep. Standing on his cot and using his thumbnail, he removed the metal screws securing the vent cover. Once it was off, he pulled himself up and squirmed into a round duct carved through granite. Like a rippling caterpillar he made his way down the tube for several hundred feet. Then he felt air pushing against the side of his head and realized he'd reached an intersection with a larger tube. He assumed the moving, fresh-smelling air came from outside the cave and turned into it. Now he could ramble on his hands and knees, somewhat in the manner of a rodent. Soon he began to smell jasmine. Then he smelled rain. He could just picture it. Not so far away, in the desert night, rain was falling on the jasmine. Freedom was that close!

Hearing what sounded like a sneeze, he stopped and listened. To steady himself, he reached out for the duct wall, but instead of stone he touched louvered metal, which immediately gave way. He tumbled through a hole and fell several feet to a soft landing. Guttural curses came from underneath him. He sprang aside and a head rose next to his—a not very large head covered with an amazing amount of dark hair.

"Do you speak English?" Candide asked hopefully.

"In the middle of the night you jump on me and want to know if I speak English?" asked a quite melodious, but lowered, voice. "Who are you and what are you doing in my bed?"

"Ernest Candide. First Lieutenant, Plunderian Army. Serial number 767–33980."

"Oy! A Plunderian military robot. What will they think of next?"

"I'm not a robot," said Candide. In the room's dim light he saw a most attractive small face. The woman had pulled the covers up to her chin. "Where am I?" Candide asked her.

She shook with soundless laughter. "You don't know?"

"That jasmine smell," he said, sniffing and looking around.

The woman lifted her wrist to his nose. "We all wear this stuff now. Moolah buys our fragrance in bulk when we're on the road."

Candide saw the room contained many beds, each with a long-haired head asleep on a pillow. "But I smelled rain."

"Some of us take showers before we crawl in. Helps us sleep."

The only conclusion Candide could draw was that he had happened upon a women's dormitory of some kind. Was the Moolah running a college for beautiful young women? That seemed odd in the middle of a war. And what might he be teaching them?

"You still don't know, do you?" said the woman.

"No," admitted the naïve soldier.

"Let me spell it out. Apparently without intending to, you managed to break into the very well-guarded harem of Moolah al-Razir. If you get caught, fool, slow castration will be the least of your punishments. More important, you'll get *me* in trouble."

Thus did Candide learn, from one of the cutest bearers of ill tidings ever, what an awful pickle he'd gotten himself into. Now the harem door swung wide and a tall guard entered with a large curved sword. He looked around in the dim light, probably trying to determine where the voices were coming from. Candide's bedmate pulled him flat to the mattress and drew the covers over them. The two moved close together, very close, with her amazing hair exposed and Candide's blond flattop hidden, as they attempted to simulate a single rather large cactus flower.

The guard was checking every bed as he came their way. Poor Candide, unable to move for fear of detection, found his face pressed into a most distressing locale, the soft bosom of the lovely-smelling young harem dweller. This contact, or perhaps his warm breath, activated the little doodads on the ends of the beauty's mammary glands, and these pressed into his face through her nightdress. Entirely against Candide's will and defying every silent command he screamed at it, his jubilant appendage began to rise through the zipper he'd inadvertently left open in his haste to depart his cell. Mr. Eager slipped thoughtlessly under the lady's nightwear. Soon, in the midst of its trek, it abutted something soft and furry. Whatever it was appeared sensitive, because the woman to whom it was attached reacted with a small intake of breath.

Candide heard the guard's heavy footfall close by and held himself as still as he could. Yet the part of him currently in rebellion continued doing its thing, expanding and pushing inside the warm spot it had found. As the guard moved away, the lieutenant began to slowly rock his hips, trying to free himself from the thrilling trap. The woman seemed to be trying to free herself too, but somehow they stayed stuck together. Neither heard the door click as the guard exited the room, so far gone were they in their vigorous unsuccessful extrication...

Afterward they lay quietly together, catching their breath.

"Boy," said Candide, "What was *that*? It was like quicksand. I couldn't shake it off."

"*Quicksand?* Shake it off? I thought we were making love."

"I was afraid that's what it was! For some reason I couldn't stop."

"Me neither," said the woman ruefully.

"Oh my gosh! Now we've got to get married! But how can I marry you? I'm betrothed to another!"

"You can forget the wedding stuff. I'm Moolah's newest wife. What you need to worry about is how we're going to escape now that you've turned me into an adulteress."

"Let's crawl out through the air duct."

"With your sense of direction?" She handed him a pillow. "Here. Tie that to your middle."

So it was that Moolah's lovely bride and Lieutenant Candide (disguised as a mother in labor) made their way through the harem guards. Once they were beyond prying eyes, the unlikely duo crept downstairs to the main floor and snuck out through the service entrance into the desert night.

16

WITH the sun as their compass, Candide and the young woman he came to know as Delilah hiked north two days over mountain passes and through high valleys. The lieutenant's strength-hormone apparatus was still on the mend, so he barely possessed the power of 2.6 men by the time he and Delilah crested a high pass and saw below a small, perfect valley, its snow untracked by the machines of war. There they found a habitable cave. Candide's plan was to rest, recover his strength, and when he could fly again, take them into Pockistan.

A search of the cave turned up flint in the floor rubble. This and the lieutenant's wilderness wisdom soon provided fire to warm them and to melt snow for drinking. As for food, Delilah from the first supplied an abundance. A rock thrower of remarkable accuracy, she could kill a snow rabbit with a head shot at 50 meters most every time. Even more surprising, her rock velocity was sufficient to bring down a mountain yak. Candide's contribution was to carry home the larger carcasses on his strengthening shoulders.

During the winter evenings the lieutenant constructed ergonomic furniture for their home, including two beds. He'd thought initially one bed might be enough, because it seemed prudent to conserve warmth on the cold Ragistani nights by Delilah and himself sleeping together. But she insisted on her own bed. "I shared with you before," she pointed out, "and look what happened. That was my first time too, you know."

Candide was incredulous. "How could it be your first time? You're married."

"Sure, Moolah came to me—that smelly old camel! I was his new bowl of candy after all. But I tricked him."

"How?"

"I ordered a device advertised in the back of one of his Plunderian magazines. The Electropump 500 Honey Box. He never knew."

Delilah asked Candide to build walls inside their cave, so she could have her own bedroom. Eventually two separate apartments evolved, one for each. They continued to hunt together and in the evening joined for supper. Delilah cooked while Candide washed and dried the stone dinnerware. The lieutenant found himself growing quite fond of his petite but scrappy hunting partner. She was normally in excellent humor and nothing seemed to frighten her. One day, caught out in a snowstorm, they sought refuge in a cave which happened to be the den of a Ragistani cave bear. The huge beast attacked, bellowing bloody murder. Delilah—standing her ground—drilled it with a streaking rock between the eyes and the great body flopped dead at her feet. That night bear steaks roasted under the stars, stinking up the whole valley. As the nauseated hunters choked down the revolting flesh of their kill, they tried not to think about the 93 remaining bruin strip steaks cooling in the snow. Candide took a break from chewing to ask a personal question. "Delilah, do you love Moolah?"

"Me love Moolah? He bought me from slave traders."

"As you know, I am betrothed to the Baroness Cunegoody, the finest lady I ever hope to meet, but sometimes I wonder if I love her enough."

"If you wonder, you don't."

"Can't I wonder?"

"Not about that, bumpkin. Not unless you both accept it's a marriage of convenience."

"Maybe I shouldn't marry her until I'm absolutely certain I love her enough. Wouldn't it be tragic for her to love me like crazy but not get as much love back?"

"Like crazy she loves you?"

Candide missed the question. "Someday I might meet a woman *I* love like crazy," he fretted. "If I was already married—gosh what a mess!"

"Lost in the wilderness and surrounded by enemies, who ponders the finer points of love?"

"Who?" asked the soldier.

"An idiot, that's who."

17

ONE afternoon game was sparse and the winter sun low in the sky. Candide and Delilah were about to call it a day when they flushed a big rabbit. It bounded away over the crusted snow. Delilah fired a rock and, for once, missed. Before she could reload, the rabbit was out of range. Candide, whose hormone production was bouncing back fast, saw the perfect opportunity to show his stuff. Humping his bullet, he blasted off on blurring legs, kicking up a long cloud of ice crystals. In seconds he overtook the hapless rabbit and grabbed it by the ears. He broke its neck and bounded back to Delilah in easy 30-foot leaps.

Her eyes were wide. "Oy, bumpkin! How *did* you *do* that!?"

"Do what?" He wanted to hear how amazing he was from her shapely lips.

"You *are* a robot, aren't you?"

"I'm just a man," the lieutenant said. He squatted to clean the bunny. As he peeled back the skin with his knife, he related the history of his great gift—without getting into any classified information. As usual, he took little personal credit.

Delilah looked concerned. "Shooting yourself in the head seems to have done wonders for your body. But didn't it—ummm—affect your thinking?"

"Nope. My IQ's the same as before: one hundred. Exactly normal."

"What can you do besides run and jump?"

"With my full powers I can whip sand into glass. I can bench press a jumbo jet. I can fly."

"You can fly, bumpkin? No."

"Someday, when I'm really strong again, I'll fly us out of here. You can ride on my back."

"It's a nice offer but I want to see you fly first."

"No problem," said Candide nonchalantly. He ran his blade through the snow to clean it, then began to gut. "Delilah, there's something I wonder about."

"Yes?"

"I've never seen anybody throw a rock like you. How did you get so good?"

"Well, when my parents and I emigrated from the Soviet Confederation to Zionia, we were assigned to a Zionian settlement in the Gaza. Most of my friends there were Shrinkistanian, and those kids learn to throw rocks at an early age. I simply picked up their habit."

"How *could* you be friends with Shrinkistanians? They're terrorists."

"Not usually as children."

"You're wrong. I've seen them on TV throwing rocks at Zionian tanks and helicopter gunships. Those bad kids don't care who they hurt with their rocks."

"Well, if those kids had tanks, they'd use tanks to fight. But all they have is rocks."

"Tanks are necessary when you're dealing with terrorists. You never know when they're going to blow themselves up."

Delilah sighed. "One man's terrorist, bumpkin, is another man's freedom fighter. Weren't the founders of your country called terrorists by their oppressors?"

"I've heard that, and it may be true. But the founders of my country weren't suicide bombers. A suicide bomber intentionally kills civilians, even women and children. That's evil."

Delilah looked frustrated. She tugged at a tuft of her beautiful but unruly hair. "I wish you could talk to my friend Hashim. Koala we called him back when we were kids. He had big gentle eyes and ears that stuck straight out, a sweet-natured boy. When he was nine he made us stop blowing up anthills with firecrackers. Said we were being mean, that ants had a right to live just like us."

"Hashim is Shrinkistanian?"

"You bet."

"I always thought *some* of them must be good apples."

"True. Now when Hashim was eleven, his father was assassinated by Zionian Intelligence—and it was all a mistake. The Zionians thought they were killing someone else, a Fuzzbalah student organizer."

"How tragic! Hashim's father would probably be alive today if it hadn't been for that bad apple the Zionians needed to take out."

"When Hashim was thirteen, he lost his little sister, shot through the head by one of the men in our settlement, I'm pretty sure. The Zionian Army investigated, but never found a suspect."

"What was the girl doing when she got shot?"

"Playing kickball in her schoolyard."

Candide frowned.

"One day, when Hashim was fourteen, he hitchhiked into town looking for a job. On his way home he was picked up by Zionian Security and learned he'd just become the prime suspect in the shooting of a settler a few miles away. For days the cops beat him and used water torture to try and make him confess. They kept him naked except for a heavy black hood that cut off his light and air. He came back to us with broken ribs and different eyes, humiliated eyes. I think the police did things to him he couldn't talk about."

"Those cops were dead wrong. And it just goes to show, there's a rotten apple or two in every barrel."

"When Hashim was seventeen, the Zionian Army bulldozed his house, looking for terrorist tunnels, they said. Hashim's grandmother, watching the only home she'd ever known turn to rubble, had a heart attack. When the ambulance taking her to the hospital was turned back at a Zionian roadblock, she died."

Candide, busy assimilating the tragic homily of Hashim and his vanishing family, suddenly developed a revealing picture. "Hashim became a suicide bomber, didn't he?"

"Wouldn't you?"

The lieutenant raised his finger to object—when the oddest thing happened. His athlete's brain, rusted almost solid by years of concentration on foot speed and positive thinking, squeaked and clanked and even popped. But in the end—lo and behold!—the human smartbomb formed an idea entirely his own. "Well, I might blow up some *soldiers*. A guy can only take so much."

Delilah's eyes softened and a big smile lit her face. "Sometimes you surprise me, bumpkin."

Candide loved it when she smiled. When she smiled (and oh what a smile it was!) a warm sun rose in the young man's heart and lighted his world. The rabbit was by now cleaned. Strips of meat lay side by side on the snow, ready for packing. Candide washed the blood from his hands.

Delilah, with an impish look, challenged her pupil again. "Zionia has one of the most powerful militaries on earth, equipped with top-of-the-line Plunderian weapons. This superarmy is being used mainly to fight teenagers with bomb belts and children with rocks. How does that strike you?"

Hoping for another smile, Candide forced his brain to squeak and clank some more as he produced a second homegrown notion. "Children and soldiers shouldn't be fighting each other. It's not fair."

"That's what I've always thought."

They continued discussing these matters for some time, until the lieutenant's cerebrum began to ache from the unfamiliar exercise. "Can we rest a little?" he asked.

"Of course. Thinking's not so easy at first. But you're getting it." Delilah looked into the distance. The sun was almost touching the snow. "Bumpkin?"

"Yes?"

"That strength hormone you mentioned. It could be used for the good of mankind, you know."

"That would be cool. I'd much rather help people than wipe them out with my superpowers."

"Do you know the chemical composition?"

"Technical stuff like that they don't tell me," said the bumpkin cleverly. He knew exactly what it was.

18

CHAIN Dickey's trench-coated handlers watched the vice president's rotating body complete its microwave thaw. With a metallic clunk, the impeccably clothed corpus locked into position face up, red tie fallen over its shoulder.

"Juice him," said the taller agent.

His compatriot threw the switch and Dickey's corpse shuddered, sparks flying. When it was over wisps of smoke rose from the vice president's nostrils. The body lay absolutely still. The eyes remained closed.

The taller agent reached into the casket and felt Dickey's carotid. He looked concerned. "No pulse."

"Jesus. What now?"

"Zap him again."

"Should we up the voltage?"

"That might cook him." He stooped and adjusted the dial. "We'll buzz him twice as long."

The switch was thrown again. Dickey throbbed and jiggled for a full minute. Finally he was quiet. His eyes snapped open—very,

very wide—almost popping out of his head. He kipped himself out of the casket like an acrobat and initiated a jig on the vault floor. "*Oooweee!!* I feel *good! So* good!" He danced up to the shorter agent and grabbed him by the shoulders. "No bad news on the president's health, I trust." He was grinning.

"CWAP is meeting."

Dickey twirled on his heel and launched into a dramatic one-man tango. A flaming fart ripped loose from his excellency's posterior, scorching the vault wall ten feet away. "HA HA HA HA HA!" he roared. "You cannot imagine how good I feel." He danced up to the taller agent and boogied in front of him. "I haven't been this wired since I was eighteen. How about, after the meeting, we hit some strip clubs and troll for a buzz."

"Let's talk about it then. Sometimes you wind down."

19

PARSON Weed held a brandy snifter on his fingertips as he reposed in a low-slung chair that called to mind Picasso's most daring work. Behind him a glass wall showcased a panorama of Baltimore and its harbor in fading twilight. Vice President Dickey, ever on the move, was executing a solo Macarena on the polished floor, his thin hair tossing in a halo above his head as his coattails flew in abandon.

Weed rested his drink on the coffee table. He picked up a Cuban cigar and a metal statuette of Joan of Arc. With his thumb he depressed the saint's nose several times, producing sparks from Joan's hair but no flame. The twinkle-toed VP, seeing the parson's distress, danced over and snapped his fingers under the cigar, making a big spark. A blue flame rose from Dickey's index finger. He held it for Weed as the holy man puffed.

"I've been meaning to ask about your wading pool," said Dickey, shaking out the flame. He thumbed the balcony, where red velvet drapes covered all but the end of a shallow tile pool.

"Not a wading pool," said the parson, staring into his brandy.

"Hot tub, whatever."

"Baptismal font," said Weed, annoyed. The VP looked confused. "Who do you baptize up here?"

"Oh, you never know…"

"Yeah?" said Dickey, interested. He stopped in the middle of a complicated Mashed Potato move. "Gimme a hint."

"Well, let's just say a few of the chosen."

A lopsided smile grew on Dickey's face. "Ones with a true vocation, I take it."

"Yes, they all have the calling."

"Boy," said Dickey, contemplating the possibilities. "Ever do doubles?"

"Definitely not," said the parson, looking sour.

Dickey, unfazed, was off again in a graceful waltz. The doorbell rang and he pirouetted over and opened to Clayton Minefield.

The Secretary of Defense regarded the VP "cutting the rug" Viennese style and shook his head. "You don't get out enough."

"Tonight could be my lucky night," Dickey riposted, waltzing away.

"You're late," complained Parson Weed from across the room.

"Traffic was awful," said Minefield.

The parson smiled. "What a waste. VIP magazine's Sexiest Man in the Administration cooling his heels in traffic, all alone in the back seat of his cushy limo."

"Not quite alone. My personal assistant was taking dictation." He made a face.

The three men guffawed, Dickey without breaking the rhythm of his amazing limbo.

"Will you watch it, man!" the parson yelled. "You're about to knock over my drink."

The vice president terminated his boogaloo and came out from under the coffee table. Straightening his clothes, he walked to the space-age couch and lowered himself into it, his eyes sinking below his knees. Minefield, at the wet bar, finished fixing drinks and carried them to the couch. He handed one to Dickey, then sank down beside him.

"I called this meeting," said the parson, "because to me the time seems ripe."

"Ripe?" said Dickey. "Ripe for what?"

"Phase two."

A sudden chill settled over the room and the shadows deepened. "Think so?" said Minefield in a hushed voice.

"Look where we stand. We've bombed the crap out of those mountains and probably killed most of the terrorists. We've beaten back the warlords, deposed the sitting government, and installed our puppet administration. Most important, we've won concessions for the oil and gas pipelines and awarded the pipeline project to our most patriotic oil company. Once we finish choosing the patriots for the reconstruction projects, there'll be nothing left in Ragistan to do."

The vice president screwed up his face and affected a mock-liberal stridency. "*Oh, oh!* But if we pull out now the whole countryside will descend into medieval combat among the biggest warlords. Bloody chaos will ensue!"

"Democracy is messy," offered Minefield beaming. "Part of the process."

Again Dickey squealed in the Chicken Little voice. "But poor Ragistan will be even worse off than before! What about freedom? What about robust elections and women's rights and a spunky press?" The veep began to snicker, unable to maintain his hilarious ruse. Soon all three men were howling. Dickey began to cough, face going red. Minefield slapped his back.

"Okay. Phase two," Minefield said to Weed. "Invasion of Qroc. What's our case to the president?"

The parson raised his long fingers and began ticking off talking points. "One, his father lost the election for not taking out Madmahn Badassi when he had the chance. Two, we know for a fact that Madmahn has weapons of mass destruction. Three, now that Moolah al-Razir has escaped Ragistan, he's no doubt teamed up with Madmahn to attack us again. Four, Qroc's huge oil reserves must be protected from Badassi's greed and placed in trust for the Qroci people."

"And *don't forget*," Dickey quipped, "we must usher in gay marriage and the humane treatment of trees!"

The triumvirate laughed loud and long. When the hilarity finally tapered, Weed spoke again. "So we're all on the same page?"

20

EVERY day Candide more strongly felt his oats (in scientific terms, his pineal ur-hormone). He'd been conducting flight tests in secret and figured he was ready to airlift his cave pal out of the country. Knowing that Delilah needed a little convincing, he decided on an impromptu air show to establish his credentials. She was tenderizing yak steaks on their cave porch as he began swinging his arms in the looping crawl that provided most efficient propulsion. He rose from the snow, ascended steadily to 800 meters, did a somersault and went into a power dive. Down from the sky he plummeted at 300 knots, 400 knots…until, mere meters from disaster, he threw his arms into reverse at tremendous RPM, buzzing like a million pissed-off bees. He decelerated abruptly, flipped, and landed on his feet in front of Delilah.

"Oy! You *can* fly, bumpkin. A lie to get in my pants is what I thought."

"Heck, anyone with my superhuman strength could fly, with the right training and enough commitment. Want a ride?" He got down on his hands and knees in the snow.

She smiled. "Why not?" Descending from the porch, she climbed aboard, seating herself in front of his hips. He stood and she gripped his shoulders. Then he began moving his arms, keeping them away from his body so as not to hit her. Slowly they rose—in a wide spiral just for the heck of it. "Come on. Do your stuff. I don't break easy."

He took her at her word, leveling out and accelerating to 150 knots. Delilah flattened herself against him to prevent the rushing air from tearing at her face. As she did, the front of her torso (doo-dads and all) pressed into the lieutenant's back. He soon found this particular contact, from this particular individual, distracting. Her lustrous hair with its lovely smell whipped his face—and that didn't help one bit. The testosterone-enriched young soldier developed a terrific case of heightened alert. It mightn't have been a problem but for wind resistance. The proud sail his mizzenmast raised in his fatigues caught the rushing air in a manner most painful.

He slowed and descended to earth, putting down on his hands and knees.

Delilah was laughing. "What fun, bumpkin! Why did you stop?"

"Got a cramp," said Candide, face wrenched.

She climbed off and looked. "Oy. I see the cramp. How did that happen?"

"Maybe if you wore more clothes, a lot more clothes, and tied your hair back—maybe that would help."

"Sure," she said, rubbing her eyes.

"You need goggles too. I'll make some tonight. We can leave in the morning if you want."

She looked down at him with sympathy. "Still can't get up?"

"In a minute."

21

EARLY the next morning Candide awoke primed with splendid visions of Delilah riding him for the next several hours. He dressed and hurried next door to present her with the stylish goggles he'd crafted. He found her door thrown wide. Inside, furniture was up-ended and the whole place ransacked. Most of her things seemed to be there, but she was gone—along with the snow rabbit coat he'd so carefully pieced together. The lieutenant was devastated. The woman he admired above all others (save one) had been torn from their cave and carried off god knows where. Disarmed of her rocks, Delilah was perhaps even now being...no, no, not the way to think, he told himself. Focus on finding her and executing a daring rescue.

He attempted to pick up a trail in the snow, but every footprint he examined belonged to either Delilah or himself. He deduced that the kidnappers had entered and departed the valley using old footprints, so as not to leave any of their own. Somehow they'd even managed to duplicate the pattern on the soles of Candide's army-issue boots. Who, he asked himself, was capable of such a precision caper? His answer should surprise no one: Moolah al-Razir, the little lady's viperous husband.

OPERATION SUPERGOOSE

Lieutenant Candide, without his radio equipment or his hunting partner, was now truly an army of one. Yet he felt no fear. It was the haunting face, etc. of Delilah that drove him into the teeth of death like a moth to a flame. Flying top speed he retraced in minutes the two-day hike north they'd made earlier. Soon he spotted the ridgeline overlooking Moolah's cave and put down on a snowy peak.

He surveilled for an hour without seeing any sign of life, then glided down and into the cave mouth. Flying at forty knots through halls and up and down stairways he searched the complex and found it empty of both people and furnishings. Back outside, he saw that recent snow made tracking impossible, and at that point was forced to acknowledge he'd reached a dead end in his search for Delilah. Immediately his duties as a Plunderian Army superweapon reasserted priority. He knew he must fly into Pockistan and seek out his safe house in Peshawar.

He winged south by southeast over the Hindu Kush. It was deep winter everywhere and a blanket of white covered all except the sites of recent bombing. Candide couldn't help noticing that in burned-out vehicles and collapsed homes lay the corpses of many women and children, and a lot of old folks too. He wished he could believe that terrorists had committed these atrocities, but the detailed evidence provided by his telescopic vision revealed people butchered by cluster bombs or turned to charcoal by depleted uranium. Such high-tech modes of death and dismemberment had Plunderland's fingerprints all over them. To Candide, this was quite confusing. Why on earth was his country slaughtering so many civilians?

His befuddlement doubled as he neared a band of scraped-clean earth that cut through the blanket of snow in a straight line. Soon he was flying over the beige band, perhaps thirty meters wide and stretching from horizon to horizon. Sections of steel pipe bigger than he'd ever seen lay on the dirt next to the snow. Down the center of the bare soil ran a ditch, and in the ditch teams of fitters worked aligning sections of pipe. Welders were busy sealing joints. All the workers' hardhats bore the logo of Plunderland's biggest oil company, Petroking, and so did the trucks and heavy equipment.

On the perimeter of the project, Plunderian Army troops stood guard. Candide couldn't help wondering what it was all about. Were the Ragistanis going to pipe their oil to the Pockistanis, who'd just helped defeat them in war?

Later the lieutenant passed over Plunderian mechanized troops, battalion after battalion, all in orderly retreat. Army vehicles were moving from villages and farmland toward a huge airstrip in the south dotted with transport planes. One transport was landing while others loaded troops and equipment. As Candide watched, a plane lifted off, banked, and flew toward Pockistan. Minutes later another followed.

To the north of him, Candide saw something else interesting. Armies of native Ragistanis on horseback were pouring down from the mountains and entering the areas vacated by retreating Plunderian forces. If the lieutenant could believe the evidence of his eyes, his military was giving back its recently taken territory to the warlords. These warlords, he knew, had in the past terrorized the rural population and managed Ragistan's opium industry.

A fundamental psychological law holds that a mind at rest will remain at rest, while a mind in motion will continue in motion until it arrives at a conclusion. Candide's mind, previously goosed into activity by Delilah, now lit up like a klieg light. The soldier realized that despite President Twofer's golden promises, Moolah and his men had escaped, many civilians had been killed, and most of the long-suffering Ragistani population had been abandoned to the mercy of rogue armies. The only progress in evidence was the pipeline. The hasty development of this project—as well as the many Plunderian soldiers devoted to its protection—suggested to Candide that the pipeline might well be the real reason for the war. Much as Moolah had said.

Near the border with Pockistan the lieutenant was distracted from his pessimistic thoughts by ghastly screams. They seemed to be coming from a small encampment on a creek. He glided down to investigate. In the creek ravine, he saw a big Ragistani goon with a knife torturing a tall man in safari gear tied to a post. Two thugs with automatic rifles watched from the sidelines. Much of the victim's face was gone, but Candide was able to identify General Pangloss by his distinctive dress and by the powerful baritone curses interspersing his ungodly soprano shrieks.

The flying trooper dropped into a power dive, arms whirling at full extension. Making fists, he swept into the campsite and pulped the heads of both guards before they could lift their weapons. Then he flew at the torturer, who'd postponed his flesh sculpting to see what was going on behind him. His turning face probably didn't have time to register the approaching death blur. Another headless body slumped to terra firma as Candide landed on his feet in front of the general, stripping black hair and brain tissue from his manual bludgeons. Old Nut Cracker looked down from his station on the post, smiling through a bloody, dripping mask. "Bravo, Goose! Couldn't have done it better myself."

Candide untied his friend, trying not to look below the general's hairline, where not much remained but oozing bone. The left ear was gone, his left eye as well—and the nose. Most of the left side of Pangloss's mug had been carved down to the grinning skull. "The savages!" cried Candide.

"All's fair in love and war, Goose. Damn, it's a rush being back in the fray! Running on adrenaline. Heart in my throat. I was kicking major booty till I hit this little snag."

"How you must have suffered! I heard your screams."

"Not screams, soldier. Samurai battle cries—targeted on the enemy's eardrums. They were just beginning to work when you turned up."

"But your eye!"

"Hell—I've got another. And a black patch is the ultimate babe magnet."

"Your ear, your nose."

"Hardly distinctive, either one. If they ever put me on a stamp, I want to look like I belong there. *MacArthur*...now that's a stamp. One thing though."

"Sir?"

"*It hurts!!! Oh Lord it hurts!!* Get those little morphine doohickeys out of my first aid kit and step on it!"

22

AS President Buzz Twofer II spoke to the nation, his incisive gestures, dazzling smirks, and well-annunciated sibilants trumpeted a confidence never before seen in him. Riding high on an 80% approval rating, he was indeed the apple of his own eye and, more important, had most of Plunderland eating out of his acquisitive hand.

"That is why, tonight," he continued, "I am officially proclaiming a complete and awesome military victory in Ragistan. Most of the terrorists are dead, and the few survivors are wounded or dispirited, therefore powerless to attack our flags. Moolah al-Razir is dead or wounded or dispirited. We have kicked out the evil Ragistani government and handpicked a posse of good guys to foster forth democracy, freedom, and a spunky press. A new day is dawning robustly in Ragistan as the fine people of that land go forward into dignity and hope. All thanks to us.

"But I must remind you, my fellow citizens, the world is still a dangerous place. Evil lurks in every dark nooky and cranny. We learn from our best intelligence sources that Madmahn Badassi, evil dictator of Qroc, gasser of his own people, buddy of Moolah al-Razir, is at this very moment arming thousands of biological, chemical, and even nukaler weapons. Why? The answer is clear. For an all-out surprise attack on Plunderland. We have asked the World Congress inspectors to find and destroy these weapons, but they keep bumbling the job. Is this incompetence—or something with a worser smell? We don't know.

"Here's what we do know. The shadow of Madmahn Badassi is stretching forth across our motherland licking his bloody choppers. Madmahn's assault aircraft, ladled with nukes and bird flu, soon will be knocking on our borders. We cannot wait for the foot-dragging arms inspectors. And we can't listen to any more hand wringing by our so-called European allies—who seem perfectly willing to let us wage war for world peace all by ourselves. As your beloved president I will not, I cannot, and I must not stand idly by with my thumbs in my britches while that rape-room cowboy Badassi swaggers our way, openly fondling his gun. That is why, tonight, with all the powers implanted in me, I have declared total war on Qroc. Operation Prophylactic Attack, a preemptive military jugglenut of overwhelming bombast, is set to go forward.

"I have ordered the immediate encirclement of Qroc by a floating flotilla of aircraft carriers. In order to defend the honor of little Qtip, our intimate ally, we are inserting a phalanx of two hundred thousand battle-hard troops. Over a period of months we will swell Qtip's belly with our potent ground forces, allowing us to deliver Operation Prophylactic Attack on or about the due date. What date that is is mine to know, yours to find out, but understand that it will be the right date, the best date, the good date fated for us to go forward to total victoriousness. In the process of making the world safe for Plunderland, we will of course liberate the Qroci people, lockbox their oil reserves, and usher in a new era of pro-life rights for the little Qroci woman. God bless you my fellow citizens! And God bless Plunderland!"

Candide and General Pangloss were watching the CNN broadcast from the emergency room of a hospital in Peshawar. Pangloss was in a wheelchair, his whole head wrapped in gauze except for the staring, lidless right eye. Candide sat beside him.

"Makes you proud, doesn't it lieutenant, to see a president willing to stand behind his guns?"

Candide was about to agree when his mind shifted into gear. He began frowning. "What he said about Ragistan isn't really true, sir. The warlords are taking control again and the only thing we're liberating is their oil."

"Bullshit," the general snapped. "Where'd you pick up that load of crap?"

Candide explained what he'd seen with his own eyes.

"Son, you're going to be debriefed soon and you're talking like a terrorist. I sincerely advise you to disinsert your head from your dark region. What's got into you?"

"I like to think about stuff now. It's kind of fun."

"*Think*? Some people should never think. It's disaster!"

"I don't see what's wrong with doing a *little* thinking, kind of as a hobby."

"Did I get where I am today by thinking?" The general's eye was blazing. "Hell no! I owe everything to *not* thinking."

"According to Delilah—"

"—Delilah? Did you say Delilah?"

"You know her? Isn't she wonderful? We made love but it was an accident. She's so smart and such a fine person—brave too. Once she saved both of us from a cave bear. But she's impressed that I can fly. Oh, we found ever so much to talk about, Delilah and me."

"You idiot! You've fallen in love with Delilah Jihad!"

"Delilah who?"

"Shrinkistan's number one spy—the most dangerous woman on the face of the earth!"

"Wrong Delilah. Mine's kind and sweet and—"

"—She's small, beautiful of course, lots of black hair, big green eyes."

"My Delilah's eyes aren't always green. It depends on the light. Sometimes her eyes seem almost gray or even lavender. But what I'd mention first about her eyes is how expressive they are."

"Hopeless," said the general, shaking his head. "Absolutely hopeless."

"She's a good person. I say that with confidence because we bared our souls to one another many a time."

"Lieutenant, get a grip! Tomorrow morning intelligence is going to crawl up you with an electron microscope. I've seen men less compromised get five firing squads. You've got to watch what you say."

"No one can make me speak ill of Delilah."

"Jesus H. Christ. You're doomed."

23

"YOU are all familiar with the parable of the widow's mite," sermonized Parson Weed. "She gave all she had, though it was but a pittance—and God judged it to be the greatest gift of all." The most devoted members of the White House staff were convened for the president's prayer breakfast. Trays of bagels and donuts rested on white linen. Leavings of scrambled eggs, French toast and Canadian bacon could be seen on plates. Everyone looked a little sleepy.

"I want to examine that parable again, because beneath the obvious and rather trite lesson is another more fundamental truth. We all know the widow had only a mite, but we don't consider the fact she had that mite to give. I want to tell you, friends, there are a lot of poor widows out there, and if you can pull in just one penny from every widow—say once a week—you'll be a millionaire in no time. Especially we who prosper on donations must never forget the widow and her mite." Mild applause rippled.

"Now let us pray," said Weed. The listeners bowed their heads. "Our Heavenly Father, on this bright morning of your creation we are gathered joyfully in your worship, ready to go forth and reap profits by the sweat of our brow. Bless our endeavors, but bless not those we endeavor against or those who endeavor against us. For thine is the power, and the glory, and the truth forever. Hollowed be thy name. Amen."

"Amen," repeated those around the table. They stood and began to file from the room. Soon President Twofer and Parson Weed sat alone at the head of the table. High on the president's left cheekbone glowed a shiny raspberry poorly concealed by makeup.

"Somethin' I want to ask you," said Twofer.

Weed was examining the presidential bruise. "Who clocked you?"

"Nobody. I choked on a pretzel. Now what I wanted—"

"—A pretzel?"

"Yes," said Twofer, defensive. "I saw something funny on TV, which made me choke on a pretzel, then I fell forward and hit my face on the coffee table. Hasn't that ever happened to you?"

"Not going to fly, Buzz. The media will eat you alive. Anyone can see you got smacked."

"I'm the president. Nobody smacks me."

"Have it your way, sir. You were mugged by a pretzel. What did you want to ask?"

"I need some spiritual advice."

"I'm your man."

"As you know, the stock market keeps goin' down and down while unemployment goes up and up. Even after my brainy trillion dollar tax cut, the economy is still poopin' out, and now folks are sayin' it could be a double dip recession—just like happened to dad."

"All true—unfortunately."

"Parson, I been lookin' through my Good Book near every day, but I can't find nothin' on stimulatin' the economy. You know more about the Bible than me. What does Jesus say?"

"A very good question."

"I know it's in there somewhere, 'cause the Good Book's not gonna just leave us hangin' on important stuff like that."

"Perhaps to understand what Christ would say, we need to consider what Christ did."

"What?"

"Remember when he threw the money changers out of the temple?"

"Yep."

"Why did he do that?"

"Well..." Twofer said, scratching his stomach. "They say money carries bacterites. Maybe that's what he was worried about. Fatalistic diseases."

"Maybe. But think about what money changers do. They change the money of one country or denomination into something different—and in the process they take a little fee, a little tax, you might say."

"I guess."

"So what was Christ saying through his action?"

Twofer furrowed his brow and strained hard, activating a fart. Deep, deep in the dull eyes twin sparks began to flicker. "I got it! Christ was sayin' no to taxes! He hated taxes same as me."

"Shed any light on your current predicament?"

Twofer looked uncertain. "Maybe I should go for another tax cut?"

"Seems obvious, doesn't it? The first one wasn't big enough to get the job done."

The president's face already was relaxing. "I sure feel better, parson, when I know Christ is behind me."

24

CANDIDE was inside a cell, pinned to a steel table with thick steel bands. There were bands everywhere bands could be, even around his forehead and neck. He couldn't move much more than his eyes. A tall man wearing desert safari gear came to his cell door and looked in. Strangely, he had the face of Madmahn Badassi! Candide wasn't sure what to think.

"Don't let the mug fool you," said the voice of General Pangloss. "This is my temporary. The James Coburn is being detailed in Bethesda and should arrive in a week."

"Why do you look like Madmahn?"

"Turns out he's popular here in Pockistan. These were all they had in male, extra large." The general smiled Madmahn's toothy smile. "Didn't take my advice, did you?"

"I've been charged with collaboration. They say I'll get at least three firing squads."

"Before I spoke up for you, they were going to hang you twice, too."

Candide, silent, apparently wasn't feeling grateful.

"I pointed out that you, of all of us, actually made contact with Moolah al-Razir. If you hadn't got sidetracked screwing his harem, you could've brought back a nice trophy."

"Only one woman was involved, sir. And it's not called screwing when the partners respect one another."

"Lieutenant, even if you do escape the firing squads, the hangings, and the electric chair, you're going to spend the rest of your life glued to a steel table if you don't get with the program. Keep your feelings about this woman to yourself."

"Yes sir."

"Concentrate on your volunteer mission."

"Mission, sir?"

"The one I proposed to get your sorry ass out of the soup. Operation Supergoose II. You will enter Qroci air space, seek out Madmahn Badassi, and effect a decapitation of the leadership. This time you cannot fail. If you do, you end up back here with all present penalties in place—and no doubt many new ones."

"I appreciate your faith in me. I won't let you down."

"Any questions?"

"When you say 'decapitation of the leadership'…"

"They want his head in a box."

25

AFTER his release from custody, Lieutenant Candide found himself with a few free days in Peshawar. He used the opportunity to phone his dearly beloved some 43 times at all hours of the day and night. As luck would have it, he got her machine every time. Since Solange was a homebody, her absence was puzzling. Deprived of his loving support, had she become discouraged and retreated to Nebraska to sulk? But why hadn't she left a message on her machine? It bothered him.

A week later the baroness was still on Candide's mind as he rode in the belly of a stealth bomber. More accurately, both Solange *and* Delilah were on his mind—his bride to be and his best buddy. Two stunning women—yet what a difference! His thinking about them seemed much the same (he was concerned for their safety) but only one haunted his heart, making it ache like a pecan in a nutcracker. Inexplicably, the lady causing him cardiac distress was not in the least blonde.

As he stood up, his knees popped. From time to time they did that now and Ernie wasn't sure why. He did stretching exercises to loosen his powerful muscles then made his way forward into the cabin. The pilot, a major, pointed down excitedly. "Looky there, Goose. Anyone we know?" Spread out over the desert hardscrabble in fast advance, kicking up dust, were mobile units of the Plunderian Army's 101st Airborne. The lieutenant felt a surge of pride. Here were some of Plunderland's finest, hell-bent for Baghdad. Would they beat him to Madmahn, he wondered. Would they, instead of himself, relieve the cruel tyrant of his you-know-what?

Candide noticed the troops were bypassing a city of about 100,000 which lay below hills containing a huge reservoir. This recalled a scenario Pangloss had laid out while training him. Some of Plunderland's war planners feared that Madmahn Badassi, desperate to preserve his own hide, might blow up dams to create unmanageable human catastrophes as distractions. Why, Candide wondered, were no troops being deployed to secure the dam? Didn't the city and its inhabitants matter? I guess we'll do it later, the loyal soldier told himself. Before all else, Madmahn's genocidal fingers had to be slapped away from the chemical, biological, and nuclear triggers.

The stealth whispered on past the advancing troops. Candide was about to go aft to check out his equipment when something else on the desert floor caught his eye. The plane had begun to pass over an oil field, a huge one, with derricks and cricket pumps for miles on end. The field bustled with activity as a full division of regular army combat troops went about establishing what appeared to be permanent positions. Swarms of Navy Seabees were framing a vast complex of barracks. Earthmovers scooped trenches and raised berms. Supply roads were being asphalted and huge power generators installed. It seemed strange to Candide that so many fighting men were defending an oil field. Was oil more important to his government than protecting the people below the dam? He filed these matters away to think about when his mission was complete.

Soon they were passing over Baghdad—a spread-out metropolis burning with a hundred fires. The size of the city amazed Candide. It just went on and on. Eventually though it gave way to suburban farmland, then rocky brown desert again. The bomb doors of the stealth opened and a human cannonball dropped through. The compact package fell for a thousand meters then opened into a flying man. Operation Supergoose II was under way.

26

EVEN the bravest of hombres has his hour of weakness, his whistling stroll through the valley of the shadow of doubt. So it was with the leader of the free world, alone again in his sagebrush think tank, the six-guns on his hips ready to rock. The guns were ready, but not so the gunslinger, who appeared wilted and tentative. Without a single practice draw, Twofer slouched to the mirror and muttered:

> *"Buzz Twofer's been a baddy.*
> *Who's my daddy? Who's my daddy?"*

From deep in the mirror the image of Rod "Cowpoke" Raygun swam into view:

> *"Search no more, little buzzer.*
> *I'm the bloke who buzzed your mother."*

A bright smirk broke out on Twofer Jr.'s face as he dipped and swirled, drawing his weapons. Four revolvers blasted away at crash test dummies—labeled this time TAXES, SOCIAL SECURITY, MEDICARE, and LABOR UNIONS. The room filled with smoke.

"Heh heh heh heh," chuckled Twofer. "Wish all problems was that easy to solve. Don't you?"

Raygun smiled back but didn't answer.

"Oh, yeah. Gotta rhyme, don't I?"

Raygun smiled amiably.

Twofer furrowed his brow, looked at the ceiling and chewed his lip. Finally a couplet hatched:

> *"Mirror, mirror, hear my plea.*
> *How can I goose the economy?"*

Rod Raygun's lips moved again:

> *"Taxes are the sticky wicket.*
> *Another tax cut is the ticket."*

"Bingo!" said Twofer, smirking with assurance. "Me and you and Jesus all see eye to eye to eye."

27

LIEUTENANT Candide spent the afternoon of his first day in Qroc establishing base camp north of Baghdad. Knowing he might be in the area for some time, he built three underground rooms and 1.5 baths, laid tile floors, wired and plumbed. After a night of sound sleep on his new innerspring mattress, and with an all-bran breakfast under his belt, he overflew Madmahn Badassi National Highway into Baghdad. He took it slow, scanning the interior of every vehicle with X-ray telescopic vision—just in case he got lucky.

On the outskirts of the city he began to pass over sites of recent bombing. Some were military installations, obvious targets in any war, but others bothered him. The municipal waterworks had been heavily bombed. That was no military target. Both of Baghdad's sewage treatment plants had been bombed as well, and as a result the raw sewage of the city was pouring into the Tigris River. Every power station Candide saw had been turned into a blackened snarl of wire and blown transformers. Four big public markets lay flattened by bombs. In all these cases it was clear the destruction had been aimed not at Madmahn and his army, but rather at Baghdad's civilians.

Candide remembered a seminar from his last year at Westport: "Practical Theories of Warfare." It had been a bit of a yawn, but the little he'd learned began to make sense now. His teacher had explained the reasons for inflicting severe damage on civilian infrastructure. If you could destroy the enemy's society and commerce, you cut the legs out from under its military, forcing quick surrender. One case cited by Candide's teacher was that of General Sherman turning Georgia into a Yankee bonfire during Plunderland's Civil War. An example taken from the more recent past was the firebombing of Japan's cities, climaxing with the big bangs over Hiroshima and Nagasaki. Candide's prof then had turned to even newer techniques. "These days we do it much less crudely, of course, and out of public view. We bomb city waterworks and sewage treatment plants and let disease do the rest. You can kill a million people with a few well-placed conventional bombs. And if you think I'm just talking theory, go to Qroc and see for yourself. It's all part of our so-called economic sanctions."

Well, now Candide was seeing for himself. And he knew how the scheme played out. With no running water, people were forced to go to the rivers laced with common sewage. Typhoid, typhus, cholera, dysentery—take your pick, all hellish ways to die. Children were most vulnerable, but that wasn't really a problem because dead and dying children happened to be excellent sappers of parental morale.

Candide's teacher had done his best to be objective but couldn't help revealing that, to him, this "total war" school was barbaric. It seemed barbaric to Candide too, especially now that his nose was being rubbed in it. All day long, as he flew sectors searching the bunkers and catacombs of Baghdad for Madmahn Badassi, he was continually distracted by the hundreds of dead civilian bodies he saw, many mutilated in ways beyond the most insane imagination. It was with a heavy heart that the supersoldier flew north toward camp that evening.

As he neared his base, he saw bright lights to the west, glowing against the evening sky. Employing his binocular vision, he determined that a huge crowd had gathered. He flew over for a closer look. From several klicks away he could see it was a stage show of some kind, and then he made out a USO banner. Behind the stage were several luxury RVs. Bright flashing lights on the largest of these spelled out "Private Coach of the Baroness and Jellyroll."

Candide used the cover of falling darkness to glide down silently behind the crowd, alighting on a small rise near the camp perimeter. On stage, a comedian with a mike was teasing the massed Plunderian troops. "So tonight, lonesome campers, whether you're a soldier boy or soldier girl, we have a little eye candy for your solo sack time. Without further ado, let me introduce two of the brightest stars of the new millennium, fresh from their triumphant world tour—the Baroness Cunegoody and Jellyroll Conklin!" The comedian bowed as the curtain behind him rose to reveal five musicians flinging their hair in abandon as they pounded out the thunderous lead-in to their rousing anthem, "Short Man Blues."

OPERATION SUPERGOOSE 87

Solange was lead vocalist, backed by Webner "Jellyroll" Conklin on keyboards. The guitarist was Basque, the bassist Arapaho, and the drummer a Sikh from the rhythmic region of Punjab. Their music was a most innovative fusion of forlorn C&W and driving boogie-woogie. The complex melody enthralled Candide, and indeed everyone within earshot. The lyrics, flowing hauntingly from the Baroness's perfect lips, cut into the listener's heart with pitiless pain, leaving an invisible tattoo:

> *Always starin' at people's buckles,*
> *bearin' all the sneers and chuckles,*
> *we be livin' the short man blues,*
> *the short man blues...*

As the chorus built in intensity, Webner jumped up on his bench and danced a mad jig while tickling the ivories. A raw compelling sound poured from the gigantic speakers, weaving its magic upon the audience, enticing many to sing along:

> *For we be livin' the short man blues,*
> *the short man blues...*

Candide was boggled by the vast improvement in his fiancée's warbling style. Her voice had somehow acquired a smoky throatiness, a luxurious sad wisdom of life that suggested, without actually betraying, deep reservoirs of passion. Whizzers, he said to himself, she sure sounds sexy. The songs that followed were, if anything, even more captivating, and their variety hinted at the broad spectrum of talent possessed by these musical maestros. In "Givin' Jim His Dues" the tune and message were harsh and disquieting. Jellyroll's instrument moaned with oppression as the Baroness, in an icy soprano, expanded ironically on each nuance of smoldering rebellion:

> *Smile when you han' me that bale, my man,*
> *an' I'll be smilin' on your little woman...*

Candide's favorite though was the foot-tapper "Stand by Your Jellyroll," with its pure-as-moonshine back country melody fused to a sub-Saharan beat. After a few infectious bars and with Solange's encouragement, the whole audience rose and joined in. Candide sang along too, popping with pride for his girl. She'd pulled it off just like she always said she would—and she'd done it *her* way. Somehow she'd even found a place in her act for little Webner.

The wowed lieutenant, the thousands of happy soldiers relaxing, the sentries refusing to be left out of the fun—and all so caught up in the magic of the moment they neglected to notice the hundred thousand or so Qroci Republican Guard troops surrounding them and even now cutting through the concertina wire on the perimeter. Soon enemy soldiers were pouring onto base, the sounds of their ambush covered by joyous singers recommending fealty to a stuffed pastry.

A shot rang out. Then a burst from an automatic weapon, followed by more bursts. The Plunderian soldiers stopped singing as they realized they were under fire. They stampeded in all directions, looking for rifles, cover, or both. Enemy troops stormed the amphitheater, guns blazing as they mowed down the largely unarmed Plunderians.

Candide's first thought, naturally, was to rescue Solange. And he saw she was much in need of rescue. Three enemy officers were on stage—one of them a dead ringer for Madmahn Badassi, the other two closely resembling his murderous sons Olay and Parquet. The certified bad guys were skulking in kidnap formation toward the Baroness, who stood stunned and oblivious, microphone in hand, gawking at the panicked audience and the fighting.

Candide was not alone in noticing the threat to the Baroness.

Webner was advancing nimbly across the stage, whirling his mike at a ferocious clip on ten feet of cord. The height-challenged musician came in under Madmahn's line of sight (fixed on Solange's beautiful, gaping face), and thus the keyboard man was able to kneecap the Murderer of Baghdad with a mighty whack. Badassi's bellow of rage and pain burst over the sound system, echoing across the plains of Qroc even as his tall, pot-bellied body went down. Olay and Parquet tripped over their father's writhing corpus and fell on top of him.

Webner's silver mike flashed like a scimitar under the stage lights as he moved in to finish the job. Candide knew he had to act fast. The lieutenant threw his arms into rotation and took off at maximum thrust, accelerating like a Skud missile. He glimpsed something white below him an instant before he met his match in a terrific explosion and blinding flash of light. The unlucky soldier, mortal after all, fell to the uncaring sand and passed into oblivion.

28

"YOU'RE kidding," said Chain Dickey.

"Afraid not," said Secretary Minefield.

They were seated across a White House conference table from Parson Weed, who smiled cynically. "I'll bet it's true, because the man is...well, himself. He certainly is himself. Pennies of Joy, did you say?"

"Pennies of Joy, Pennies for Joy...something like that," said Minefield grinning.

Weed lifted a hand to his eyes and began to laugh. The others joined him. Soon they were roaring. The door opened and in ambled the leader of the Western World, swinging a rawhide briefcase, brow furrowed. "What's so funny?" asked Buzz Twofer II, glancing with a confused smirk from subordinate to subordinate. "Somebody cracked a good one. Let me in."

"I'm afraid we were having a little chuckle at the expense of former President Beavers," said Parson Weed smoothly. "Not worth your valuable time, sir."

Twofer looked a bit put out, but let it go, seating himself. "In that case, boys, let's get down to brass knuckles. What do you have for me?"

The three glanced at one other, nonplussed. The vice president spoke. "You were going to give us your ideas on economic stimulation today, sir. We're here to offer feedback."

"Of course. Just wanted to clarify that." As Twofer fiddled with the combination on his briefcase, the cover popped open and a car alarm sounded. A big apple and a blue baseball cap rested inside.

The president quickly closed the briefcase, cutting off the alarm. "I decided not to bring any handouts. It's all up here." He tapped a finger on his forehead.

"More secure that way, sir," said Minefield. "No paper trail."

Twofer nodded, serious. "Ready for the nitty-gritty?"

"We're ready."

"The main dish of my economic miracle is my new trillion-dollar tax cut. It's 'specially designed to give hard-earned dollars back to our deservin' citizens, jump start the economy, manufacture jobs, boost tax revenues and move us forward with robust confidence."

"Hear, hear!" shouted the VP.

"Fearless policy making," said the secretary of defense. "And they said it couldn't be done twice."

Parson Weed appeared lost in thought. "I'm not sure," he said. "I'm not sure I like it."

Twofer looked hurt. "What's wrong?"

"Well, if a trillion-dollar tax cut is good, why not two trillion to make twice as sure the economy gets stimulated?"

Twofer wrinkled his brow and worked his lips—mimicking a chimpanzee almost to perfection. "You're forgettin', Reverend Weed, I'm a fiskile conservatory. I got my finger in the wind and it tells me two trillion is simply too much. We might overstimulate the economy—and blow a gasket or somethin'."

"Didn't think of that," said Weed.

"You didn't," said the president, "but it's okay because you're not paid to. You're not the top banana."

"Sir," said Minefield, "isn't there more to your miracle? You said the tax cut was the main dish, but that implies side dishes, or maybe a dessert."

"Of course there's more. You didn't think I'd shot my wad, did you? There's also my Pennies of Joy campaign."

"Promising name," said Vice President Dickey.

"You see, my new trillion-dollar tax cut will cover the military expenses of the Qroc war. But our relief effort for the bombed-out, starvin' population will cost money too. Where's that gonna come from?"

"True," said Dickey. "It's not been budgeted."

"Durin' my speech I plan to ask all the children of Plunderland to give one penny a day to the children of Qroc. Accordin' to my raw figgers, if all our kids did that, then their kids would be fed. And besides, our little shavers would learn a valuable lesson: Moslems eat food just like we do—that is, if they have it."

"An idea with both vision and compassion, sir," said Parson Weed.

"And quite fiscally sound," added Clayton Minefield. "Won't cost the taxpayer a cent."

"Might even give our war on drugs a boost," said Dickey. "Because if our kids are strapped for relief payments, there's less scratch for a buzz."

29

CANDIDE woke in a field hospital with IV drips in his arm and bandages on his chest. He felt like he was floating in a dream world. The camouflage pattern on the tent above him rippled psychedelically in the desert breeze. Seated next to him was a smiling blonde female apparition.

"Welcome back to the living," the apparition remarked cheerfully, staring at him through thick lenses.

"Feels like I'm under water."

"That's the morphine, sir." She stood and saluted. "Corporal Babs Nerdette. I'll be your orderly during recuperation."

"Something white hit me. I think."

"The troops are still talking about it, sir. You shot off that hilltop like you'd been goosed by the great cosmic finger. You triggered one of our Patriot missiles."

"Baroness Cunegoody? Her butler?"

"Jellyroll was rescuing the Baroness when the Patriot blast knocked him down. After a terrible fight with Madmahn and his evil sons, Jellyroll was overpowered and tied up in his microphone cord. Those slimy bastards fled with Mr. Conklin and the Baroness in a jeep headed for Baghdad."

"He's taken them as human shields!" cried the lieutenant. "Maybe to his rape room!!!" He yanked the drips from his arm, threw off his sheet, and heard a gasp from the corporal. Realizing he was naked as a jaybird, the lieutenant quickly covered his legs, etc. "Sorry," he said.

"Not a problem, sir." The corporal's eyes were shining. "Things like that happen in war."

"Where are my clothes?"

"Classified information."

"Don't be ridiculous."

"My orders are to make sure you don't leave till you're well."

"Nothing really wrong with me. My many wounds are all superficial."

"You're not a doctor," said the corporal firmly. "Besides you're high as a kite."

Lieutenant Candide pulled his top sheet out from under the mattress and worked it around his body, tucking and tying. In mere seconds he was dressed in the manner of a Roman senator in sumo hot pants. He stood up on the bed, threw his arms into swift rotation and ascended, ripping through the top of the tent.

He flew south at 420 knots along the Badassi National Highway—X-raying all jeeps. He reasoned Madmahn would most likely take his hostages to some bunker deep beneath Baghdad, so, when he arrived over the Qroci capital, he focused his X-rays 100 meters underground, taxing though it was to stare through so much dirt. He began plumbing the urban bowels near city center and worked outward.

Early in the afternoon, beneath the Tigris and not far from a presidential palace, Candide thought he detected movement 82 meters down. He circled the spot, peering and probing. Yes, definitely something was moving deep under the riverbed, something human, a female judging by the curvy torso. The abbreviated movements suggested constraint. "It's Solange," he decided.

He executed a streaking dive into the Tigris, swam down through water spiked with sewage, and began burrowing into the river bottom like a bionic worm. At first he had it easy, digging through mud, then sandy dirt. Fifty meters down though he struck hard clay, which slowed him considerably. Twelve meters of clay, more dirt, then at 65 meters he hit poured concrete—and knew he'd found the bunker shell. He spun like a high-speed bit, tearing at the reinforced concrete with his fingernails. After boring in this manner for half an hour he broke through the bunker ceiling and poked his head into the chamber. He saw not the Baroness, but rather—surprise of surprises!—his buddy Delilah. She was strapped cruelly to a cement altar in her unmentionables and seemed to be either asleep or unconscious. The chamber was otherwise empty, except for two dozen suits of European armor, each holding some ghastly medieval weapon.

Candide dropped to the floor and walked to the altar where Delilah appeared to be coming around. She rolled her head from side to side in a lustrous pool of black hair as the lieutenant traced with fascination the exquisite line of her nose, the delicate neck, the collarbone so perfect, the brown pipe-stem arm that somehow threw rocks with the force of a grenade launcher. Now the big green eyes came open—oh, so full of expression! "Bumpkin," she screamed, "look out!" Reflected in the two loveliest peepers of the lieutenant's acquaintance was a huge spiked mace sweeping toward his reverently bowed head with lethal speed.

30

THE year is 1956 and the place is Texas, a football gridiron populated by young boys in uniform. The day is hot and so are the little butt kickers, who happen to all be white. Many a ruddy cheek glows inside many a sweaty helmet. The boys, being boys, could of course knock off, drink soda pop, unwind in the shade and make rude noises with their armpits—but no, actually they can't. Didn't you hear me say Texas? 1956? Football? The competition is cutthroat (in preparation for the Texas bidniss world), consequently nobody can knock off, nobody can acknowledge any weakness or bodily need, and no camaraderie can occur unless feigned to get an edge.

To make sure of all this, here comes the coach of the Richardson Horny Toads—gangling, boyish, phony in the manner of the glad-hander. He's a guy with a toothy grin and a handshake like a cricket pump, then a quick knife in your back some night when you're looped. He's an oilman and budding politician. He has a football in his hands and looks uncomfortable holding it, but here he is because this is what good dads do if they want to score big in life.

His son, named after him, has been pressured to try out for receiver. Always the poor kid is being pressured to do something or other, and now it's football, in an effort to wean him from his extended fascination with dolls and tea sets. The last place on earth Jr. wants to be is here on this grassy battlefield crawling with mean little chipmunks, but here he is—terrified of making an ass of himself.

"The pass reception is probably the easiest skill in football to master," the coach is saying in a loud, confident voice. "All you have to do is hold your hands up over your head, bring them together in a pincer motion to trap the incoming pigskin, then run like the blazes. Let me demonstrate." He tosses the ball to his son. "Put some pepper on it, Buzz."

Little Buzz Twofer works the awkward ball between his hands as his father lopes downfield in a high-kneed, long-legged gait, attention grabbing to say the least. Picture Ichabod Crane hotfooting it through a rattlesnake ranch. A rainbow wobbler is launched and Pop cuts under it, throwing up his arms. The ball beans him on the pate and bounces away in the grass. The team hoots and howls. Wherever Buzz Jr. turns, he sees ruddy faces berating his father. The elder Twofer elects to ignore this rampant disrespect. With forced jauntiness he scoops up the ball and trots back toward the team. He points to his son. "Okay, Buzz, you get the idea. Run out for one."

Buzz Jr.'s ungainly stride, too much like his father's to be believed, sets his teammates to snickering as the ball is thrown high and long. Jr.'s arms fly up. The football drops between them, bops him on the helmet and bounces away. Again the team howls. Even more than cheap shotting one another, these pint-size gridsters love mocking their fool coach and his wimpy offspring. When the hilarity dies, a cackle draws young Buzz's attention. It's a tall woman standing near the bleachers in a blue dress the size of a tent. Why, it's Goosey Twofer, his own mother. She shakes her head, points a thumb at the sod and redoubles her cackling.

The leader of mighty Plunderland woke from his nightmare and sat up in bed. He turned on his lamp to introduce more reality into his world and found he'd sweated through his Spiderman PJs. Next to him, fast asleep, lay his beautifious first lady. She wore a full-face sleep mask depicting Freddie Kruger. Looking at it, the president shivered. "Don't know why you insist on wearin' that damn thing to bed. Shrivels me up like a raisin."

31

CANDIDE regained consciousness lying facedown on the stone floor of a dank cell. He rose to his hands and knees, feeling strangely weak. Massive pain in his head was centered above his left ear and when he felt there he found blood congealed thickly in his hair. Fortunately, it seemed to be merely another scalp laceration. Slowly he stood up—amazed by his weakness. The cell door swung open and two big guards entered. They yanked him forward like a cloth doll and pushed him stumbling into the hallway.

He was shoved and slapped along a maze of corridors in what looked like a catacomb. Passing through an ancient wood door, the lieutenant and his escorts entered a new concrete hall and proceeded to a stainless steel door standing ajar. A guard kicked Candide in the butt, propelling him into a steamy room containing a gold hot tub. Seated in the tub with water to his chin and a cigar in his mouth was the most evil bad guy of contemporary times. Even brave Lieutenant Candide felt a little intimidated as he confronted, up close and personal, the famous snake-eye gaze of Madmahn Badassi. Without a thought to the needs of his guest, Badassi puffed on his cigar then took a sip of margarita. "How's it going, tough guy?" he sneered. The strongman, to Candide's complete consternation, spoke excellent English—with a slight lisp.

The lieutenant, swaying, pointed his finger angrily at the

murderous potentate. "I demand you release Ms. Delilah Jihad! Keeping her tied to that altar in her unmentionables is, well, unmentionable."

"Then don't mention it. Hardly matters anyway. We'll soon be sending her pretty little head back to Zionia in a box. And the same to all Zionian spies!"

Candide's heart clutched at the bloody threat to his darling cave pal, but he'd only begun protecting his women. "And what have you done with my fiancée, the Baroness Cunegoody?"

"I'm treating her with the courtesy and respect befitting the concubine who will soon become my fourteenth mistress. As to the little hothead they call Jellyroll, I've discovered he makes an excellent assistant butler. He's been assigned to dress the lower half of my body. I don't believe there's ever been a butler named Jellyroll. Has there been, do you think?"

"You're evil."

Badassi smiled so broadly it stretched his moustache. "Thanks."

"You're not even ashamed."

"The only thing to be ashamed of, lieutenant, is failure. Speaking of which, weren't you on a mission?"

Candide found himself at a loss for words. He brushed sand from his hastily constructed cotton crib suit, filthy with Tigris River loam and dried blood from his many wounds.

"Look at you. Even your own mother wouldn't claim you. Is this the man who was going to take away my head in a box?"

Candide wanted to grab Badassi by the neck and yank him out of his fancy bubble bath but lacked the strength to wipe his own brow. It occurred to him this new weakness wasn't accidental. "What have you done to me?" he demanded.

"You've been shot so full of estrogen it's punked you out. Another week and you'll have a rack most women would die for."

This low point in Candide's career as superhero thankfully did not drag him down into despair. On the contrary, the true Plunderian in him rose defiantly into his mouth as he began to lecture the errant foreigner. "I may be a failure, but you're a bully. Gosh, I'd hate to be a bully like you."

Badassi threw back his head and laughed, showing gold molars. "Good one, Lieutenant. You Plunderians, unprovoked, invade my sanction-wracked third world country with the most powerful war machine in history—and *I'm* the bully. Love that Plunderian righteousness."

"You were about to attack us with weapons of mass destruction."

"Ah, yes. My famous WMDs. The same ones nobody can find. Maybe they're invisible, like your stealth aircraft."

"We know you have them."

"Of course Qroc *had* weapons of mass destruction. And yes, Plunderland certainly knew about them because your people came here and built the factories that produced those weapons."

"Why would we do that?"

"So that my soldiers could defeat our enemy and yours—the Ayatollah Panatela and his Persian horde."

"Well, using WMDs against armed combatants is one thing. But you used WMDs against civilians. How evil!"

"Just imitating you guys."

"Liar!"

"Careful who you call names, Punky. Want a cigar tattoo on your gearshift knob?"

"I was merely pointing out that my country doesn't use weapons of mass destruction against civilians. Against civilians, we use kinder, more considerate weapons like missiles, rockets, artillery, napalm, cluster bombs, and white phosphorus."

Badassi grinned around his cigar. "Tell that to the Japanese."

Candide sensed he'd hit a dead end, debatewise. With Mastodon cunning, he shifted to character attack. "You don't really care about civilians."

"Never claimed to. It's you Plunderians who care. Right?"

"Oh, you think you know us, but you don't. You hate us so blindly you can't even *begin* to know us."

"Who knows you better than me? For many years your government and I were like two peas in a pod. Plunderland helped me gain power, kept me in power, sold me high-tech weapons and loaded me up with WMDs. Whenever I pulled some badass stunt, your leaders turned their pious faces away and pretended not to see. Really we were more than friends, your government and I. We were bosom buddies."

"I don't believe that for a minute. Being free ourselves, we bolster freedom and elected leaders—not tyrannical dictators."

"Puppets and puppet governments is what you bolster here in the Middle East."

"Poppycock!"

"Your leaders want to control world oil supply. The puppets are a means."

Candide suddenly recalled the Plunderian troops he'd seen occupying the Qroci oil field. But it tended to undermine his argument so he put it out of mind and focused on shifting blame. "Who are you to point fingers? You invaded little Qtip to steal her oil."

"Look at Qtip on a petroleum map some time. It's a tiny nation, but it sits on as much oil as we have in all of Qroc. *And* it blocks our access to the sea—like a cork in a bottle. A punk country like that was never meant to be."

"It came from somewhere."

"The Western powers that won the First World War created a lot of Qtips throughout the Middle East. Tiny, fake nations sitting on huge oil fields. And all these Frankenmidgets have conspired with the West ever since to keep oil cheap. In return, the West enriches the puppet leaders and protects them from their own angry populations and from badasses like me." Badassi rudely flicked his ash on Candide's bare foot then partook of margarita.

Candide tipped the ash off his foot. "You make Plunderland sound evil. But I know we're not."

"Your country is the only superpower right now. I think your leaders want things to stay that way."

"Maybe it's natural."

"It's even more natural for empires to fall, and when they do everyone gets hurt, not just the emperor. But you Plunderians are going to have to learn that all over again—because you're such arrogant *nincompoops!*" Madmahn clapped his hands and the guards entered and seized Candide. The dictator blew a smoke ring at the lieutenant. "Once we've socked you in a triple-D bra, we'll turn you out in Abu Ghraib Prison. Our most brutal criminals will take their fill of you, then your chatterbox will be detached and mailed back to your president wrapped like a Christmas ham." Badassi flipped his hand and the guards whisked Candide from the room.

The cruel despot climbed from his gold hot tub and wrapped a towel around his waist. He walked, dripping, to a full-length mirror and spoke:

> *"Mirror, mirror on the wall*
> *who's the baddest ass of all?"*

In the reflective surface appeared a burly, graying man with a thick salt-and-pepper mustache. It was the former leader of the Soviet Confederation, Joseph Saltine. Saltine smiled, then his lips began to move:

> *"You're the baddest, Madmahn Badassi,*
> *Badder than Buzz Twofer's posse."*

These two world leaders so often vilified—one living, one dead—regarded each other with frank admiration.

32

BACK in his primitive, smelly cell Lieutenant Candide attempted to eat supper. The entree, a large heavy biscuit, was so stale he could barely score it with his teeth. He tried breaking it against the stone floor and failed. He was soaking it in water to try and soften it a little when his guards entered, one with a big hypodermic. They forced him to his cot and yanked down his pants. Candide struggled until he felt the needle go in. As the hormone entered—it took a full two minutes—the guards talked together in their language. One said something in a mocking voice and they laughed. When they were gone, Candide checked his biscuit. Still too hard to eat.

At lights out, Candide removed his makeshift clothing in preparation for bed. He was chagrined to see in the dim light, beneath his nipples, pink fleshy mounds. Already he had the chest of a teeny-bopper. His chagrin doubled when he noticed two brown eyes peeping through his food slot. He recognized the bushy eyebrows percolating with excitement as those of the larger, more brutish of his guards.

The lieutenant slept with one eye open, which is to say he slept not at all, because nobody ever slept with one eye open. In the early morning hours he heard a key inserted, very quietly. His cell door swung open. With a sick twist in his gut, the neutered super-soldier readied himself for a fight he didn't feel up to. His one chance he believed was to punch his attacker in the temple hard enough to put him down. Coiled for this purpose, he waited. The guard, advancing on tiptoe, looked very large in the dark.

A sound came from the hallway—*kapock!*—followed by a thud. Candide's attacker ceased his advance and stepped back to the cell door. He stuck his head out to see what was happening. The strange sound—*kapock!*—was repeated as the guard's hair flew sideways and his body dropped to the floor, inert. A nimble figure stepped over the fallen hulk while Candide rose from his cot.

"Let's go, bumpkin," said a voice that sent a thrill straight up the lieutenant's spine.

"Delilah!"

"Shhh. Can you carry these?" She handed him a sack of prison biscuits.

He saw another biscuit in her right hand, ready to fire. Naturally, the lieutenant was all for swift departure but something nagged in the back of his mind, something that needed doing. Ah yes: "We must rescue the Baroness Cunegoody and her butler and take them with us."

"Forget it. They escaped an hour ago, creating such a hubbub I decided we should go too. My guards couldn't stop talking about it. Everything's in confusion."

"What happened?"

"This amazing man they call the Jellyroll. With one bold move he accomplished what an army couldn't, writing a new chapter in the history of Qroc."

"What did he do?"

"According to my guards, Madmahn Badassi picked this night of the full moon to induct the Baroness Cunegoody into his harem—if you catch my drift. He ordered Jellyroll to lay out his wedding silks. The devious servant took the opportunity to steep the dictator's shorts in flame accelerant. Later, when the dipped skivvies were in place, Jellyroll struck a match and lit up Madmahn like a birthday cake. The Lion of Baghdad, roaring in agony, was wheeled away to the bunker infirmary with severe burns on his most sensitive parts."

"Serves him right."

"We'd better get moving."

Candide, dressed as a jail guard, escorted Delilah, with hands tied behind her back, through the long hallways of the bunker. Her comment about confusion proved accurate. The whole underground society was like an anthill stirred with a stick. People hurried this way and that, eyes wide with panic, not seeing much of anything. The escaping pair ascended to the bunker mouth and exited through a manhole onto a back street in a poor residential neighborhood. All the lights were out everywhere, but the moon was shining through heavy smoke, giving a little illumination. They stepped carefully through rubble as they made their way along an avenue between apartment buildings. In time they came upon a donkey and cart parked conveniently at a hitching post and commandeered this rude conveyance.

Their plan was to get as far from Baghdad as possible under cover of night. Luckily they encountered almost no traffic on the narrow old highway they chose. Ten kilometers or so south of the city they entered a village and began hearing screams. As the cart rolled forward, the high-pitched shrieks got louder. Soon the chilling sounds came from beside them—where stood a small brick police station. Candide, looking worried, halted the donkey.

"Let's go, bumpkin," said Delilah. "None of our business."

"I'd know those screams anywhere," stated Candide firmly.

"Oy! He knows them." She threw up her hands.

"That's one of my superior officers. The man who taught me desert warfare A to Z."

"Too bad he didn't know how to keep from getting caught."

"I must try to help him."

"If he's your comrade and you have to—that I understand. Let's see what's possible."

They peeked into the station through an open window. Three policemen were torturing General Pangloss with a hand-cranked generator hooked up to his gonads. One Qroci cop spat out questions in poor English and, whatever Pangloss answered, a second cop cranked the generator with enthusiasm and a big grin. A third cop cradled a Kalashnikov as he watched the fun.

"Bumpkin, that man they're shocking is a Plunderian movie star, isn't he?"

"That's a disguise." Horrific screams poured again from the general. "We've got to stop this!"

"I can take out the guard," said Delilah. "Can you get his weapon?"

"Leave it to me."

They entered through a window in the building rear. Using General Pangloss's shrieks as cover, they stole into position behind a doorway next to the torture chamber. When they rushed, Candide went first. Delilah fired a biscuit over his shoulder. It cracked into the gunman's forehead, snockering him. The lieutenant dove for the released assault rifle, snatched it up and trained it on the torturers. They looked quite surprised.

"Good show, Goose," exclaimed General Pangloss. "Bully good show."

"Thank Delilah too. Couldn't have done it without her." Candide turned, smiling—but she was gone. "That's funny. She was right behind me."

"The little viper knows I can expose her," said the general.

Candide made one of the torturers untie his commander. Between poor Pangloss's legs was an extensive blackened area burned down to the bone. To distract his friend and himself from the hideous wound, the lieutenant posed a question that was troubling him. "You claim that Delilah's a spy for Shrinkistan. And Madmahn Badassi says she's a spy for Zionia. Who's right?"

"Who's right—me or Madmahn Badassi? For God's sake, soldier, listen to yourself. Consorting with that wench has you talking treason again."

33

PARSON Rupert Weed was on stage with a mike speaking to a large audience and three television cameras. He paced back and forth, forehead shining with perspiration, free arm gesticulating freely. "For who can it profit to win the worldly race, yet lose the kingdom of heaven? On the eve of Armageddon, why be shortsighted? Soon you'll be receiving your tax cut sent by President Twofer. Have you thought about how you'll spend it? A Reno weekend for you and the mate? An exotic pet?

"Carefully considered, such are temporary pleasures. We know in our hearts we should be seeking more permanent attainments, ways to improve ourselves as people, thus easing our passage into the Eternal Kingdom. That's why Parson Weed and the Sunshine Network are offering, for a limited time, a thirty percent discount on a Weed Prayer Direct to God. Want to boost your magnetism at church socials by kayoing that bad breath? Does carcinoma hamper your verve? Let God zap your bummer with His wondrous power. Your Prayer by Weed comes with a lifelong guarantee and a certificate of authenticity. Our online tracking system allows you to follow your message in real time upward through the hierarchy of angels to the Lord Himself. And because each prayer is individually sprinkled with cybernetic holy oil, not one has been lost in transit or hijacked by the Devil."

The parson crossed the stage to a young man in a wheelchair, now spotlighted. The thin little fellow looked lost inside his cheap brown suit. He looked sad and hungry too. "Folks, meet Little Jimmy Jeeters. Mr. Jeeters was an aspiring tap dancer when he was mowed down by an MTA bus in Van Nuys, fracturing his spine in twenty-seven places, paralyzing him below the hairline." Parson Weed reached forth his arm dramatically and seized Jimmy's brow. "Lord, clasp this deserving young man to your universal soul and heal his affliction. Put him back on his dancing feet so he can tap out a tribute to your infinite mercy. Heal! *Heal*!!" As the parson removed his hand, Little Jimmy rose miraculously from the wheelchair and his taps began clicking on the stage. He swung his arms and grinned. Dipping and whirling, tears of joy streaming down his face, Little Jimmy tapped like a machine gun, circling Parson Weed as a crawl appeared low on the screen giving an 800 number for prayer signup. The TV went dead.

Lieutenant Candide dropped the remote beside him on his cell bunk. He was incarcerated in the army base stockade at Pearl Harbor. Enough time had passed that his chest had lost its feminine developments, and in part to celebrate his resurrected masculinity he now wore a handsome blond goatee. Not all was well with him though. He faced multiple death sentences again. In part to take his mind off that, he picked up a book entitled *A History of South Vietland, 1900–1975*, opened and began to read.

A whirring became audible. Soon an automated wheelchair came into view bearing General Pangloss in a new safari outfit. A confident smile lit up the charismatic James Coburn mug. "How's it going, soldier?"

"As well as can be expected, sir," said Candide. "Getting some reading done."

"Admit it. You're beating your meat and going stir crazy. What's that on your face?"

"A beard, sir."

"Enchanting. I did a pro in Amsterdam who had one just like it—between her legs. And oh my was she proud of it."

"When did you get out of the hospital?"

"I'm still in the hospital but the end is near. My integrated package arrives from Bethesda late this week. After they hook it up there'll be some therapy, then I'm on my own."

"What kind of, uhh, package did you choose?"

"Extra large, high speed. More bang for the buck."

"Will you be able to feel anything?"

"No. But as a man gets older, he comes to understand it's not how much pleasure he gets. It's how much he gives."

OPERATION SUPERGOOSE 105

"Nice philosophy."

"I didn't come here to discuss my love life. I'm here to spring you." He frowned at Candide. "Hopefully."

"Yeah?"

"You can fly again, can't you?"

"Be able to soon. Why?"

"Because, despite all the commie-terrorist propaganda you spouted at your debriefing, I've found a way for you to prove you're a patriot after all."

"How?"

"By demonstrating heroic commitment to the national cause."

"I need specifics."

"As you know, we invaded Qroc in order to destroy their biological, chemical, and nuclear weapons."

"That's what we claimed. Now it looks like there were no weapons."

"Damn it, soldier, we know there were weapons! We know there *are* weapons. But the sneaky Qrocis have hidden them so well we can't find them."

"You want me to find them?"

The general was silent for a time. "Not exactly."

"What then?"

"We want you to fly them in."

"You want me to sneak WMDs into Qroc?"

"Just a boxcar of nerve gas, a silo of anthrax and three briefcase thermonukes. Enough so's we can nail them good."

"No thanks."

"And why not?"

"Because that would be an idiotic way to serve my country," Candide said to his own surprise.

"You ungrateful little shit! It's the goddamn best way to serve your country. The men you will be helping are true patriots with unblemished reputations. They are at the highest levels of government. They'd be *very* inclined to help someone who helped them."

"The highest levels of government? Sounds like you mean the president."

"All he wants is proof you love the fatherland. His generosity will surprise you."

"And Secretary Minefield?"

"There isn't much he wouldn't do for a loyal army man—like you used to be."

"General, that ignorant bumpkin I used to be is no more. I'm not going to bring you any heads in a box, and I'm not going to plant any WMDs."

"You've become a terrorist, haven't you, Candide? That little Shrinkistanian whore has you in some kind of Arabian peter lock. She's turned you against your country and the men who run it."

"My country and the men who run it are two very different things."

"I truly pity you—a trooper with so much promise—and now you're going to submarine your own career. Your life, for that matter. Why did I ever waste time on you?" The general did an abrupt about-face in his wheelchair and whirred away at full power, not looking back at his former protégé.

Candide shrugged and picked up his book.

34

NO president in the history of Plunderland ever lusted after downtime more fiercely than Buzz Twofer II. He was thus in fine spirits as he strutted the barnyard of a Maryland milk farm, sucking in balmy spring air and sashaying around fresh cow pies. He approached and entered a big barn and strutted forward on straw. In the shadowy interior, he saw a farmer behind a cow, milking. Clearly audible was the pish, pish, pish of the nourishing liquid you'd better not be without. "Howdy!" said Twofer to the rustic.

The brim of the farmer's straw hat rose to reveal the friendly supersized face of Willy Beavers, former president of Plunderland. "Hi, Buzz. I'd shake your hand but I got a good rhythm going."

Twofer looked taken aback. "I'm positively scandalated that a deposed president of our rich land hasta milk cows in retirement!"

"Naw, Buzz, this is just to relax. Moneywise, I bop with you fat cats now. Got my twelve million dollar book deal to tell how I shot up the Oval Office with my pocket rocket. Rake in one hundred grand per speech. Directorships by the dozen, often at companies that financed my political campaigns. Consulting jobs. And, for a capper, I'm negotiating with the makers of Vigorim for a billion-dollar ad campaign. *Man* do they ever want me to stand up for their product!"

"Money's wonderful stuff," Twofer said with a smirk. "Wouldn't be without it. But I got somethin' money can't buy. An eighty-three percent approval rating."

"That why you came? To gloat over a temporary bump you got out of starting two wars?"

"Simply statin' a plain ordinary fact. A president can't get more popular than me."

"Seems like I recall your dad saying something like that right before his tires went flat. Voters tend to forget about military victories when the economy tanks."

"The economy again. Why do people keep harpin' on that?"

"It's important to them."

"You pulled the plug on the economy. Right before you left office it was fine. Then I step in and boom it falls over like a dead cow. What did you do to screw it up for me?"

"Buzz, you've been president almost three years. At some point don't you have to take responsibility?"

"I'm doin' all I can. My tax cuts and my attacks on other countries should have the economy hummin' like two-bit hooker, but it just lays there."

"Maybe the tax cuts and invasions aren't helping."

"They're helpin'. We know they are."

"You *think* they are. You can't know."

"We do too know because God says so."

The rush of milk against the pail ceased. "Pardon me?"

"God's behind everything we do. Parson Weed is our contact man. The Lord comes to him in visions and the parson, who is awful smart, memorizes every word. Bet you never thought of puttin' God on your team, did you? Heh heh heh heh heh." Smirking,

Twofer kicked at the straw, then discovered something stuck to the toe of his shoe. He tried to shake it off, unsuccessfully. He bent down, picked up some straw and wiped it off.

Beavers began milking again. "How can you be so sure God talks to Weed?"

"The parson says so."

Beavers looked skeptical. "I see."

"Men of honor take each other at their word. And that's because we're honorable men. But I guess you wouldn't know about that."

"Look, Buzz, you came here to pump me about the economy. Think I'm going to help if you insult me?"

Twofer worked his lips and glanced around the barn. "Nice barn you got here."

"Belongs to a buddy."

"Nice overalls."

"Appreciate you saying so, Buzz. I favor these because just two buttons opens you up front or back." He winked. "Man, if I'd had these in the White House, I'd never have got caught with my pants down."

Buzz Twofer's mind was elsewhere. "When you say my tax cuts aren't workin'. Well, heck, what's wrong with 'em? Not that I agree."

"I don't know what God would say, but to me they're creating a time bomb of debt. At the end of my administration we were running a budget surplus and using it to bankroll Medicare and Social Security for the retirement of the baby boomers. Now all that's come apart. The way you've got it set up, when the boomers retire we'll have to hand them IOUs. Stuff like that spooks investors."

"If I hadn't cut taxes, you Jackasses would have just spent all that money. Spend, spend, spend—it's your answer to everythin'."

"Sometimes spending *is* the answer; sometimes it isn't. You can't be so one sided, Buzz. You have to remember that the president represents *all* the people. He has to think for everybody, then kind of blend the ideas together and come up with a mix that pleases most of the voters. It's called triangulation."

"I suckered in enough voters to get myself elected, didn't I?"

"No, you didn't. You were appointed by the Supreme Court. But I got elected the old-fashioned way. And I did it through triangulation."

"How's it work?"

"All right. Say, like me, you got the Plunderian worker behind you and trade unions too, and those folks give you money. As we know the unions and the workers believe in keeping good jobs here in Plunderland, for obvious reasons. You with me?"

"So far."

"Now I also get campaign money from big corporations that want to ship all their production jobs overseas, so they can pay lower wages and make bigger profits. And these corporations give me *huge* contributions, a lot more than the blue-collar folks. So what do I do?"

"What?"

"I triangulate. I cooperate with congress to pass laws allowing our companies to ship their good-paying jobs overseas. Then I tell the workers how lucky they are that we have more jobs in this country all the time. I don't need to mention that nearly all the new jobs are part time or minimum wage."

A smile lit Buzz Twofer's face. "That's slicker than shit."

"To be fair, Buzz, you've been doing the same thing. You just didn't know it."

"Slick Willy they call you. Now I see why."

"I could go on and on. I triangulated on welfare, I triangulated on the environment, and I triangulated on world peace. I triangulated on so many things I got elected twice and left the members of my Jackass Party with absolutely no sense of what they stand for except triangulation."

"Don't forget your love triangles," said Buzz Twofer, smirking. He drew himself up straight and raised his hand in the posture of a man taking an oath. "I swear on a truckload of Bibles I did not poke that woman."

"Leave it alone, Buzz. You can't speak for those of us burdened with sexual charisma. Which reminds me. Time to unhook the milking machine." Beavers reached inside his overalls and a soggy pop was heard.

"Machine? I thought you was milkin' by hand."

"I'm doing the cow by hand. The machine's for me." He held up a small flask half filled with white liquid. "My wife and I finally agree on how much fun I can have."

Twofer's brow furrowed. "What's one of them suckers cost?"

35

SQUIP, squip, squip, squip—the peculiar sound caught Candide's attention once again. Though he'd had many days to get used to it, it still drove him up the wall. The noise was coming from his attorney, Captain Sparsby, seated next to him nervously sucking the business end of a blue ballpoint pen. This habit probably helped the captain relax. It also explained why his lower lip was stained blue.

Weeks earlier, during Sparsby's first visit to see Candide, the attorney had projected calm confidence and professionalism throughout their interview. Oddly though, he'd made no reference whatsoever to his custom-colored lip (just as though it wasn't there) and this bothered Candide greatly. Was the captain nuts, he wondered, or just totally devoid of social sense? Either way he inspired no confidence. The supersoldier immediately requested a change of counsel through the stockade administration and was refused. A day after the refusal, Sparsby visited again, this time with trembling hands and shattered aplomb. He leveled with Candide, explaining that a few months earlier, after losing his eighty-seventh straight JAG case, he'd been busted back to latrine duty. The opportunity to defend Candide, sent his way by a friend, represented his ticket out of the crappers.

Sparsby actually got down on his knees and begged with clasped hands. "Just give me a shot, pal. Who's more desperate than me to win this one? I'll come through like gangbusters. Swear to God."

Did Candide have a choice? It was Sparsby or no counsel at all, so he accepted the captain as his attorney and for the first time in his life experienced having his shoes kissed. Ever since that day, he'd watched his legal beagle sleep through depositions, make stuttering confused objections, kiss up to the tribunal, kiss up to the witnesses, kiss up to the prosecution, apologize if challenged by anyone, and dependably through it all *suck that damn pen!* True, there were good reasons for Sparsby to feel pressure. The members of the tribunal were impressive, intimidating even, being the uppermost tier of the military feeding chain: Secretary of Defense Clayton Minefield; Chairman of the Joint Chiefs, Melvin "Brick" Gracy; and Commander of the Army, Jerry "Swamprat" Beanway. With such high-powered judges, Candide needed a strong and vigorous defense to stand a chance. Instead Sparsby had whipped out one all-purpose argument for every occasion—namely, that his client was dumb as tree sap, therefore easily duped. Candide suspected everyone else was as sick of hearing this as he was.

The trial was over except for the reading of the verdict, and now Secretary Minefield rose for that. He gave the defendant a look of extreme contempt and began. "Lieutenant Ernest Lafitte Candide, it is the unanimous finding of this tribunal that you did willingly collaborate with enemy spy Delilah Jihad, compromising your country's military secrets in time of war and in a war zone. By your own admission, you undertook sexual relations with Ms. Jihad the moment you met her, thereby falling into her snare. During subsequent trysts she nibbled your ear relentlessly, plying your sex-crazed brain with terrorist propaganda until you were thoroughly brainwashed. Once she had you in her power, she pumped you freely for state secrets, troop positions, and much else. With your mind up her skirt, you wantonly betrayed the land of your birth."

The very mention of Delilah aroused in the ardent young soldier a rush of poignant memories: their single act of intimacy seared into his brain with the force of a blowtorch; the thrilling cave bear episode; their flight from Baghdad culminating in the daring rescue of Pangloss; and above all, Delilah's lessons in how to think. Where was she now, he wondered. What she was doing? Was she safe? Her face hovered before him like a will-o'-the-wisp, smiling the smile that tumbled his heart. He could almost hear her call out to him: "Bumpkin, pay attention! They want to shoot you full of holes."

This imaginary warning pricked Candide's daydream. He reopened his ears to the cutting tones of Clayton Minefield, who had arrived at the most absurd of the charges. "And thus, with malice aforethought, you did on two separate occasions hesitate to intervene in the torture of your superior officer. You watched as his face was pared away and his manhood fried to a cinder. No tribunal member—or anyone with a heart—will ever understand how you could twiddle on the sidelines, unmoved by the anguished but manly appeals of your comrade in arms. Through callous delay, you conspired indirectly in his torture."

Candide was sickened by the general's betrayal, hard to fathom given that he'd saved Pangloss's life twice. Add to that Captain Sparsby's stunning incompetence *and* the obvious bias of the tribunal (who'd, in effect, joined the prosecution in railroading him)—together these warred severely with the young man's notion of Plunderian justice. Surely even kangaroos got fairer trials. Candide felt anger, yes, but deeper down, beneath it, an almost bottomless despair. Something had happened to his country since the attack on Screaming Eagle Flagworks. The rule of law had been braided into a noose to string up anyone his government chose to label "traitor." His own traitorous act had apparently been to tell the truth.

Candide heard Minefield say, "The prisoner will rise." He stood, mechanically, in the posture of a soldier, shoulders back, chest out. "For your grave infractions against the military code, it is the unanimous decision of this tribunal that you be put to death by firing squad. We further order that you be stripped of rank and discharged from the Plunderian Army with maximum dishonor." Minefield walked to the defense table and ripped off Candide's insignia, theater ribbons, stripes and bars. When the shirt was clean of decorations and somewhat tattered, the secretary averted his eyes from the defendant and spoke to him one last time. "*Mr.* Candide, I now remand you over to the Department of Justice for sentencing on civil charges. Be seated."

Candide sat down, wondering what the heck was going on. Sparsby had told him Attorney General Zombus would be in court to witness the sentencing, but there'd been no mention of new charges. Did these mean more punishments? What punishments could you add to a firing squad?

Zombus, seated at a table with Justice Department staffers, slowly stood up. He shuffled papers and cleared his throat. "The defendant will rise." Candide did so. "Ernest Lafitte Candide, the violations of military law you have been convicted of carry civilian penalties as well under the Patriot Act of 2001. In the perpetration of your battlefield crimes, you did on many occasions give material support to terrorists, which the act specifically forbids. Therefore, by the authority of my office, I hereby strip you of Plunderian citizenship and of all rights pertaining thereto. Henceforth you will be a man without a country and without human rights. You will be confined at Camp Zircon in Guantanamo Bay until such time as the Army chooses to execute you. And may the Lord have mercy on your wicked soul. Be seated."

Candide sat, discouraged. He tried to focus on the one positive he saw. Although he'd lost his service commission, his income, his citizenship, his rights and his freedom, at least he wouldn't have to rot in Guantanamo for long—because they were going to shoot him soon.

Then a question arose. Why Guantanamo? Gitmo was for interrogation, not execution. Why send him there? It just didn't make sense.

36

BUZZ Twofer was hard at work at his desk in the Oval Office trying to stack three Diet Poopsie cans on a round paperweight, quite a challenge as you may know. There was a knock. "It's open," sang out the pres, "and so's your fly." Chain Dickey entered with a sheet of paper and the president looked up at him. "Chainman, wassup?"

"Sir, I'm here to present the findings of the Commission on the Plunderian Infrastructure."

"The who?"

"The committee appointed to determine the condition of our

country's permanent assets. My staff boiled down the commission's report to that six-page summary I brought you last week—"

"—Oh yeah, but it was too wordy," said Twofer, cutting to the chase. "Important stuff like that belongs in a paragraph so's I can linger myself on the grist instead of readin', readin', readin'."

"Would you like to read the paragraph, sir, or should I read it to you?"

Twofer waved his hand magnanimously. "You read and I'll linger."

The VP took a chair and began. "The commission finds that our interstate highways, after decades of heavy use, are breaking down. Most secondary roads need repair, as do many bridges, water systems, sewers and schools. Hundreds of the nation's older reservoirs are beginning to fail—a threat to both life and property. Dozens of major airports require expansion to remain safe. In large parts of the West the water supply is running out for both people and farming. And inadequate electrical generation is driving up prices, bankrupting small businesses and leaving many poor without power. In short, the infrastructure of Plunderland is crumbling, and at an accelerating pace. Bottom line—unless something is done soon, severe economic and physical catastrophes can be expected."

"Good report. Very frank."

"The commission is terribly alarmed and they wanted me to communicate that clearly and forcefully."

"What do you think we should do?"

"Well, first we should consider the source," said the vice president. "President Beavers appointed the commission."

"Bunch of liberals and Chicken Littles are they?"

"That would be my assessment."

"Any right-wing, born-again Christians among 'em?" asked the president.

"Not that I know."

"Well, then naturally this interfructure thing has 'em peein' their pants. They got no faith in the good Lord. Us faithful ones trust in Him to watch over the interfructure. Chain, as you know, if our bridges need fixin', He'll fix 'em. And if folks need electrical juice,

He'll shoot us down some lightnin' or somethin'. No way He's going to let his chosen people go without. Hell no."

"How should we respond to the report?"

"Well, doggone it, let's wear our faith proudly on our sleeves. *Cut fundin'* for bridges, airports, highways and all them other things. Then God will have to step in sooner—savin' us billions."

"If I may be blunt, sir. That's the sort of bold, right-lobe thinking you're known for far and wide."

Twofer turned in his chair and looked out the window. He adopted a pose resembling George Washington on his horse. "It comes from my faith, Chain. My faith in the Big Fella upstairs—and my faith in my ownself."

"Amen."

37

AFTER his first full day at Camp Zircon Candide was still in the dark about many things, but did understand why he'd been sent to a facility for interrogation. Those who had convicted him, it appeared, wanted him to sign a confession to all the crimes he'd been convicted of, and the rules at Camp Zircon permitted a wider array of persuasive techniques than was available almost anywhere else. Some of these techniques involved pain. Others humiliation. In the aggregate, they were designed to break a man.

It began when Candide debarked at Gitmo airstrip. He had to walk a gauntlet of Plunderian Army troops as they cussed him and urinated on his legs. At Camp Zircon the four guards who escorted him to his cell threw a housewarming party by jumping him and beating him brutally. Candide didn't fight back, but did call on his superpowers to help him absorb the blows. In time he pretended to lose consciousness. The guards manacled his hands behind his knees and left him contorted on the cell floor.

In the middle of the night he awoke to find himself being feasted on by mosquitoes and ants. Rolling to change position, he was stung on the arm by a scorpion. For 18 hours straight he suffered a posture that became more and more excruciating. His back burned, his hands throbbed and his wrists were chaffed raw. He was sorely tempted to break the cuffs, but knew it would be a bad idea.

This was his welcome. Soon his days took on a routine. Up at six for a breakfast of rotten fruit. Six-thirty to ten-thirty, torture by water boarding—meaning he was strapped to a board and suffocated with a wet cloth again and again, but not quite frequently enough to stop his heart. Candide was able to lessen the effects of this torture considerably by breathing through his ears, one of his minor superpowers. At ten-thirty, he got a break of sorts as they sat him down at a table with a copy of his confession and a pen. Eleven to one, more water boarding, followed by a lunch of foul porridge served in a dirty bowl. Hooding from two till seven. For that a three-foot-tall black plastic cone was placed on his head, weighing him down, cutting off his air and wrapping him in a rancid stench that made him want to throw up. For Candide, who hated close confinement, this torture was the worst—and his special powers helped not at all. The high point of his day came when the hood was pulled off in the evening and he was taken back to his cell for his daily beating, then chained into the pretzel of the night. Strobe lights and loud rock music had been added to his cell to help him sleep. Eventually he learned to.

After three months of this, Candide felt he was handling it not so badly. Then one morning he woke to find his cellmate, Kamal, suspended from the top of their cage. Kamal had woven strips torn from his prison blanket into a rope. Taking him down, Candide for the first time felt desperation clutch. When his friend's body had been bagged and carried away, the ex-soldier sat dejected on his cot, considering his own bleak future. Suicide, somehow, was beginning to make sense. Why was he preserving his hide? So the government could take it?

Deep in his sullen funk, Candide noticed a man in a dark blue suit coming his way. The guy was sixty or so, tall and thin with a vaguely familiar face. Finally it clicked who he was—Plunderland's premier defense attorney and social activist. Wonder of wonders, the lawyer who'd never lost a case seemed to be stopping at

Candide's cell. "How you doing, Ernie?" the flaming liberal asked through the wire. He managed to smile and look concerned at the same time.

Candide, suspicious of the familiarity, especially under the circumstances, stared coldly. "Been a bad day," he said.

"Could be looking up. I've got a writ for your release."

Candide stood and walked over. "Nathan Rader, right? How'd you find out I'm here? That's supposed to be secret."

"I'm Arab-Plunderian, so I've been keeping a close eye on who gets shipped here. I help when I can."

"I'm not Arab-Plunderian."

"No, but your case has big implications. The government violated six amendments to the Constitution in railroading you. We'd like to use that to dismantle this fascist court system they've set up."

"But my execution…"

"Can't happen. The army brass forgot something in their stampede to punish you."

"Yeah?"

"They can't execute civilians. And you've been discharged."

Candide had to laugh. He was feeling lighter at heart all the time. "Does this mean I'm free? What about my citizenship?"

"You're free for now. And the Ninth Circuit Court of Appeals has decided your citizenship can't be taken away without a civilian trial. But we expect Attorney General Zombus to charge you with treason soon."

"I see," said Candide, somewhat deflated.

"There's something else, Ernie. When you go stateside it won't be easy. The media will dog your every move."

"The media?"

"Yes, and I mean the world media. You're the biggest story on the planet right now."

38

"THE biggest story on the planet" expected journalists at Miami International, but none did he see. Nashville was another matter. As his descending plane passed over the interstate he saw dozens of news vans with their rooftop transmitters in the bumper-to-bumper traffic. And the gate area was packed. Cameras flashed as questions peppered the returning prodigal.

"Mr. Candide, what secrets did you divulge to Madmahn Badassi to save your skin?"

"How does it feel to sell out your motherland?"

"Is it true you infiltrated Moolah al-Razir's harem to seduce archspy Delilah Jihad?"

"What does it feel like having sex with sexy Delilah?"

"During your sexcapades, did you witness any of Delilah's murders?"

Candide, reeling from the assault, held up his arm to block the flashes and made his way quickly through the feeding frenzy. He exited the terminal and climbed into a cab, hoping for a little peace. The cabbie glared at him with hostility in the rearview mirror. "Where to, sucker?" As the taxi jerked away from the curb and joined traffic, a flock of news helicopters rose from a nearby parking lot and began to pursue. Candide could hear the choppers beating the air above them all the way to Murfreesboro.

After paying for his ride, the ex-soldier trotted across his front yard through another gauntlet of blinding flashes and probing questions. On his porch, he fumbled with his keys, finally got the door unlocked and entered. The first thing he did, with a thrill of anticipation, was phone his fiancée to let her know he was back.

"What a surprise!" said Solange. "I haven't heard from you since you left all those phone messages. But I know you've been busy. Boy have you ever!"

"There's so much to tell you, darling. I'm not a traitor like they claim, but I think differently now. That is, I think, therefore I am a thinker—which I wasn't before. You still don't know how to think, but that's okay, because I can teach you. Then we can do it together like…ummm…like some couples do. Well, I mean if you even *want* to think, because sometimes it kind of backfires on you and then, oh golly—"

"—Ernie," she broke in, "can you come for dinner tonight? We'd both love to see you and we'll all get caught up."

Candide took a long shower. With a towel wrapped around his waist he lay down on his bed. He was basking in the knowledge that the woman who had so often soothed his body would soon be soothing his troubled mind, merely with her gracious presence and undying love. Imagining Solange's talented fingertips massaging his temples, he fell dead asleep. It was evening when he awoke. He dressed, combed and recombed the matted hair he'd slept on wet and peeked through his blinds to see what his media friends were up to. The hungry herd seemed to have thickened. Though it wasn't yet dark, lights were now trained on his front porch, awaiting his reappearance.

When Candide exited, bodies surged forward. A hundred questions seemed to come at once, accompanied by a hundred flashes. The newsworthy young man leapt nimbly to his porch roof and took off. Since he hadn't flown for months, he was rusty. Intending to soar straight up, he instead veered sideways, skimming over reporters' heads and bumping a satellite dish atop a news van. He quickly got the hang of it though and rose 50 meters. He leveled out and sped west through the darkening sky. Behind him the helicopter flock crested apartments and pursued.

Evasive maneuvers were in order. He flew outside town, descended into woods and found a creek he knew. Flying below the banks and just over the water he made his way undetected (except for two startled fishermen) toward Solange's ranch. When he sensed he was close, he lifted above the trees and, sure enough, there was the old plantation house much as he remembered, its downstairs windows glowing under a purple sky. In the driveway stood an RV he recognized as the private coach of the Baroness and Jellyroll. No newspeople were about, much to his relief.

Webner, in a smoking jacket, answered the door. "Hi, man," he said. "How you doin'?"

"Better all the time, Webner. Good to be home."

"Come in and rest your wings. I'll get the Baroness."

Candide, though surprised by the servant's concerned friendliness, was thankful for it. It was the first time Webner had been anything but hostile toward him. And yet, was such familiarity really appropriate in a butler? Didn't servants need to know their place? Candide seated himself in a chair in the drawing room. Soon Webner and Solange entered, holding hands, and sat down together on the couch opposite him. Yes, Candide decided, it was definitely important for servants to know their place. Even more important than he'd thought.

"Ernie, we have something to tell you," said the Baroness.

Candide was trying hard to understand what it was all about. *Something* had changed.

"Jellyroll and I are married—have been for more than six months."

"No!" shouted Candide. "You can't do that! We're betrothed!"

"I broke it off, Ernie. A long time ago."

Candide felt like he'd been mugged. He'd heard about soldiers going away to war and having their girls stolen by a guy named Jody, but never expected it to happen to him. He was completely at a loss—and suddenly felt very alone. As for Webner, what a sneaky little Jody he was!

"Nobody planned it," said Solange. "It was the music. We started writing songs together, then Jellyroll joined the band, and pretty soon we had our heads together day and night. Our relationship flourished."

Candide's whole world had been flipped—again! When was that going to stop happening?

The Baroness stood. "I think we could all use a mint julep. And, Ernie, let me warn you. We put in julep now, so tell me if you want it non-alcoholic."

"Make mine a double."

Solange departed.

"Sorry, man," said Webner. "Like she said, it just happened. Nothing against you."

Webner's concern took the sting out of Candide's pique. After all, how could he blame the keyboard man for loving someone as lovable as Solange? "It's okay, Web. The better man won, I guess. I just don't understand how it happened. We were betrothed."

"Mind a little advice?"

"Got nothing else going for me. Shoot."

"If you love a woman, Ernie, you need to pay her attention. Make her the center of your world—at least some of the time."

"But the Baroness knows how I feel. She's everything to me. I put her on the very highest pedestal."

"Now there's part of the problem, that pedestal business. She's way up there, you're way down here. What's that all about?"

"An angel like Solange deserves to be elevated."

"No woman wants to be *that* elevated. Also, don't think she's going to love you just because you're strong and can fly."

"No?"

"What two folks got to have is things in common. All you and Solange ever had in common was being the two coolest kids in your high school. But school days are over, baby. Better put 'em in your rearview."

It was as though a gong had sounded inside Ernest Candide's cranium. Things in common! He was suddenly ten thousand miles away in Ragistan, remembering what General Pangloss had called Delilah: "The most dangerous woman on earth." Since Candide was surely the most dangerous man, didn't he and Delilah have a lot in common?

Delilah, Delilah, Delilah, why did he always vibrate to the sound of that incomparable name? Why was she the last thing he thought about before he fell asleep and the first thing that occurred to him in the morning? Why, when he reflected back on their adventures, did his heart gallop with such a thrilling happiness? Could it be he'd developed a bit of a thing for his old cave pal? A whole new world of love's possibilities was opening in Candide like a field of blooming sunflowers. He jumped to his feet and swept up one startled Jellyroll in his arms, hugging him. "Thank you, Webner. Thank you thank you thank you—from the bottom of my heart!"

Jellyroll straightened his shirt and tried to reestablish a little dignity. "No problem, man," he said.

Solange entered with the drinks on a tray and regarded the spontaneous embrace. She smiled brightly. "To see you two breaking down barriers is simply the loveliest thing."

39

CWAP's three philosopher kings were convened in Clayton Minefield's living room. "Fire it up," said Minefield to Parson Weed. Weed uncuffed a briefcase from his wrist. He set the combination tumblers, popped the lid and lifted out a disc labeled

TOP SECRET—FOR CWAP'S EYES ONLY

Weed handed the disc to Minefield, who shoved it in the player. Chain Dickey, on the couch, picked up a remote and snapped on the screen. Rod Raygun in cowboy duds swam into view. He smiled and began to speak:

> *"Fear not nukes, son of Twofer.*
> *Show mankind our Godlike power."*

Grinning, Raygun drew his six-guns and blasted away. When he was done plugging the air, his image faded.

CWAP's elite sat silent for a time. Finally Weed spoke. "Well?"

"Not very subtle," said Chain Dickey.

"As we know," Weed replied curtly, "anything subtle goes right over his head."

Silence again.

"Twofer and power don't rhyme, do they?" asked Minefield, squinting.

Weed looked peeved. "You try and find a rhyme for Twofer. Goofer is the only one there is—and obviously that's out. Besides, near rhyme is acceptable poetic practice nowadays. I checked with some English profs over at Johns Hopkins."

"To me," said Dickey, "it just needs to be snappier. Remember, it's got to stick to that lamentable brain of his like a nicotine patch, to reassure him in his hours of doubt."

"Exactly," said Minefield. "More snap."

"Okay," said Weed with a sigh. "I'll give it back to my producers, see what they can do." He rose, walked to the player and ejected the disc. "Talking points?"

"Here's one," said Minefield. "The rats we need to kill hide in holes so deep only *nuclear* bunker busters can root them out."

"Two," said Chain Dickey, "our existing nukes were designed for the Cold War. We need new weapons and a new nuclear policy for this dawning era of Plunderian preeminence."

"Like it," said Minefield.

Parson Weed went next: "Plunderland needs a nuclear arsenal so large and so flexible it will discourage our primary enemies from developing their nukes."

"Not logical," objected Dickey.

"Our subject lacks logic," said Weed. "He'll buy it."

"Sure, *he* will. But remember the arms race we had with the Rooskies? Want a new one with the Chinese?"

"Why not?" said Minefield. "We'll use it to sell the public on our Star Wars Laser Defense Shield."

The veep chuckled, wagging his finger. "You bad."

"Here's something to think about," said the parson. "We established clearly in Ragistan, and even more clearly in Qroc, that we can attack nations that have not attacked us. What about a nuclear first strike? Doable?"

Minefield didn't need to think. "If we can start wars without being attacked, as we've just done, and if we can use nukes during war, which we did back in 'forty-five, then we can strike first with nukes."

"Absolutely," Dickey said. "If it comes to a nuclear dust-up, you don't want to be a counterpuncher."

"I'm curious," said Parson Weed. "What kind of losses might we take in a nuclear war?"

Minefield answered. "Best estimates I've seen give us twenty million dead tops if we get into it with anyone except the Rooskies. So we'd get cut up a little, but we'd survive and win. Whoever rumbled with us would be reduced to radioactive grit."

"And if we get into it with the Rooskies?" asked Chain Dickey.

"Not possible," said Minefield. "They're weak as kittens now."

"I'm just asking. What if?"

"There is no *what if*," said Minefield. "We've got their economy by the short hairs. They'll do pretty much anything we tell them."

"Nuclear war between us and the Rooskies would wipe out life on earth," said the parson.

"That right?" Dickey asked Minefield.

"Theoretical, but correct."

"Can we risk that happening?" asked the vice president.

"If we pull in our horns now," said Minefield, "the competition will think we've gone soft. We need to keep them rocked back on their heels."

Parson Weed smiled benignly. "Even the worst case scenario shouldn't frighten those with faith. There's been a prophecy, you know."

Dickey, looking concerned, said nothing.

40

ATTORNEY General Zombus stood at a podium, his face deathly pale (as usual). On the wall behind him a slogan in gold letters was repeated many times: Death to Traitors, Death to Traitors, Death to Traitors, etc. He looked down at his notes. "I have this morning, in federal court, filed charges of high treason against Ernest Lafitte Candide, a man of unequalled physical gifts who might have chosen to serve his country honorably in her hour of need, but who chose instead to expose her bosom to the enemy. Our indictment contains seventy-nine separate counts, nineteen of which are capital offenses punishable by lethal injection." Zombus looked up. "I'll take a few questions." Hands rose and he pointed to one. "Yes?"

"Pierre Lucland, Le Monde. This is double jeopardy, is it not so? Mr. Candide was already tried on these same charges in another court."

"The defendant was tried and found guilty in a top-flight military court. Since then, due to the legal chicanery of his lawyer, that legitimate decision has been overturned. Now our country must go to the expense of convicting him all over again." Zombus pointed.

"Alex Drivelle, Faux News. Judging by his name, Ernest Lafitte Candide is of French extraction. Can this explain his cowardly acts of treason?"

"There has been much speculation at Justice on that point, but the question remains open." Zombus pointed again.

"Maria Buttafarco, Inside Scoop. Is it true Delilah Jihad was a hit woman for the Polish Mafia before she became a spy for Shrinkistan?"

"Yes, Mr. Candide could not have poured our nation's critical secrets into a more compromised ear."

Zombus pointed to a man in his 50s sporting a sleeveless leather jacket, shaved head and dog collar. "Rocky Muskals, Lonesome Biker Magazine. A two-parter. First, don't you find it difficult convicting traitors while being hounded by the liberal media? Second, can Mr. Candide possibly be as fierce as reports make him out?"

The television mounted high in the corner of Candide's cell on the thirteenth floor of the D.C. Federal Courthouse blinked and went dead. The ex-trooper, seated on his bunk, shook his head in disgust. He picked up a book—*Blowback* by Chalmers Johnson—opened to a page mark and began reading.

41

PARSON Weed was seated across from the president in the Oval Office. Twofer, behind his desk, was multitasking: folding a paper airplane even as he ran his mouth. "He keeps bitching about my cuts to his education budget. Can't seem to get it through his thick skin that I'm a fiskile conservatory."

"I warned you he was big trouble when you appointed him. He's got a doctorate in education."

"But I looked into his soul and saw a good man. What happened?"

"Can't say for sure. But we know the Dark Prince loves to control powerful people."

Twofer was taken aback. "The Devil got in him!"

"I don't like the man's eyes. Check them carefully. I think you'll see what I mean."

There was a knock at the door.

"It's open and so's your zipper," said the president. "Heh heh heh."

Secretary of Education John Castle entered, a harassed-looking man in his fifties.

"What's up, Johnny boy?" said Twofer with an unfriendly stare.

"Certainly not funding for public schools," Castle said bitterly. He remained standing and crossed his arms, since he hadn't been offered a chair.

"You can't improve education by throwing money at it," snapped the president. "We need innovative solutions. And for that, cooperation with private bidness is the ticket."

"Yeah, cooperation with business, exactly what I wanted to discuss with you."

"You got one minute," said the pres, smirking. He leaned back in his chair.

"I'll keep it simple so you can understand. Under your Every Child Goosed to Excellence Act, all school children have to be tested on a regular basis."

"You're wastin' your minute, fuzzbutt—'cause I already knew that."

"Here's my question. Why do *all* the testing materials for *all* the schools in the country come from just *one* publisher?"

"Well, I reckon it's the best publisher we got. Nothin' but the finest for our little steers and heifers."

"That publisher happens to be one of your biggest campaign contributors. I checked it out."

Buzz Twofer stood up, palms on his desk, eyes narrowed. "What are you sayin'?"

Secretary Castle looked a little less sure of himself. "I'm asking for clarification, because there seems to be a conflict of interest the size of the Swiss Alps."

"You callin' me a crook, numbnuts?" said Twofer with menace.

"Okay, that's it. Let's settle this like men, right here, right now. Bowie knives or six-guns, your pick." He opened a drawer, rummaged inside and produced a red bandana. "Glom your chompers down on that. I'll bite the other end and we'll go for the whole bag of chips. Game?"

Castle smiled. "Don't make me laugh. I was a marine PT instructor."

Twofer's smirk wilted as he dropped the bandana back in the drawer, slammed the drawer and locked it. "Don't have the stomach for it, huh? I shoulda known."

"Every Child Goosed to Excellence is little more than a bag of goodies for your corporate pals," said the secretary. "It's also the most destructive education bill ever devised."

Parson Weed, looking serious, cleared his throat and spoke quietly. "I'd be careful if I were you, John. Without proof, such charges amount to slander. And slandering a president in wartime is tantamount to treason."

"Yeah, Johnny boy, where's your proof?" sneered the president. "Lay it on the line or we'll ship you out to Gitmo for a witch's hat and some water sports."

"All the proof I need is in the act itself. Every Child Goosed to Excellence sets up testing standards that become harder for the schools to meet every year. After 2010 the standards become so outlandish most schools will fail—and therefore be subject to closing, the teachers fired. You and your corporate pals are out to destroy public education. It's as simple as that."

Twofer pointed at Castle. "Your minute's up and so's your job. I hereby can your sorry butt."

"You can't fire me because I already quit. I left my resignation with your secretary so she could read it to you." Castle turned and departed.

Twofer yelled after him. "With all the powers invested in me as president, I hereby officially *veto* your resignation, you overeducated noodle! And now I officially can you again—for the second and last time. Nobody quits on me before I can fire his ass. Nobody!"

"Let him go," said Parson Weed. "Good riddance."

The president was breathing fast, face red. He swung some air punches, the last a low blow, then sat down. "You're right about the bastard. The devil's in him."

"Did you see his eyes when he lost his temper?"

"They glowed like a furnace. And I smelled brimstone on his breath."

"He's right about one thing," said the parson.

"What's that?"

"Every Child Goosed to Excellence will shut down the public schools."

"It will?"

"That's the whole point, Buzz. Then we can replace them with goodly Christian schools, schools that combine the best teaching of our Lord with sound business practices."

"How come nobody told me?"

"You were at the meeting when Chain Dickey laid it out. You don't remember?"

Twofer slipped his fingers inside his shirt and scratched his stomach. "You know, parson, way back in grade school I developed this special knack for sleepin' with my eyes open. Helps me focus on the big picture by shuckin' off all the confusin' details."

"Rod Raygun, they say, was blessed with the same laser focus on the big picture. He knew, as you do, that the president's hand belongs firmly on the flagpole of command. Presidents can't be bothered to count beans and the like. That's for subordinates."

"Christian schools, huh?"

"What better way to imprint sound moral values on Plunderland's youth?"

"Damn right," said Twofer. "Give all them little shavers the same educational benefits I got: sound moral values." He picked up his now completed airplane and, showing his tongue, threw it toward Weed. The malformed craft spun into the carpet.

42

NATHAN Rader was being interviewed on the "Charlie Peters Show." Peters, with mussed platinum hair and a brash voice, blasted his questions. "YOU REPRESENT THE SLEAZIEST TRAITOR IN THE HISTORY OF OUR COUNTRY. PEOPLE WONDER HOW YOU CAN LIVE WITH YOURSELF. WHAT DO YOU SAY TO THEM?"

"Ernest Candide undertook two hazardous missions for the army. On both he acquitted himself bravely and with honor, suffering enough wounds for a dozen purple hearts. He should be receiving decorations, not a treason trial."

"AND WHAT MEDAL WOULD YOU PIN ON OUR HERO FOR FEARLESSLY BANGING A TERRORIST?"

The TV blinked, changing channels to "Ambush." On this debate show two combatants from the Mastodon Party confronted two combatants from the Jackass Party around a table and took potshots by turn. Roger Nitpick, the Mastodon regular, was questioning Nathan Rader in a voice dripping with insinuation. "Mr. Rader, I've long been an admirer of your hand wringing and tree hugging. This case is right up your alley, isn't it? Another lost cause?"

The channel switched to "The McNaughton Report." James McNaughton, the moderator, queried his three panelists sequentially in Uzi-burst style. "Question! Should-Ernest-Lafitte-Candide-be-excuted-for-selling-out-his-country-in-return-for-sex? JACK GOURMAND!"

A heavyset balding man with intelligent brown eyes came on camera and began to speak. "Well, that's what his trial is supposed to—"

"—Don't give me that old pap about the sanctity of jury trials, Jack. New days are dawning. You need to read the Patriot Act. ELINOR ROBIN, snuff-or-no-snuff?!"

Again the channel changed. A middle-aged man in a brown western suit and white hat stood on a car lot full of enormous glass and steel behemoths raised on tractor-size tires. He spoke into a mike. "Neighbors, Pal Dillingham down here at Pal's Blunderbus

Acres. All this weekend we're having a fire sale on these pre-owned beauties. I'm just *burning* to give you a *hot* deal!"

"Take this cherry number," he said, lifting his arm as the camera pulled back. "Three bedrooms, two and a half baths, a triple X adult playroom with wet bar all included in this 2001 Guzzler for under thirty grand. Too bulky for speed, you say? Guess again. Each wheel is independently powered by a 394-horsepower engine. The little beast turns 190 in the quarter mile with a top end of 255. An excellent all-terrain vehicle, with superior gas economy for its class: 3 mpg on the highway, 1.7 in the city. And trust the 300-gallon fuel tank to deliver hours of worry-free driving between fill-ups."

Candide was watching from his bunk. "For *this* we go to war?" he snorted. "Insane!" He killed the TV and picked up the book lying next to him. It was Noam Chomsky's *Media Control*, a brief, clear explanation of how Plunderland's press had been muzzled over the years. Such works were easier for Candide to understand all the time. Guys like this Chomsky helped him fathom what had happened to his country's leadership to turn them into such dangerous bullies, intent on (among other things) squashing him like a bug. Soon after his initiation into the art of thinking, Candide had read to improve his mind and for the fun of it. Since his court-martial and Guantanamo, he read primarily for survival.

43

ON the first day of his civilian trial Candide looked around the courtroom and saw a full house. In attendance were journalists, sketch artists, crime authors and curious citizens of all stripes, even a Hasidic Rabbi packing a Torah. The judge, Santiago de la Cruz, was a Vietland war hero and rising star in the Mastodon Party—someone Candide had long admired. It made the cashiered soldier sad each time de la Cruz's eyes met his own and filled with contempt. It was exactly the look a war hero might give a cowardly skunk who'd betrayed his homeland.

The opening statements were in the book and now the first witness for the prosecution, Major John Sniffert, was being put through his paces by hotshot lead prosecutor Melanie Mezey. "You were Mr. Candide's chief debriefer after his Supergoose operations, were you not?"

"I was," said Major Sniffert, looking a little uncomfortable.

"Why did your team decide to charge him with collaboration?"

"We had no choice. He asked us to believe that while captive he conducted civilized debates with both Moolah al-Razir and Madmahn Badassi—preposterous lies to save his skin. It's well established that Moolah and Madmahn are total savages, incapable of civilized anything. Clearly, they tortured the boy and he spilled his guts."

"Did Mr. Candide divulge information that endangered our troops?"

"He did. On his missions in Ragistan and Qroc he learned our troop positions as he overflew the battlefield. These he surrendered fully to the enemy."

"You have proof of this, major?"

"Army Intelligence has calculated his damage with precision. The casualty rate in Lieutenant Candide's sectors was 68.73 percent higher than in other sectors."

"How many soldiers did he cost us?"

"Ten dead, forty-six wounded, give or take fractions."

"And what did you learn about the defendant's relations with archspy Delilah Jihad?"

"On that subject we caught Mr. Candide in more stark lies—lies which enabled us to deduce additional treasonous activity."

"I really must object," said Nathan Rader. "This is nothing but rank speculation."

"I'm going to allow it," said the judge. "Speculation it may be, but the witness was in an excellent position to assess Mr. Candide's truthfulness."

Candide had heard the silly charges concerning himself and Delilah so many times they made him weary. She'd never seduced him, never brainwashed him, never drained him of any information. All she'd done was show him how to think. Had it become illegal to think in Plunderland? Apparently.

After Ms. Mezey finished showcasing the major's fantasies concerning Candide's superhuman sex life, Nathan Rader approached the witness. "Major Sniffert, all the evidence of treason you've presented is either hearsay or speculation—correct?"

"I've given the facts as I know them."

"Do you have one shred of material evidence to support any of your claims?"

Sniffert squirmed and looked peeved. "No."

"Witnesses?"

"I'm sure there *were* witnesses. Ms. Jihad likely neutralized them all."

"Any evidence she did?"

"Who had better reason to neutralize them—or better means?"

"Did Mr. Candide ever admit during debriefings that he'd given up classified information to Ms. Jihad—or to anyone inappropriate?"

"No."

"Now, major. You testified the Plunderian Army's casualty rate was higher in sectors my client overflew."

"I did."

"But wasn't Lieutenant Candide assigned only the most contested sectors—the very ones where casualty rates would naturally be highest?"

"Perhaps."

"Only perhaps, major?"

"I suppose he was."

Rader smiled. "That's all I have for this witness, your honor."

"Please step down," said Judge de la Cruz.

Melanie Mezey called Dr. Daniel Clapperman. A nondescript fellow of medium height took the stand.

"What is your occupation, Dr. Clapperman?"

"Analyst supervisor for the Central Intelligence Agency."

"And your duties?"

"I direct the bureau which monitors the crimes and conspiracies of Delilah Jihad."

"A whole bureau devoted to one woman? Why?"

"The agency recognizes Ms. Jihad as a great menace to our national security."

"How many analysts work under you?"

"Twenty-seven."

"My, my, twenty-seven. You and your subordinates must know more about Ms. Jihad than anyone else—other than Ms. Jihad herself."

"I'm sure we do."

"Help us form a picture of her. Who is she? Who pulls her strings?"

"She's a twenty-two-year-old Shrinkistanian intelligence operative and terrorist. She works for the SIA."

"SIA?"

"Shrinkistanian Intelligence Agency."

Candide was listening fascinated—and dismayed. Clapperman was saying much what General Pangloss had said. Boy, thought Candide, if Delilah's a spy for Shrinkistan, she sure told me some whoppers.

"Could you acquaint us with her criminal activities?" Ms. Mezey asked.

"Certainly. She's headmistress of three terrorist training schools in the Gaza. She's suspected in forty-nine murders, mostly of Zionian politicians and military officers. Twice she tried to assassinate Zionia's Prime Minister, Airbus Shalom, and both times nearly succeeded. She has smuggled conventional *and* nuclear weapons into nations hostile to the democratic free world. I can introduce you to victims of her torture chamber, to those who survived her ambush bombings, and to a broken man she held captive for a week and raped without mercy. I can list crimes attributed to Ms. Jihad from here to the Middle East and still not do full justice to her destructive capacities."

Candide wanted to laugh out loud. Delilah a rapist? Such a rap sheet as had just been hung around her neck would challenge Beelzebub to pull off. This Clapperman guy was obviously full of it.

"What can you tell us about Ms. Jihad's childhood?" asked the prosecutor.

"Most of what we know was taken from news accounts, in connection with a particular incident. When Ms. Jihad was fourteen, her family, illiterate farmers in the Gaza—incapable even of reading a map—carelessly planted their olive grove on acres destined for a Zionian settlement. When the bulldozers came to push over the invasive olive trees, Delilah's kin and their neighbors resisted with their bodies and some illegally thrown rocks. A helicopter gunship was sent to quiet the dangerous revolt. As the gunship hung protectively over the crowd, wiggling its cannon to make any terrorists think twice, Ms. Jihad was seen by many witnesses firing a rock that clanged into the chopper's rotor blades, snapping one off. Unbalanced, the gunship spun out of control, crashed into a nearby hillside and caught fire. Three ZDF paratroopers died. Thus did Ms. Jihad become a fugitive from justice and mortal enemy of Zionia."

To Candide, some of this had the ring of truth. He could just picture Delilah bringing down a military helicopter with a rock. But was she really Shrinkistanian? With her big green eyes, she *looked* Zionian, as she'd told him she was. Her skin was fairly dark, but that could go either way. He wasn't sure what to think. "Thank you, Dr. Clapperman," he heard Ms. Mezey say.

Nathan Rader came forward, buttoning his jacket. "Doctor, what crimes has Ms. Jihad been convicted of?"

"None, but that's only because she's never been tried."

"What crimes has she been charged with?"

Clapperman looked annoyed. "None, yet, but that's because she's never been caught. She's strongly suspected in literally hundreds of crimes. She's murdered dozens of people. That we know."

"Those are your opinions, but in fact Delilah Jihad is merely a person of interest. Correct?"

"Yes."

"Thank you. That's all."

The judge, amused, recessed for lunch.

44

MS. Mezey kicked off the afternoon by calling General Pangloss. Despite bodily mutilations and advanced age, the old warhorse made an impressive figure in his black eye patch and desert khakis robustly packed below the belt.

"General," the prosecutor began, "what is your acquaintance with the defendant?"

"I taught him desert warfare. I loved him as my fellow soldier and nurtured him like my own son, imparting gems of wisdom. Later I monitored his missions into Ragistan and Qroc."

"You spoke to Lieutenant Candide at length after both missions, did you not?"

"I did."

"And what did you learn?"

"I learned that the terrorist spy Delilah Jihad had turned him into a sex-crazed jellyfish. She had drained him of his vital juices and of all the classified information he was privy to." Pangloss went on to regurgitate the same off-base imaginings he'd spouted at the military tribunal, and Candide wondered once again why this man who claimed to have loved him was now working so hard to end his life. Was it Pangloss's distorted loyalty to his country? Or did his commitment to career trump friendship and the truth? Whatever the reason, the results were sad to behold. A true hero had managed to shrink himself into a mean, lying snitch.

After Ms. Mezey had shot every fish in the barrel, she strode past Candide with a withering look.

Nathan Rader began by taking up the general's closing remarks. "You seem awfully certain my client intentionally delayed rescuing you. Did you see him holding back?"

"Didn't need to. I inferred his malicious hesitation from prima facie evidence and a few airtight tautologies."

"Please explain your reasoning for the benefit of the court."

"A: He let the little whore get him by the dick. B: To please her he betrayed his country. C: Any man who would betray his country would also betray loyal defenders of his country. D: I am a loyal defender of his country. Ergo: He must have betrayed me."

"And this is your proof that Lieutenant Candide conspired in your torture?"

"More is not needed."

"Not by you, I guess." Rader glanced at the jury, most of whom were frowning doubtfully, then at the judge, who was astounded. He confronted Pangloss again. "I believe you testified that after meeting Ms. Jihad my client began thinking in a treasonous manner."

"No. I testified that after he met Ms. Jihad, he began thinking. For any soldier, thinking is treasonous ipso facto. When a soldier thinks, the whole military raison d'etre trembles and threatens to collapse. It's like smoking a cigar in a room full of blasting caps."

"Your career, I take it, has been based on not thinking."

"Better believe it. As I tried to get the lieutenant to see, not thinking has made me the man I am today."

"Thank you, general. You've certainly given the rest of us a lot to think about."

45

SOLDIERS accused of high treason generally have few supporters—and so it was with Ernest Lafitte Candide. His only witnesses were he, himself, and him. His attorney, having taken him through preliminaries, was getting down to the meat. Candide glanced out over the spectators and saw the Hasidic rabbi with his Torah. A new arrival was a tall Ragistani woman reporter concealed in a brown burka.

"Mr. Candide," said Rader, "you say you were bothered by what you witnessed in Ragistan. What bothered you?"

"My commander in chief, when he started that war, said our goals were to catch the terrorists who destroyed our flag factory and to free the Ragistani people. Later I found out those were lies."

"Why lies?"

"Moolah and most of his men were allowed to get away and we never even tried to free the Ragistanis. From what I've seen, we invaded Ragistan to construct an oil pipeline from the Caspian region to the Arabian Sea. I learned through army documents we're building five new military bases along the pipeline route."

"A war for a pipeline? That sounds farfetched."

"Actually two pipelines. One for oil, one for natural gas. The Caspian is rich in both."

Melanie Mezey stood. "I object to this line of questioning. The administration isn't on trial here. Mr. Candide is."

"Objection sustained," said Judge de la Cruz.

Rader glanced at his notes. "Let's turn to your service in Operation Prophylactic Attack. The war in Qroc was necessary, wasn't it?"

"No. That war was based on even bigger lies. It wasn't about Madmahn's weapons of mass destruction or terrorism at all."

"What then?"

"Hate to sound repetitious, but oil again. Our president and his administration want to control world oil—"

"—Objection!" said the prosecutor. "Didn't we decide our government is not on trial?"

"We did," said the judge. "Let's move along, Mr. Rader."

Rader flipped a sheet of paper. "General Pangloss claims you intentionally delayed rescuing him. True?"

"Not true. Both times I saved him I did it as fast as possible. I couldn't stand his shrieks. They are the loudest, most heart-rending screeches I've ever heard. They tore at my soul."

A low growl and the sound of gnashing teeth came from the audience area. Candide's eyes were drawn to the woman journalist from Ragistan who seemed to be trembling inside her burka. Odd, thought Candide. Why should she care?

"Have you ever betrayed your country in any way?" Rader asked.

"No. Not unless thinking is treasonous, as General Pangloss claims. If he's right about that, then I am a traitor, because recently I've been doing a lot of thinking. Personally though I don't see how democracy can work if citizens don't think, and that includes soldiers. You can bet our leaders are thinking. I used to trust them to do my thinking for me but boy was that a boner."

The little rabbi gave him a thumbs-up. At first Candide wasn't quite sure why. Then he realized rabbis devote their lives to thinking. Naturally he approved.

"Your witness," Rader said.

Ms. Mezey advanced steely eyed. "*Mr.* Candide, are you asking us to believe that Plunderland, one of the most benevolent nations in human history, has suddenly turned into a bully that attacks other countries to steal their resources?"

"Nothing sudden about it. We've been pulling stuff like this for centuries. It all started—"

A look of panic seized the prosecutor's face. "I object!" she shouted.

"You can't object," said the judge. "He's answering your question. Let him finish."

"It began with our genocide against the Native Plunderians. According to the best estimates I could find, we killed at least ninety percent of them, mainly for their land. We stole half of Mexico through unjust and brutal wars. We killed six hundred thousand Filipinistas to establish a Pacific military base, then turned their homeland into a whorehouse. Cubaland, Isle of Haiti, Puerta Rita, Panamaland and others were conquered by U.S. Marines and forced to pay tribute as little colonies, with fruit, sugar, cigars, naval bases and nubile women. And let's not forget the millions of Africans we turned into slaves—as well as those who died on the slave ships. All so white Plunderians could rake in the bucks while others sweated the bullets.

"These various crimes against humanity were based largely on greed," Candide continued. "Later we waged wars based on silly fears, if the justifications of our government can be believed. We liquidated four million Korealanders so we wouldn't have to 'fight communists on the streets of Honolulu.' Two to three million Vietlanders died for the same reason, along with two million Cambochians and a million Laoslanders. That's ten million Asians, many of them children, sent to heaven to protect our pineapples from countries without navies."

"Cowardly lying bastard!" yelled a commanding baritone voice. It was the Ragistani woman reporter, now standing, well over six feet tall. Something was rising under her burka just below waist level, a rod-like projection tenting the brown cloth. A loud shot rang out and a chunk of wood flew from the railing in front of

Candide. He saw smoke rising from around the imposing journalist. A small hole had appeared where the burka was draped over what Candide now realized was a gun barrel. Ernie dove from the witness stand as more shots exploded. *Budda budda budda budda!... Budda budda budda!* Wood flew from the stand and holes opened in the wall behind.

Spectators ran screaming for the exits. The Hasidic rabbi jumped to his feet, pulled something from his Torah and slung it at the trigger-happy burka dweller. The projectile struck the reporter in the head with a loud *snock*, collapsing the tall body in a brown heap. Candide was first to the unconscious form. He yanked off the burka hood, uncovering the face of James Coburn in a black eye patch. Next he pulled the burka hem high above the knees. In the badly scarred pelvic region was mounted a nine-inch Sten gun hung with two bulging magazines. The remarkable sight caused quite a stir among the rubberneckers.

When Ernie looked up it was into the face of the Hasidic holy man. Naturally the ex-soldier felt a wave of gratitude. He rose and extended his hand. "Thank you so much, rabbi. You saved my life."

"That's what I'm here for, bumpkin," said a voice too high pitched to be a man's, with a lilt that trip-hammered Candide's heart.

"Delilah!"

"Don't blow my cover," she whispered. "Pretend I'm your spiritual adviser."

Candide suppressed the hug he was about to deliver and stepped back to create space, rolling his foot on something hard. He bent down and picked it up. A stone paperweight.

"They're better than rocks," said Delilah. She opened the Torah, hollow inside, to reveal five more marble paperweights.

"Order in the court!" shouted the judge as his head appeared from behind his desk. "Bailiff, disarm that assassin before he comes to. We're recessed till I can figure out what the heck's going on in my jurisdiction."

46

WHEN the trial opened the following morning, Nathan Rader petitioned the judge to allow a surprise witness: Ms. Delilah Jihad. The prosecution objected, but Judge de la Cruz overruled, saying, "If she can't throw light on these matters, nobody can."

Delilah was sworn in and Rader went to work. "What's your real name?"

"I've used others, but my real name is Delilah Jihad."

"Employment?"

"I'm a spy. And a counterspy. Also a counter-counterspy."

"For those not familiar with intelligence work, could you explain your job titles?"

"I can, but bear with me—it goes back to before I was born. My father, a Shrinkistanian economics professor, fell in love with a Zionian pediatrician—and she with him. Because of their cross-cultural love, they were ostracized from their communities in Jerusalem and ended up tending an old family olive grove in the Gaza Strip. There I was born and raised by the most loving of parents. They taught me the ways of both my cultures, for which I'm grateful."

So, thought Candide, if she's telling the truth now, she's both Zionian *and* Shrinkistanian. He was beyond being surprised by *anything* anymore—insofar as she was concerned.

"In Gaza," Delilah continued, "I led the normal life of a Shrinkistanian child—going to school when it was open, fighting tanks when school was closed. Then I knocked down that helicopter and all of a sudden I was a Shrinkistanian national hero and the enemy of Zionia. I'd planned to follow my mother into medicine, but now only two careers were open: spy and suicide bomber. I didn't like the bomber retirement plan, so I joined Shrinkistanian Intelligence and for three years was one of their most successful agents. I got good enough that Zionia had to stop me. Their method was heartless, but effective. They kidnapped my parents and threatened to kill them if I didn't flip to their side while remaining in the SIA. I went along, because I thought as a member of Zionian Intelligence I could at times help Shrinkistan. I believed I was smart enough to play the double agent game—and for awhile I did."

"Then what?"

"Oy! Then the SIA kidnapped my parents from Zionia and flipped me again. I became a counter-counteragent, very confusing sometimes, let me tell you!"

"In your several roles," said Nathan Rader, "you must be privy to intelligence from many sources. Can you tell us anything about the man who attempted to kill the defendant in this courtroom yesterday—General Jack Pangloss?"

"Pangloss is well known in the espionage community. Early in his distinguished military career he began working as an operative and occasional hit man for Plunderland's Central Intelligence Agency. Later he became a spy theorist. His seminal text, *The Unthinking Mole*, outlines a whole new approach to spy work, requiring virtually no thought on the part of the agent, just very detailed orders from his handlers. His idiotic performance yesterday will not help advance his ideas."

"Mr. Candide is accused of divulging secrets to you in return for sex. True?"

"No. But I am a spy. It was my job to get information if I could. He's too loyal, though, to spill a single bean."

"Did you have sexual relations with him?"

"Once. The night we met. It was the result of circumstances and a certain strong attraction between us. Normally I'm not that kind of girl." Glancing at the judge, she smiled. The judge shuffled papers as a blush rose upward from his collar.

"Your witness," said Rader to the prosecutor.

Melanie Mezey pounced. "Ms. Jihad, pray tell, how do we trust the word of an admitted counter-counterspy?"

"If I lie, my lies will show like anybody else's. Would I come here voluntarily—and blow my cover—just to lie?"

"Does your devotion to the truth include admitting you're a terrorist?"

"If you're afraid of me, then sure, I'm a terrorist to you. But to myself and to those who know me I'm more like a Native Plunderian on the warpath."

"A savage, you mean."

Delilah turned to the jury. "I have a number of Plunderian

friends. I've found it helps them understand what it's like for Shrinkistanians if they can see us as a tribe going through what your so-called Indians once suffered. We are losing our land to settlers who come and build upon it. New houses rise on our cemeteries. Fences are erected that we can't get through, and the ways we feed ourselves are taken from us, even destroyed. If we protest or fight back, here come the soldiers to kill our leaders and knock down our homes. Our weapons are crude, and for that we are branded uncivilized, which somehow makes our women and children fair game. Like people everywhere we once had hopes. Now we wish only to be left alone on our reservations in the West Bank and Gaza. Yet we know we won't be left alone until all our olive trees are buried, all our fields are seized, and our whole race dries up like the desert mud and blows away. Others have decided the land, all of it, belongs to them, and they mean to have it." Delilah glanced at the judge to check his reaction. Santiago de la Cruz's face had gone stony and his somber brown eyes looked older than the mountains.

"I'm through with this witness, your honor," said Ms. Mezey.

"Court is recessed for lunch," said the judge. He rose with dignity and passed quickly into his chambers, wiping an eye.

As Delilah stepped down from the stand, two federal marshals intercepted her. They handcuffed her hands behind her back.

Candide jumped up to intervene, but Nathan Rader blocked his way. "Stay cool, Ernie."

"I'll spring you, Delilah," the young swain cried. "I don't know how but I will."

"Don't worry," she called over her shoulder. "This is just a formality."

Candide was highly doubtful.

47

MELANIE Mezey paced in front of the jury with prosecutorial zeal, waving her arms in perfect concert with the mesmerizing arguments of her summation: "Under the Patriot Act recently passed by congress, a citizen of Plunderland is guilty of treason if he or she knowingly or unknowingly gives support to any terrorist group. The wild and unsubstantiated allegations against Plunderland Mr. Candide spouted proudly here in court give support to *all* terrorist groups. It is therefore your duty as loyal lovers of your country not only to find him guilty, but also to assess the maximum penalty on each count. He must be made to pay with his life for the innocent lives he sacrificed when he sank his fangs into the nurturing bosom of his motherland."

A lesser attorney would have concluded on this lofty rhetorical peak, but Ms. Mezey plunged ahead, eyes on the stars. "Consider the world we live in since Screaming Eagle was blown up—a world full of crazed fundamentalists dedicated to the destruction of civilized mankind. Who will protect us if we do not? Who will secure our citizenry from biological, chemical, and nuclear attack? Who will defend the smaller nations of the earth from Madmahn Badassi and his ilk? And who will place the world's key resources in trust for everyone, not just the selfish few? Our planet cries out for a fair and noble policeman—a cop with a heart of gold. World Congress is too weak and too corrupt for that role. All nations but one are too puny in power. Our planet's richest nation, liberated from motives of greed by its wealth and beefed to the teeth with the most fearsome weapons the world has ever known, is the only nation that can be trusted with the sheriff's badge. Mr. Candide, by questioning our wars for freedom, would torpedo this essential mission for Plunderland. Say no to his destructive negativism by finding him guilty."

With a confident smile Ms. Mezey took her seat. Rader, looking serious, approached the jury and rested his hands on the jury box rail. He carefully summarized the lack of evidence against his client, then highlighted the key issue: "Your decision has great importance. You will determine whether a Plunderian citizen any longer has the right to criticize our government and its leadership. For here is my client facing a penalty of death, and all he did was criticize—as truthfully as he could. I'm betting you decide in line with both our amended Constitution and two hundred years of practice that a person has such a right.

"As to the prosecutor's claim that the world needs Plunderland for its sheriff—such matters are not in the least relevant to the charges against Mr. Candide. I would like to respond, however, because such an assertion can cloud the issue. There is an old saying which has proven true time and again. It goes, 'The bigger you are, the harder you fall.' Do you suppose it will never apply to us if we keep on puffing ourselves up into the big palooka who promises a new world order—a Pax Plunderiana—then looks after his own interests to the exclusion of all others? In time, bullies usually end up facing a gang of their enemies. And that part isn't pretty, folks."

Judge de la Cruz instructed the jury and then released them to their deliberations. The spectators rose and the press corps scrambled for the exit.

48

CANDIDE exited a taxi in front of the Hotel Baltimore Hillcrest in the pouring rain and ran for the entrance. In the lobby he pulled a crumpled piece of paper from his pocket and read it again, though he knew the information well. He glanced at the elevator, then took the stairs. Since his incarceration, confinement of any kind made him queasy. On the third floor he found room 334 and knocked. After a time the door opened and there stood Delilah—barefoot, wearing a bathrobe, hair up in a towel. "Oh hi, Ernie. So soon I didn't expect you." She motioned him inside. "Relax. Drinks in the fridge. I'll be right out." She disappeared into the bathroom.

Candide felt a bit foolish for having arrived half an hour early, but he was just so excited. He and Delilah hadn't had a chance to talk since they'd shared a cave in Ragistan almost two years earlier. Boy, did he have a lot to tell her! He sat down on the couch and like a good Plunderian picked up the remote and snapped on the television. Telejournalist Ralph Blister appeared, standing at his news desk. The savvy wordsmith was feeding the hungry public a little purple prose with a Blister twist: "Like a stone thrown violently into a quiet pond, the acquittal of Ernest Lafitte Candide continues to

OPERATION SUPERGOOSE 145

send out disturbing ripples. Here are some of tomorrow's headlines we will bring you this hour.

"Our first report revolves around Delilah Jihad, the sexy mole to whom Ernie Candide lost his heart and for whom he nearly lost his life. Following Ms. Jihad's capture by federal authorities, she was questioned by the FBI, the CIA, the Department of Homeland Security, the Department of Justice, Interpol, the New Hampshire Attorney General's Office, and the Sheriff of Concord. No charges were filed by any agency. Ms. Jihad was released at the joint request of the Zionian Government, the Shrinkistanian Authority, the Secretary General of World Congress and Greenpeace.

"Correspondent Audrey Satchel is on the scene of another story at the D.C. District Courthouse. Just this hour Korealand War hero General Jack Pangloss was indicted on nine counts ranging from attempted murder to carrying a concealed lethal sex toy. Audrey—any further developments?"

Ms. Sachel came on camera holding a mike, with the courthouse behind her. "We're hoping to have those soon, Ralph. General Pangloss is expected to plead guilty on all charges. Apparently he has confessed, but claims he was on assignment for the CIA. A spokesperson for the CIA, however, has denied the existence of any such assignment, or any knowledge of any such person as General Jack Pangloss."

"Thanks *so much*, Audrey. Our third story takes us to the halls of congress, where Senator James Eagle of West Virginia is calling for congressional hearings into the charges leveled by Ernest Candide against the Twofer administration during his trial. Lionel Trill, our congressional correspondent, has managed to scoop an interview with Senator Eagle and we'll have all of that for you." Candide poked the power button and the screen went dead. He yawned, scratched his shoulder, glanced at his watch. Then he noticed something strange about the satin couch he was sitting on. Its chartreuse fabric was covered with small semicircular cuts. There were so many he'd thought they were fabric design before looking more closely. Puzzling...

Candide walked to the minifridge, opened and looked in.

Behind three baby bottles filled with formula a small can of Crimson Blast tomato juice caught his eye. He lifted it out and was closing the fridge when—startled—he realized he was being watched. A toddler in diapers stood three feet away, finger in mouth, swaying slightly.

"Well," said Delilah from across the room, "I see you've met." She was dressed in jeans and a tight red sweater that revealed her interesting curves. Her hair was being tamed with a brush. The blonde toddler crossed the room unsteadily, arms outstretched, and grabbed Mommy around the legs. Delilah rested a hand on the child's head. "Ernie, this is Yonita."

"Hi, Yonita," said poor Candide with but half a voice. He felt like he'd been kicked in the scrotum. Obviously, in his absence, Delilah had married—a Caucasian by the looks of it—and the happy couple had started a family. All the wonderful things Candide had come to tell his darling evaporated in an instant. He was speechless.

"Yonita, this is Ernie. You two have a lot in common." The little girl stared at Candide with the widest, most curious blue eyes he'd ever seen. It really rankled him that Delilah's husband was apparently of his own race. It suggested he'd had a chance with her himself—if only he'd played his cards right. He felt his face pucker with resentment.

Delilah quickly lost her smile. "Oh my. Well…what did I expect? I just thought—I don't know what I thought. Sometimes women are foolish, aren't they?"

Candide then saw a sight that rocked him back on his heels. Glistening on his favorite spy's cheeks were, of all things, tears! He realized he'd hurt her feelings with his sour response. He went to her and took her by the shoulders. "I'm sorry, Delilah. I *am* happy for you, really I am. It's just that I wanted to be part of it. I wanted to be the man who gave you this beautiful child."

"OY!" exclaimed Delilah as she threw up her hands and rolled her eyes. "Can't you see this *is* your child, bumpkin? May both my Gods preserve me! You've learned to think, but now you can't operate your vision."

"You're not married to some other guy?" Candide asked hopefully.

"I'm not married. Since slavery is illegal, my marriage to Moolah was always null and void."

"Jumpin' Jiminy. If you're not married and have borne my child, that means I've ruined your reputation. We must wed immediately."

Delilah looked exasperated. "First you have to ask me. I don't want a shotgun wedding."

Candide got down on one knee and took Delilah's hand. He looked up into her eyes with love. "Will you marry me, my darling? On the night we met, you stole my heart forever—it just took me a couple of years to figure it out."

"I *might* marry you, after we talk about a whole lot of stuff we need to get straight. Now stand up. You look silly down there. What kind of example are you giving our daughter?"

Sitting on the couch together, Candide and his perhaps bride-to-be discussed their possible future. Yonita toddled to the coffee table and braced herself against it. She couldn't stop staring at Candide. It was like she was trying to memorize him. Candide felt the coffee table bump his leg and saw it rising from the floor. Up and up it went, tilting ever more until it was almost vertical. Much to Ernie's consternation, the heavy piece of furniture was being held aloft by the tiny arm of his daughter. She gurgled happily. She seemed to be looking at him for approval.

"Holy smokes," said Candide. "It's Mighty Minnie Mouse!"

"Like father, like daughter."

"But I couldn't have passed my powers to her. They aren't genetic."

"Just be glad our child is strong. There are downsides too." Delilah fingered one of the cuts in the satin couch.

"She did that?"

"Teething. I'll probably have to buy this couch."

Over the next couple of hours the young parents talked through their wedding plans, future finances, fair division of responsibilities, and miscellaneous. When little Yonita was put down for her afternoon nap, planning was temporarily postponed for a more intimate conference between the child's parents. But that we'll leave for their memoirs. Suffice to say, as Ernest Candide that evening made his way back down the carpeted hotel stairs he'd earlier ascended, he was whistling like a meadowlark. Halfway to the second floor he encountered four hulking hotel workers on the landing. One was sweeping the carpet, one polishing the banister, one changing a lightbulb, and one holding the stepladder. "Hi fellas," Candide chirped. "How goes it?"

He felt a heavy blow on the back of his head. It knocked him down but didn't quite put him out. Groggy, he felt his arms being seized and a knee pinning his head to the carpet. A needle pricked his carotid. Whatever poison it was swept over him in waves, following his heartbeats. Each wave weakened him further and took more of his consciousness. By the fifth wave he was gone to the world, slumped lifeless on the landing. Two heartbeats later the pump stopped. Ernest Lafitte Candide, a young man with so much to live for, was now dead, as dead as dead can be.

49

PARSON Weed, running late, entered the Oval Office in a hurry and stumbled, sprawling in grass, very short grass. Looking around, he saw the floor had become a putting green—complete with hillock, trough, plateau, and of course a cup and flagstick. The presidential desk with its impressive seal stood a few feet from the green under a small oak. Weed picked himself up and checked for stains on the knees of his cinnamon suit as the president's head appeared from a sand trap. Twofer climbed out, sleeves rolled, a belly putter in his hand. Strutting with a style that was his and his alone, Mr. Big Stuff approached his holy man. "How ya like it?" he asked.

"A putting green, sir?"

"To economize my time. While I'm savin' the world, I can perfect my strokin'."

"Must have been expensive."

"Naw. Paid for it with budget cuts."

"What did you cut?"

"Well, when we remodeled the White House bathrooms to match the wife's eyes, I decided instead of installin' pissers for the fellas and toilets for the gals, we could just go with pissers all around. That one little brain stroke paid for this here puttin' green and for the goldfish pond in our bedroom."

"Urinals for the ladies?"

"If they want equal rights, let 'em pee standin' up like I done all my life. Heh heh heh heh heh."

"The reason I came, sir, is to tell you…" He winked. "Mission accomplished."

"The asshole's dead? Where's the box? Where's his head? How can I be sure?"

"The head part proved undoable. But he's been fully neutralized."

"The sonofabitch called me a liar, you know. He asked for it."

The parson smiled meaningfully. "You won't have to worry about him ever again."

"What, me worry? Heh heh heh."

"Sir, there is something to worry about." He guided the president past a ball washer to more level ground. "It's the Middle East."

"Why? We're stampin' out rats over there fast as we can. We're installin' democracy and free enterprise. What more do they want?"

"It's Shrinkistan and Zionia I mean, sir. Our wars, though greatly beneficial to the countries we've devastated, have excited the Shrinkistanian fanatics to new levels of terrorist violence. The peace we've nurtured so carefully is breaking down and I'm afraid something awful may happen."

"What do you want me to do?"

"You, sir, could do so much. Your genius for peering deep into men's souls will allow you to knit together a Middle East peace accord that really gets the job done."

"Oh yeah? Let's say I'm knittin' away and some Shrinkistanian loony tune decides to blow his ass off along with half of Tel Aviv. I end up with egg on my face. Right?"

"It's not like you to think small. Consider what it will mean when you succeed. Every president before you tried to bring a true Middle East peace and failed. Even Rod Raygun and your father tried—and failed. Sir, when you succeed you'll become our wisest, most popular president ever. You'll outpoll Abe Lincoln and maybe Christ. Even the Jackasses will be kissing your caboose."

Twofer twirled his putter, frowning and working his mouth under the duress of the special form of cogitation that was his and his alone. "I gotta pondicate on it."

50

UNBEKNOWNST to Ernest Candide, who when we last saw him was "as dead as dead can be," his captors had not meant for him to die. He had been injected with a powerful tranquilizer used to knock out blue whales and not surprisingly a miscalculation had been made in dosage. The amount so carefully computed turned out to be four times what was needed to kill the superhero.

During the resulting medical emergency, a critical care unit disguised as a Homemade Mother's Bread truck tore down the interstate at 115 mph, turning heads on its way to an operating theater in the bowels of the Pentagon. Inside the vehicle, a crack team of paramedics worked feverishly to revive Candide's corpse. They injected massive doses of methedrine extract as an antidote to the tranquilizer and zapped him repeatedly with a defibrillator. They did CPR, external heart massage and advanced yoga manipulations. Nothing worked. Death—cold, absolute and ironic—had settled upon the unlucky, and now medically deceased, young man.

At the Pentagon, some of the best surgeons and cardiologists on the Eastern Seaboard undertook more extreme revival techniques—but to no avail. It had been a full hour since Candide's body last registered a vital sign. We can thus conclude without fear of contradiction that the person once known as Ernest Lafitte Candide had ceased to be. Surgical gloves lay discarded on his open chest. A stained sheet was pulled up over the bloodless face. The lights were out and the elite team of sawbones had retired to a nearby lounge to drown their sorrows and discuss the likelihood of being indicted for the murder of a Plunderian intelligence asset.

What happened next defies conventional explanation, happening as it did deep in the nexus where biology, religion, and prevarication all coalesce. Ernie Candide's will to live, floating belly up in his blood, absorbed just enough latent pineal hormone to excite his soul fire into a tiny flickering flame. This flame reignited his spark of life. Soon the rising heat in his wide-open chest tripped his sciatic thermocouple, sending an electrical impulse to his heart, kicking it over. The cold blood chugged slowly into vascular rotation and began to warm. It wasn't long till Candide could be said to be living again, and not long after that he began to revive.

He woke totally out of it. All he knew was he needed to pee. He rose from the operating table, chest gaping. Dragging bloody sheets and pulling a plasma drip system on a trolley he exited into the hallway where two marine guards stood watch. Candide politely asked one of them for directions to the men's room and the youth went bug-eyed. *"Whoa!"* he yelled as his M-16 discharged into the ceiling. He dropped the weapon and fled down the hall. The second guard crossed himself and fainted.

The doctors were paged at their watering hole, where some had managed to become well watered. They soon reassembled in the operating theater. Candide, semi-conscious and confused, was reanesthetized before he could protest. The surgeons closed his chest and began the procedure planned from the first. The top of Candide's head was shaved and a local anesthetic injected into his scalp in preparation for the delicate extraction.

Ernie regained consciousness looking up at a dawn summer sky with two pink clouds. He was lying in grass and had a vicious headache. He lifted his head (heavy as a bag of sand) and looked around. An old railroad locomotive mounted on concrete and a small duck pond told him he was in a park—one somehow familiar. He rose to his feet, his chest burning and the force of gravity seeming to have increased a hundredfold. His first wobbly steps carried him to a park bench, where he slumped down to collect himself. Sliding fingers inside his shirt, he confirmed his suspicion that the stinging in his upper torso was from a long incision and sutures. He knew then that his dreamlike remembrance of waking in a dark morgue with his chest open was probably real. He guessed the drunken doctors playing grab ass with the nurses had been real, and maybe even the marine firing squad. But what was it all about?

He now could identify the park. It was the one he'd passed on his way to visit Delilah. That meant her hotel was only a few blocks up the street. He rose stiffly and began walking in that direction. The new weakness was with him, but he was alive at least, and the reassuring summer sunlight was now touching the green water of the pond. As he exited the park an early morning bus passed on the street, empty of passengers. After three blocks Candide began to see the top of the Baltimore Hillcrest, bright with sunshine. He was feeling better by the minute.

Delilah was awake, heating a baby bottle on a hot plate. She fixed breakfast and helped Candide piece together what had happened. The key clues lay on top of his head. A swath had been shaved through his blond flattop and a bandage taped there. Lifting the gauze Delilah found sutures. When Candide felt these with his fingertips he realized the incision was directly over his pineal gland. "They took out the bullet," he said, "and that's why I'm weak."

Delilah nodded. "Good way to neutralize you. Except for one thing."

"Yeah?"

"Your strength comes from your mind now. Just keep on thinking."

Typical female point of view, it seemed to him. But he knew he couldn't complain. Physically he was as strong as the average Plunderian male. One question remained. "What did they put in my chest?"

"Hmm." Her cute little face screwed up in thought. "Maybe nothing. Didn't you say you came to with a sheet pulled over you and everyone gone?"

"Yes."

And your chest was open, right?"

"Right."

"Sounds like they opened you up to massage your heart, but they must have failed to start it."

"Then why aren't I dead?"

"I guess you came back to life. Somehow."

Candide nodded. He was used to his body doing amazing things. "What about the firing squad?"

"Marine sentries, maybe. To keep the whole thing private."

Candide looked glum. The presence of Plunderian marines established pretty clearly who was behind it.

51

WHAT troubled Candide most about the loss of his superpowers was his greatly diminished earning capacity. A superbeaver who can whip up a housing development in a week doesn't have to fret money. But the same is not true for a fledgling thinker, especially one schooled primarily in death and destruction. And now he had a family to support! Not long after his return to the living, he somewhat desperately applied to five fast-food restaurants, then waited on pins and needles for the phone to ring. Late one afternoon he and Delilah were watching TV. Yonita lay between them on her stomach shredding a cowhide dog bone with her teeth. Suddenly Candide jumped up and ran for the phone, to Delilah's total bewilderment. The phone had not rung.

"Nobody there," said Candide as he hung up. Delilah was about to say something when the phone did ring. Ernie picked up. "Hello?"

"Ernest Candide?" It was a squeaky male voice.

"Yes?"

"Tyler Ebert, night supervisor at Burger Bomb. Got a job for you."

Candide brightened. "Great. What is it?"

"Customer greeter."

"Sounds good," said Candide, a little disappointed.

"Good? This will be *fantastic*. We're going to put you in a dog collar and chain you to the tetherball pole on our playground. As you spout your traitorous lies, the customers get to swat your butt with the tetherball paddle. Every time you yelp, they win an action figure."

Candide was furious but didn't want to take it out on some sixteen-year-old kid who was probably fronting for his manager. "Thanks, but no thanks."

"Why not?"

"The job you describe sounds thoughtless and demeaning."

"Thoughtless? You prissy ass. I stayed awake five nights detailing that promotion. You just cancelled my ticket to district manager."

"Good!" said Candide, slamming down the receiver. He fumed back to the couch.

Delilah was staring. "Ernie, why did you answer the phone when it didn't ring?"

He looked puzzled. "It rang."

"It rang the second time, not the first."

"It rang both times."

They tossed it back and forth but couldn't agree.

Two days later something equally strange happened. They were fixing dinner when the ex-soldier dropped the snap bean he was snapping and dashed into the living room. Delilah followed, curious. She saw her man standing in front of a closed window with his arms spread wide and confusion written large on his face. "What are you doing?" she asked.

"Yonita was flying toward the window. Totally out of control."

"She can't fly, at least not yet. And if you saw her, where is she?"

"She was about to hit me, then she disappeared. Listen, I don't understand it either."

At that moment the flying upside-down body of their toddler swept out of the hallway toward them, her tiny limbs blurring and buzzing. Candide opened his arms as before and Yonita flew into his chest, knocking him back. Nestled in his arms, the tyke looked up at him with a multi-toothed grin.

Delilah was flabbergasted. "Ernie, you can see the future! I mean actually *see* it!"

Candide had reached the same conclusion and was a bit overwhelmed.

"Remember that phantom phone call?" she asked.

"I can hear the future too."

"Right. But maybe not always. Certainly seems to happen with things you care about. Like finding a job. Or the safety of your kid."

That made sense. How smart she was!

Delilah got a quarter and asked him to sit next to her on the couch. "I'm going to flip, and I want you to pick heads or tails. You with me?" He nodded and the trial began. One hundred times the coin was flipped. Ninety-four times Candide got it right. Yes, he could see into the future, though not perfectly.

Ernie's eyes lit up. "Hey, I can go to Atlantic City and win enough to support us."

"Probably so."

"What I don't understand is why me again? Why *another* special power?"

"You said the doctors who operated on you were drunk. Maybe when they took out the slug, they accidentally created a bumpkin Nostradamus."

Both laughed—not realizing how fateful those words would be for themselves, for their toddler, and for all the other living things sharing their planet.

52

"HIT me."

A card scraped softly.

"Again."

Another card scraped.

"Hold."

"Twenty here, Ernie."

"Two jacks and a one—I win again."

Delilah marked on a pad. "That's ten in a row. And forty-six out of fifty. Want to knock off?"

"Why not? We know I can do it." He noticed she looked worried. "What's the matter?"

"Ernie, the more I think about this, the less I like it."

"But you said—"

"I know. I was wrong."

"Give me a week. I'll be back with enough money to put us in a house."

"You admit you've never gambled."

"Doesn't matter. I can beat anybody at blackjack. Anybody, anytime."

"Maybe. But what if you win too much, or too fast, or too consistently? I heard the casinos watch for card counters and you're going to set off alarms. I don't want you coming home with bullets in your knees."

A gloom settled over Candide. "How am I going to support us?"

"Surely there are better ways than gambling. Use that brain of yours to help you find one."

He knew she was right, but it wasn't easy hopping suddenly back to square one. He put away the cards with a dark cloud hanging over him.

"I'm not asking you to do anything I'm not doing, Ernie. Can I spy now that I have a kid?"

"But your parents, won't they be…" He drew a finger across his throat.

"The people I work for know mommies don't make the best spies. When they see I mean it, they'll release my parents."

"What will you do?"

"My plan is to train as a nurse, then make money at that while I study medicine. I always wanted to be a pediatrician."

"Sounds like a great plan," he said, morose. "I haven't thought past Atlantic City."

"Forget Atlantic City. Promise me."

"Well, I don't really approve of gambling. I suppose it would be inconsistent to earn my living that way."

"Ernie, think about how you might follow your deepest ambitions and, at the same time, make the world a better place."

"Tough one."

"Well, think about it."

At that moment an idea came to him. Not a career idea, rather one for raising money. "I could sell my blunderbus!"

"You have one of those?" Delilah was incredulous.

"Back in Tennessee. Must be worth thirty thousand bucks. We can sell it, buy a small car for transportation and put twenty grand in the bank. We'll save on gas too!"

"Smart," she said. A warm glow suffused Candide, as always when his cherished one complimented his acuity.

Later that day he was able to reflect at length on Delilah's advice. He remembered that in the nearly two tons of mail he'd received during his treason trial were a couple of offers from publishers. Both had wanted him to write a tell-all book about his experiences during and after the Supergoose operations. He'd questioned the purpose of such a book at the time. Now he realized he might be able to give the publishers what they wanted, yet go beyond, probing matters much more important to himself and to everyone. He could use his war experiences to expose his government's cynical invasions for oil. He could also explain to the Plunderian people how the wars in Ragistan and Qroc were weakening Plunderland at home and abroad. And by employing his new predictive powers he could sketch his country's likely future if it stayed on the warpath it had been blazing since the Screaming Eagle attack.

His fellow citizens—too many of them—had their heads in the clouds, or maybe buried in the sand. They couldn't see, or didn't want to see, what their government was up to with their tax dollars. Taking advantage of this apathy were politicians owned lock, stock and barrel by the big corporations, many of them weapons makers, defense suppliers, or heavy-construction contractors. What a blueprint for endless wars! Somebody needed to do something about it and why not him? His book could be a wake-up call. If it sold well, it could even help support his family.

Ernie knew he wasn't trained as a writer. He could think, though, and if he could think well enough he figured the writing would follow. Wasn't writing just ideas placed in a meaningful sequence? He would need to do a lot of research of course. He'd have to bring himself up to speed on the history of the Middle East and on the fundamentals of the oil industry. Also, the more he knew about the polecats running his government the better. Reading was the key to all of these, and, happily, reading was something

Candide now did very well. The D.C. area had great public libraries. Could he write a book? Damn right he could!

Bring it on.

53

PRESIDENT Twofer strutted the holy soil of Bethlehem wearing a blue suit stuffed with himself and himself alone. He bore in his hand a parchment of incalculable significance: the Blueprint for Everlasting Peace. With his trademark smirk shining on his kisser, the president joined two other men in suits standing under the blazing desert sun. The larger of these by far was Airbus Shalom, elected leader of the Zionian people. The smaller was Fakir Bogus, a last-minute replacement for the popular leader of the Shrinkistanians—in other words, a Plunderian puppet.

Cameras flashed through a photo op. Then President Twofer led the two leaders to the peace table where they took seats. Twofer directed them to study their copies of the almost magical document. Fakir Bogus posed for the cameras. Airbus Shalom hunched over his copy and rocked like a Talmudic scholar, reading slowly and carefully every word. His face registered increasing disgruntlement until in the end his upper lip lifted in a sneer, revealing clenched teeth. Twofer motioned the leaders to rise. He indicated they should hug. Shalom tried backing away, but Fakir Bogus, too quick for him, shot forward like a magnet and attempted to encircle the Zionian leader's immense middle with his short arms. He only half succeeded.

The next day, on a dusty street in the West Bank, a Zionian helicopter gunship fired its cannon into a passenger car, killing a leader of Haggis, the radical Shrinkistanian group. Also killed were the man's wife and three-year-old daughter. As bystanders were pulling burning bodies from the vehicle, the airborne cannon fired again and four rescuers died. Haggis quickly retaliated. A suicide bomber disguised as Airbus Shalom in drag smuggled two hundred pounds of plastique into a happening disco in the Tel Aviv suburbs. The explosion caught seventy patrons in a complicated line dance—

handing the police a grisly jigsaw puzzle. To avenge this atrocity, the Zionian Defense Forces assassinated three more Haggis leaders, killed eleven more bystanders, and reinvaded the Gaza to destroy crops, olive groves and homes.

The awesome Blueprint for Everlasting Peace began spiraling out of control. Another Shrinkistanian suicide bomber blew up a crowded bus in Jerusalem. Shrinkistanian snipers began picking off Zionian motorists driving between settlements. In response, the Zionian government ordered whole West Bank neighborhoods bulldozed. More than thirty Shrinkistanians died under the tumbling walls. Afterward, all the dead, including a month-old baby, were determined by the Zionian government to be terrorists. Step by mortifying step the internecine violence escalated as Everlasting Peace, the harbinger of holocaust, stole over the blood-soaked land.

54

IN a freshly painted apartment filled with boxes and furniture, Delilah, wearing faded jeans, knelt behind the television hooking up the cable. Candide entered through the front door carrying a cardboard box heavy enough to make him stagger. He put it down on top of another box and stretched his back. Delilah came around to the front of the set, picked up a remote and pressed it.

As the picture developed, Parson Rupert Weed, Bible in hand, was seen reading from a spotlit pulpit in a magnificent cathedral. The holy man was dressed all in white—white suit, white tie and Panama hat. His urgent voice thrust into the audience like a plunging sword. "I looked and beheld a great earthquake. The sun became black as sackcloth, the full moon became like blood, and the stars of the sky fell to the earth as the fig tree sheds its winter fruit when shaken by a gale. The sky vanished like a scroll that is rolled up, and every mountain and island was removed from its place."

"Isn't that guy Plunderland's national security adviser?" asked Delilah, astonished.

"Yeah. He's also a minister."

She made a sour face.

Weed closed his Bible and looked into the camera. "Indeed, my fellow faithful, the hour of reckoning is upon us. The signs of the old prophecy are plain to see. The Beast has begun his long climb from the deep hole of his confinement and soon will walk among us. For those whose foreheads bear the mark of the Beast, the retribution will be swift and harrowing. But for those whose saintly brows bear the mark of the Lamb, verily shall we pass unscathed through the conflagration at the end of this corrupted world—and into a far better place. For our time has come."

Delilah turned the set off, shaking her head. "If your president listens to that guy, we're in worse trouble than I thought. He *wants* the world to end."

"Where's Yonita?" asked Candide, looking around the room.

"She was with you," said Delilah alarmed.

Candide smiled and pointed. "Look." A white refrigerator, hovering a foot in the air, inched into the room. The fridge eased down onto the polished oak floor and Yonita came out from behind it in diapers, grinning and gurgling happily.

A gray-haired woman in her sixties appeared in the doorway. She wore a beige uniform on her amazing body, that of a champion athlete a third her age. She smiled down upon Yonita. "Your kid?" she asked Candide.

"Afraid so."

"Here I am watching the Redskins game and I see a refrigerator floating up the stairs. Figured I'd better check it out." She extended her hand. "Corky Cochran, building security."

"Ernie Candide."

"By damned! Should have known. A kid who can juggle refrigerators? Got to be yours."

"And this is Delilah," said Candide.

"Ma'am," said Corky with a nod, then turned back to Candide. "Ernie, got to know something. In that Colorado game when you brought Westport back from thirty points down in the last quarter, did you fly over the Buffaloes' line on your eighth touchdown?"

"There's no rule against flying in football, but I didn't feel flying was fair, because nobody else could do it. That day in Boulder I long jumped fifty feet."

"Knew it! Man, I could have won some bucks on that if I'd had a way to prove it."

"You look like you might have been involved in sports yourself."

"In my own small way. Silvered in the Rome Olympics. Should have been gold, but that's a story for another day."

"What sport?"

"Gymnastics. Ever hear of the Cochran?"

"Don't think so."

"Basically it's three backflips combined with a triple gainer. I was the only one who could ever do it. Yuri Andropov tried in Barcelona and put himself in a body cast."

Candide wasn't sure what to say.

"Let me confess," said Corky. "At your trial, when the whole thing started, I thought you were guilty as sin. But by the end I went with the jury. The government tried to railroad you, plain and simple."

"Sure did," said Candide smiling. He was beginning to wonder when his new buddy would let him get back to moving.

"What you said about thinking at your trial really shook me up, young man. Haven't been able to forget it. Recently I've been devoting at least fifteen minutes a day to freestyle thinking."

"How's it going?"

"Good. Pretty good…but now and then I come up with stuff that kind of knocks me off my feet."

"That's what it's like. Sometime when I'm not busy we could kick it around."

"Sure, sure, you're busy now. And here I am yakking. Hey, how about I give you a hand?"

"Well…" said Candide. Should a woman his grandmother's age be carrying his furniture?

"I'm not exactly frail, you know. Bench-press two-fifteen. Could do more but that's all we got in our gym. Management's a bunch of skinflints—as you'll soon learn."

"Anyone who can bench-press two-fifteen can help us move. Very kind of you. But what about your Redskins game?"

"Heck, I'll be in a better mood all day if I miss the rest of that."

55

CANDIDE had created a small office along one wall of the new apartment. He spent six to eight hours a day typing into his computer. Weeks earlier he'd finished drafting the memoir section of his book and now he was developing predictions for the future of his country. He'd begun with the assumption that Plunderland was creating a lot of new enemies for itself by beating the stuffing out of two impoverished lands in order to get a chokehold on world oil. Add these new enemies to his country's old enemies and he estimated as many as two billion people—maybe a third of the humans alive—would like to see Goliath go down.

Obviously, terrorist recruitment would be booming far into the future. Some of these combatants would remain in their homelands waiting for Plunderland to invade or for Western tourists to visit. More deeply committed holy warriors would travel to Ragistan or Qroc to join the new crusades. The bravest of all would find ways to penetrate Plunderland's borders so as to strike from inside the body of the beast. Just the worry of them coming would keep Plunderians forever on edge.

Terrorism was but the tip of the iceberg, however. What if two billion consumers weaned themselves from Plunderian products and services? What if foreign owners of Plunderian financial assets—many trillion dollars worth—decided to cash in? Or what if overseas holders of Plunderian debt (more trillions) called home their chips? Any one of these scenarios combined with ballooning oil prices could plunge the world's most over-leveraged economy into a long and severe decline.

Candide also expected foreign governments to cooperate among themselves to isolate and weaken Plunderland, merely for their own protection. Economic and military alliances which excluded his nation might bring a new balance of power and a safer world.

Though Candide knew he wouldn't like seeing his homeland humbled in this way, he realized it was probably necessary. President Twofer's bull-in-the-china-shop approach to international relations had shown the whole of mankind that raw force can take whatever it wants, at least in the short run. This wonderful lesson in power politics threatened to work its way down the pecking order of nations, giving a terrific boost to the world arms trade. Most ominous of all, Plunderland's pursuit of ever-better nukes would continue to spawn imitators. If nothing changed, earth appeared poised to enter the golden age of nuclear proliferation.

Candide meditated hard upon these likely developments while descending deep in his mind to that neural wellspring which bubbled with prescience. He slipped into a trance as his hair stood on end (pretty much as usual, given his rather erect haircut). His fingers, driven by a demon energy, channeled dismaying visions of the future into his word processor. The events he recorded, when later he read them, made his blood run cold.

Two of those predictions will be disclosed here, for reasons that will become apparent. First, Candide foresaw in great and fearful detail the "capture" of Madmahn Badassi by Plunderian marines. Badassi refused to be taken alive. With the troops closing in, he turned the square mile of land surrounding him into an erupting volcano of exploding 500-pound bombs laced with sarin gas. When the cloud of death cleared, Madmahn and two hundred brave marines lay mute on the inscrutable desert sand. In a second gripping vision, Candide watched Moolah al-Razir hijack Plunderian televisions and threaten to turn a nation of couch potatoes into French fries.

56

TERRORISM. Sure enough, one night on the evening news Candide heard that two surface-to-air missiles had barely missed a Zionian passenger jet as it took off from Addis Ababa airport. Soon more skilled havoc slingers took the field. A Plunderian Airlines jumbo jet lifting off from Dallas-Fort Worth was brought down by a SAM, killing everyone aboard. A Zionian 747 was

SAMed (as the technique came to be known) while landing at Charles de Gaulle. Luckily, that plane was low on fuel and didn't catch fire, so the pilot was able to bring it in, but eight passengers died from the missile blast.

Embassies were bombed. Night clubs were bombed. Hotels were bombed. Resorts and nooky massage palaces were bombed. Wherever on earth Plunderians gathered—or Zionians gathered—bombers from a variety of hard-line groups threatened to blow out the party candles at any given moment. For the targeted ones, life abroad became a process of always guessing.

A calamity resembling Candide's most horrific prediction was foiled only minutes from perpetration. A shrimp boat flying Plunderian flags and carrying five bearded fishermen in yellow slickers motored up the Potomac almost to central D.C. before a coast guard cutter ordered it to stand fast. When it tried to flee, the cutter shot tracers over its bow. Small arms fire from the shrimper initiated a brief but violent skirmish. The coast guard officers who boarded learned they had machine-gunned not patriotic fishermen but a crack squad of ASP suicide bombers, minutes from wiping out Plunderland's institutions of government. Under the captain's raincoat, strapped to his gut, was a shiny plutonium nuke armed and ready to blow.

On the economic front, the worldwide boycott of Plunderian products Candide had forecast was now fact. Burger Bomb, 47 years old, reported its first quarterly loss in company history. Poopsie Corp., 105 years old, reported its first quarterly loss. Both companies cited weak foreign sales as the problem. Booing Aircraft for the first year since WWII failed to close a single overseas deal, and Euro-Mousepark was bleeding losses like a Ronald Tramp casino. Underage Japanese hipsters plugged into Tokyo Cube instead of Eminem. Aging Italian Romeos left Vigorim on the shelves and rose to the occasion with the German generic Tunderdikk. Movie buffs everywhere pirated Hollywood flicks almost as a patriotic duty. And so on and so on and so on.

Irony of ironies: Plunderland's wars to grab oil provoked sabotage against Middle East pipelines, putting a serious crimp in oil supply. As production decreased, price increased—oh my, did it ever! The resulting inflation kicked the props out from under the Plunderian economy. The dollar fell in value against the Euro and the yen and most other currencies—then fell some more. Swelling unemployment, stagnant wages and anemic corporate profits sapped tax revenues even as the Twofer tax cuts kicked in automatically. Strapped for money, the federal government cut back funding to the states, forcing many states, in turn, to terminate essential services. Foreign investors, noting the expanding disarray in Plunderland, began cashing in their Plunderian assets with a vengeance, speeding general collapse.

Mighty Goliath had fallen and couldn't get up. It didn't help one bit that the bully was bloated with fast food, boogie nights, and blunderbus living. Enemies of every stripe were discovering that a toppled giant is easy to kick, especially in the pocketbook.

57

THE four most powerful men on the planet were in emergency session in the Oval Office, seated at a patio table next to the presidential putting green. Buzz "Who da man?" Twofer was war ready, propped up by his carrier group deck hat, his pearl-handled revolvers, and his belly putter, which he fondled with abandon as the weight of the world bore down upon his woolly persona. Chain Dickey, looking plain scared, held a red telephone receiver, mouthpiece covered. He spoke to the president with urgency. "Talk to him at least. He claims it's a rogue strike. Says the Chechens hijacked one of their mobile ICBMs and targeted the MIRVs on the Denver metro area. Exactly what our satellites show. To make up for Denver, he's offering any Rooskie city we want to take off the map. They won't hit back."

The president glowered. "The chickenshit is stalling. Wants to lullaby us into a false sense of security then kick us in the nuts again."

Secretary Minefield shook his head. "They would have hit us by now. They've got something else up their sleeve."

"How could the bastard do this to me?" wailed Twofer. "We talked man to man. We played catch with a baseball. I stared deep into his very soul—and it was pure and good. What happened?"

"If he's telling the truth," said the vice president, "it was beyond his control. The Chechens are Moslems, after all. Maybe they'd like for their two biggest devils to take each other out."

"Ragheads is too dumb to come up with somethin' that cute," said the president. He pointed the shaft of his putter at Parson Weed. "Parson, you been mighty quiet. What are you thinkin' with that great big brain of yours?"

"Nothing fancy, Buzz. Just trying to put two and two together. You looked into Pooty's soul and it was pure, right?"

"Right."

"And if his soul was pure, then Christ dwelled within—at least at the time."

"True."

"But would Christ drop five one-megaton nukes on a city full of innocent skiers?"

"Nope. Not unless he was tryin' to knock out some evil dictator or somethin'."

"No question of a dictator here. Just the freedom-loving snow bums of Denver. Would Christ smoke two million of them?"

"Not hardly."

"Then we can assume Christ no longer dwells in Pooty's soul. And if Christ, who was once in him, is no longer there, what does that mean?" Parson Weed raised his eyebrows expectantly.

"The Devil's in him!" said Twofer, alarmed.

Weed nodded. "I just don't know what to do about it."

"Wipe out them Rooskies before they hit us again, that's what! You can't reason with the Devil! He's as evil as they come!" Twofer stood up, knocking over his chair, and strutted to the presidential desk. On his unstained blotter rested a black box—and in the center of this box was a bright red button. Twofer, lost in thought (such as it was), stared at the button, wrinkling his brow. The stress began to agitate his mouth and ears.

"Sir, you can't," said Chain Dickey. "They'll see our missiles coming on their radar. They'll be forced to launch their whole arsenal back at us before they get hit. We'll be wiped off the map."

"Personally I doubt it," said Parson Weed calmly. "The shock and awe of our daring all-out strike will probably freeze them up. Basically, the Rooskies are chokers. Their misguided economic system rotted them out like a barrel of apples."

"Claypoo?" asked the pres.

"Question of balls, isn't it?" said Minefield sternly, hands behind his back. "I'm betting they come up short on critical load. Here's another consideration. Once we wipe them out, we don't have to worry about them ever again."

Buzz Twofer II, straining under the intense heat and pressure of the crisis, was at this moment transformed from the lump of godliness he had been into a marvelous shining zircon—as the biggest decision of his life coagulated inside his fuzzy coconut. He pulled himself up to his full erectness, saluted himself, and commenced to talk the talk as only he could talk. "I'm top dog around here," he barked, "and so the decidin's mine to do. I'm lookin' at the big picture, and I hear it tellin' me if I don't kick some Rooskie butt over this Denver thing, people are gonna say I'm plain chicken."

"Please, sir," said the vice president, "think of our families. Think of your lovely first lady."

A devious look stole over the president's smug features. "Heh heh heh heh. Now she's gonna find out once and for all who wears the nut cup in this house." With no further reflection and using his stubby thumb, President Twofer pushed the red button all the way down into the black box.

Chain Dickey went pale, unnerved by the president's virile action. Parson Weed smiled an enigmatic smile and tented his fingertips. Clayton Minefield grimaced with bravado. And Buzz Twofer walked the walk of war from his desk around the edge of the putting green to the patio table. He took the phone receiver from Chain Dickey's hand and lifted it to his presidential smirk. He did not notice that his VP was in the throes of a coronary event. "Poot Poot. Wassup?" Twofer listened, then spoke again. "Yeah, so we noticed. Wasn't very nice of you, was it? I'm sure I speak for all the good folks of Denver when I say shame on you. Heh heh heh." There was another pause, then Twofer continued: "Well, you can see how it makes me look. You pretty much put me in a position where I gotta show my balls to the Plunderian people or they'll think I don't have any."

Twofer paused for more than a minute, a smirk playing on his lips, finally spoke again. "That sounds fair. Moscow for Denver sounds more than fair. Wish I hadn't been so hasty. Heh heh heh... No, no, just a joke. Hey Pooty, can you hold for a sec? Be right back." Twofer covered the mouthpiece with the heel of his hand. He looked at Chain Dickey, who was sitting quietly with glazed eyes, dead as a doornail. Then he looked at Minefield. "Claypoo, hop on your cell and order me up a club and a can of Diet Poopsie from the kitchen—would you? This negotiatin' makes my tummy rumble." He winked at Parson Weed and returned to his conversation with the Rooskie premier. "Still there, Poot?"

Candide felt an earthquake. It stopped, then came again as he realized somebody was shaking him. He was in bed, it was the middle of the night, and the woman he loved was shaking his shoulder.

"Sorry to wake you, Ernie, but you were yelling and thrashing around. Nightmare?"

"Sure hope so," said the young Nostradamus. "Otherwise I just saw the end of the world."

58

LATE one morning Candide was answering email. Delilah came to him, worried. She showed him the message on her Palm Secretary:

> YOUR FAMILY IS THREATENED.
> WE MUST TALK. MEET ME BY
> THE LAKE IN STILLSETTER PARK,
> 2:00 P.M. TODAY. LOVE, WIDAD

"Who's Widad?" asked Candide.
"Widad Babylonia, a Qroci spy."
"You trust her?"

"Like my own sister."

"Is it really her?"

"There's the problem."

"I'll go with you," he said.

"And Yonita?"

"We'll leave her with Corky."

"I don't know, Ernie. Corky's okay when we go to the movies, but for this?"

"Exactly for this. What better babysitter than a black belt in tae kwon do who can bench-press two-fifteen?"

"Someone a little less, well, proactive."

"Corky will do fine."

"Guess we don't have a choice."

The park was a block away so they walked. It was a cold, bright, windless day—a beautiful winter day, if only they could have enjoyed it. Entering the park grounds they passed under bare trees on earth raked clean. Candide felt his mate's hand on his arm and stopped. She was looking across the water at a woman in a blue coat sitting on a bench feeding ducks from a paper bag. "That's her," Delilah whispered. "But we don't know her—right? And keep your lips zipped."

They exited the trees, walked around the end of the lake and approached the bench. Widad ignored them, and they ignored her, even as they found resting places for their posteriors on her bench. Candide was utterly taken aback. He'd naively assumed that only in movies and pandering novels were all the lady spies beautiful. Here was reality slapping him up the side of the head yet again—for, if anything, almond-eyed Widad was even more gorgeous than Delilah!!!

With her perfect lips perfectly still, Widad spoke in a soft and melodious voice. "Pick up the bag of whole grain bread crumbs and feed the ducks. It's good cover—and good for the ducks." Candide found the bag next to him. He began distributing crumbs to the fickle fowl that seemed willing to abandon Widad instantly and eat from any hand that kept forking over the no doubt delectable dried bread crumbs.

"You said we were in danger," Delilah asserted through unmoving lips. Candide realized the two had communicated in this manner before. Probably it was a standard espionage technique.

"Powerful people are scheming to kidnap your child," said Widad, firing up a cigarette and exhaling even as her words flowed. "They want to take her young so she can be raised in their sick ways. Eventually they'll deploy her as a weapon for their cause."

"Who are they?"

"Don't know. Sorry."

"If you don't know who they are, how do you know the other stuff?" asked Delilah with maternal concern and perhaps irritation.

"Sister, you've been off the grapevine. That's why I knew I had to come. I've never heard more chatter than we're getting every day now on Yonita. Naturally there are many rumors. I could name a dozen groups I've heard mentioned, but would that help you?"

"What *can* you tell us?"

"They'll come soon. And you should assume they'll kill to get her."

"Oy! Why am I so surprised? Nebbish that I am, I've been living in some happier world that doesn't even exist. Thank you so much for warning us, dear friend. What do you need? Money? A safe house?"

"All I need is a safer planet for our children—but I don't expect to see it soon. These days the warmongers are in power almost everywhere. For peace lovers like us, it is a dangerous time." These passionate words sent a chill up Candide's spine. In his eagerness to agree with Widad he almost began flapping his lips, then realized the danger to them all. He continued feeding the greedy ducks. Amazingly, the more crumbs they ate, the more they seemed to want.

Now out of the windless lake climbed a straggler duck, moving forward with not quite the familiar duck waddle—rather a smoother motion suggestive of wheels. And what was that humming? This very odd duck continued in their direction releasing from its rear a faint trail of blue smoke. Blue smoke? Ernie realized it was probably more bomb than bird. As it closed in, he dove to smother it with his body, intending to absorb the blast, but the nimble creature shot out from under him and went straight for Widad. She flipped her cigarette at her attacker and began running. Candide and Delilah watched in horror as the beautiful Qroci operative sprinted across dead grass with the fatal fowl closing fast. The duck leapt into the air and flew the last few yards with a loud buzzing, striking Widad in her lower back.

A tremendous explosion erupted in fire and smoke. White feathers and bits of blue fabric drifted down from on high. Candide and Delilah ran to their friend, lying in the grass. She was blown almost in half, her legs turned at an angle to her torso. Blood was pooling. One didn't need a medical degree to know that the brave woman had only moments remaining. Those moments were spent holding hands with a trusted old friend and a very earnest new friend—not the worst way to go. Widad coughed, then spoke, her voice pinched. "Don't let this discourage you. I lived for what I believe in—and died for it too! How many can say that?" She smiled.

"Please don't talk," said Delilah, eyes watering.

"But there are things I want to tell you—both of you." Widad cleared her throat. "Although they've killed me, it's not their world. Not theirs only. The warmongers didn't make it and they don't own it. It belongs equally to those of us who just want to live in peace and cultivate our own gardens."

Now that the ladies were motating their lips, Candide felt he could speak. "That's what we believe," he said, excited. "That people should just hoe their own gardens peacefully. Live and let live."

Candide felt Widad's hand tighten on his. "You two have been chosen," she said, straining. "A special trust has been placed in your care. All of us who work for peace have such high hopes for your child. Raise her right and she'll lead her generation to a better world. Maybe the world we dream about, dear ones." With that, the beautiful spy breathed her last. Her staring eyes lost the passion that had filled them to the last and the muscles in her blood-splattered face went slack.

Delilah leaned forward and closed the staring eyes. A tear fell on Widad's cheek. "Ernie, maybe you'd better check on Yonita," she said. "I'll stay here."

Candide sprinted home, discovering in the process how out of shape he was. Gasping, he climbed the stairs to Corky Cochran's second floor apartment and knocked. The door swung open unassisted. Corky lay on the floor bound in duct tape from neck to foot, a strip of tape over her mouth. Fear gripped Candide. He knelt and pulled the tape from Corky's lips.

"Please don't tell your wife about this," said the security guard, abashed.

"Our daughter's been kidnapped and you don't want me to tell her *mother*?!" Candide scowled as he began to unbind Corky's wrists.

"Nobody's been kidnapped. Your little perp did this."

"Yonita?"

"I was helpless. How could I use my arsenal of deadly blows on a baby girl? She overwhelmed me."

"Where is she now?"

"From the sounds I've been hearing she's next door tormenting the neighbor's dogs. If you hurry maybe you can save the poor beasts."

Candide did indeed hurry—downstairs, outside, and over a tall white fence bearing two big signs: BEWARE OF VICIOUS DOGS and ENTER AT YOUR OWN RISK. He saw on the winter lawn three huge mastiffs lying on their sides, immobilized by duct tape. They lifted their wrapped muzzles, stared at him with frightened eyes and whimpered. Yonita ambled out from behind the doghouse holding a depleted roll of tape. Seeing Candide, she grinned brightly. "Daddy home!"

59

EARLY the next day Ernie visited the hardware store. He spent the rest of the morning kidnap proofing their apartment. He installed bolts in every window frame, taped strip alarms on the windows and put a heavy-duty deadbolt on the hall door. In the afternoon, guys from a security company came and installed motion detectors on the walls and pressure-sensitive plates under the throw rugs. Both systems were connected to a network of lights and alarms.

OPERATION SUPERGOOSE

When all was done, Candide considered their apartment as secure as it could be without a live-in bodyguard, which they couldn't afford.

The television news that day was full of the capture of Madmahn Badassi—an event totally unlike what Candide had predicted! Madmahn had been dragged from a "spider hole" with no loss of life whatsoever. The Lion of Baghdad, armed with a pistol, had not resisted according to the account, perhaps because he was hampered by "half-healed burns throughout the groin area." Watching someone pick through Madmahn's bushy hair and beard on TV, Candide almost felt sorry for him. The deposed potentate looked like an aging homeless man, crazy as a loon, eyes fearful and confused.

Then it dawned on the veteran torturee what he was really seeing—something no journalist seemed to notice, though the story played big for several days. The dark spots on Madmahn's cheek and forehead were quite recent scabs. And the dictator's wandering, jumping eyes weren't insane. He'd been shot full of some powerful hallucinogen, LSD or the like. Madmahn was being tortured physically and mentally, probably around the clock. He's getting it worse than I got it, thought Candide, and so far he's holding up.

It upset Ernie that his prediction about Madmahn's capture had been so dead-ass wrong. He'd seen in his mind just how it would happen; yet none of it had been right. His predictive powers were more flawed than he'd suspected. And this made him question whether he'd be able to protect his daughter. While he was stewing, the phone rang.

"Ernie, Nathan Rader here. How goes it?"

"Not so good."

"Oh?"

"A friend of ours was assassinated yesterday. She came to warn us about a plan to kidnap Yonita."

"My God. Let me think. Want me to get you a number at the FBI?"

"And if the kidnappers are part of our government?"

There was a long silence before Rader expelled his breath.

"You see the problem," said Candide.

"Sure do."

"Our apartment's like a fortress now. I think we'll be okay."

"Ernie, maybe I can help another way. Would all of you be safer in Nebraska?"

"Nebraska?"

"That's your home state, isn't it?"

"Yeah."

"How'd you like to run for governor?"

"You must be kidding."

"Not a bit. We're forming a new political party—a grassroots progressive party, national in scope. Our aim is to represent everyone not represented under the current system."

"Well, that's pretty much everybody," said Candide. "But third parties always fail, don't they? Plunderland's got a two-party system."

"The Mastodons and the Jackasses want us to believe third parties always fail. However, look at history. Major parties tend to grow from splinter groups which keep getting bigger because they represent peoples' needs. It can happen again. Only a couple of elections ago Russ Peru and his Reformation Party won eighteen percent of the national presidential vote and put a governor in office. We believe we can do better. We plan to become a major party."

"Mr. Rader, I'm flattered you'd consider me, but there's no point in stringing you along. I'm no politician. Besides, I need to stay closer to home right now. Hoe my own garden, you might say."

"Will you at least think about it?"

Candide knew he owed Rader that much. "Okay."

60

IN the wee hours, after even the mice had hit the sack, a faint high-pitched whine could be heard at the front door of Candide and Delilah's apartment. It stopped, then started again. In the crack between door and doorway a thin blade was licking in and out so fast it appeared to be unmoving. It's teeth, eating steadily downward through the deadbolt, finally cut through. The door opened a few inches into an apartment filled with laser beams burning through the dark at many angles. A gloved hand holding what looked like a TV remote eased into the room. The device clicked once and the beams vanished.

A tall figure entered, followed by a much shorter figure. As the two passed a window, illumination from a streetlight revealed their flowing black Bedouin robes, baggy headdresses and enormous noses. They crept down the hall and entered Yonita's room. Inside, the larger man poured something from a bottle onto a folded cloth—ether from the smell of it. The man walked to Yonita's crib, lowered the cloth and pressed down hard with both hands as a struggle ensued, violently shaking the crib. In time the shaking ceased and all was quiet.

"Open the valise," whispered the ether merchant to his partner a moment before steel-like clamps gripped his wrists. A mighty jerk that almost separated his hands from his arms yanked him off the floor at tremendous acceleration and drove him through the wall next to the crib, shattering a stud. He landed in the neighboring bedroom on top of the suddenly very awake and incensed Ernest Lafitte Candide, trained to master level in every martial art known to man. The school of hard knocks opened advanced classes for the hapless kidnapper as he received in quick succession seven roundhouse swivel kicks, six Portuguese head butts, five driving uppercuts, four low blows, three Dutch rubs, two shots to the Adam's apple, and a blinding two-fingered jab to the eyeballs courtesy of Larry, Curly and Mo.

"Give him hell!" yelled Delilah from the floor, where she'd been pitched by the heaving mattress. "I'm going to get Yonita." On her way out she grabbed the heaviest thing on the dresser—an old cologne bottle.

Candide's overmatched opponent, wounded in virtually every vulnerable zone of his body, rolled off the bed, unconscious. The instant he hit the floor, the lasers reactivated, setting off clanging alarms, flashing lights, and a howling air raid siren. In the brilliant illumination and deafening clamor Candide noticed that his blows had torn off the Bedouin's face. A closer look revealed that the wart-covered nose and thick snarling lips were parts of a rubber mask knocked askew. Ernie removed it and saw the slumbering head of Chain Dickey's taller handler. Candide didn't recognize the guy personally but knew from the stylishly cropped gray hair he was probably Secret Service. All of them went to the same barber, it seemed. Maybe shared the same mistress. As the agent began coming around, Candide leaned down and yelled in his face. "Your boss sucks cow pies!"

The shorter intruder now sprinted past the bedroom door, headdress blown back, an airborne Yonita in close pursuit. Next came Delilah, cologne in hand. Candide heard a crash at the front door, then someone tumbling down a flight of stairs. Not long after Delilah shouted from outside. "Yonita, come back here!"

With Ernie's attention diverted, the taller agent rose to his knees and began crawling. Candide flattened him on the living room carpet and swiftly administered another multifaceted comeuppance. He clamped the guy in a neck lock from behind, ready to cut off his air if he so much as peeped. Corky Cochran, in a robe over pajamas, chose this inopportune moment to enforce building security. Candide looked up just in time to see her coiled body in the open doorway of the clanging, flashing apartment. Then Corky flew into action. With a mighty hunnggYAAH! she whipped off three backflips at great speed, morphing the last into a mega-bicycle kick delivered with devastating force to Ernie's left forearm. The precision blow (unfortunately mistargeted) snapped Candide's ulna, causing him to release his prisoner.

"Ow!" Ernie yelled. "Kick him, not me!" In the confusion, the agent scrambled through the front door.

Not long after a car was heard pealing out.

Candide, cradling his injured arm, and Corky, apologizing profusely, made their way downstairs to check on Delilah and Yonita. They all met on the porch. "Oy!" said Delilah, hands on her cheeks, "They broke your arm."

Corky hung her head.

"It's a clean break," said Candide. "You two okay?"

"We're fine. I got their license number for the police."

Candide looked troubled. "Don't think the police can help."

"Course they can," said Corky. "This sort of thing is definitely police business."

"These guys have real juice at the top, Corky," said Candide.

Delilah stared at him, her face tight. "We'd better get you to the hospital. Corky, can you drive?"

Corky perked up. "Sure."

61

ONE cold January afternoon Candide found in his mail a letter forwarded from his old Tennessee address. The return was Leavenworth Federal Penitentiary and the seven-page outpouring inside was written longhand in safety pencil by General Jack Pangloss (ret.). It was a passionate plea to be forgiven for having ratted Candide out to three national intelligence agencies and for trying to assassinate him with .45 caliber depleted uranium hollow points. A document so moving should be made public, at least in part, for the betterment of humanity. So here are the most salient nuggets:

> When the powerful men I risked my life for many times and whom I trusted to do my thinking for me—when those same men turned their backs on me, denied even knowing me (and remember, Goose, I'd given my very balls for their sick causes) I finally saw the light. I realized those conniving bastards weren't really my friends. And I knew I needed to begin thinking for myself ASAP.
>
> Today I declare with pride, along with the remarkable French philosopher Rene Descartes, 'I think, therefore I am.' And truly, the 'I' that I am through thinking is hardly the 'me' that I was. I have unearthed a whole new fellow inside me, a gentle, caring spirit in tune with the changing seasons. Under his guidance I have powwowed with my feminine side and converted to Buddhism. Meditating like a beaver, in only a few weeks I've clarified my karma, bringing

my yin and my yang into harmonious balance. In short, guided by a new moral compass of my own devise, I have forgone the path of selfishness, dedicating myself to the vigorous upgrading of my fellow man, woman, or sexual deviant.

As you know, Goose, even the strongest belief has small meaning without embodiment in action. Hence I recently volunteered as a candy striper in our prison infirmary. I also devote six hours a week to the inmate truck garden, where I'm cultivating a crop of gasless pinto beans to improve prison air quality. Recently I petitioned to add nine cannabis sativa plants to next year's plantings, so as to bring a little relief to our glaucoma and terminal cancer sufferers. I doubt I can get that, but I have to try. In my spare time I founded a Unitarian church here in my cellblock and wait patiently for it to swell from its current congregation of one.

What I want to say, Goose, is that I was dead wrong. Constructive rational thought, i.e. logical cogitation, is life's greatest blessing. More importantly, a friend is a friend all the way. When I tried to blow you full of gaping holes with those fragmenting bullets I thought I was serving my country, but in fact, in vain ignorance, I was committing treason against both my motherland and the sacred bond of friendship. Please forgive me if you can.

Your former desert squadmate,

Jack (Starseed) Pangloss

Candide was thrilled that his old pal had managed to pull his soul up by its bootstraps. He sought out Delilah, folding diapers on their bed, and read her the entire letter in a passionate voice, waving his casted arm gracefully in rhythm with the masterful prose. Delilah proved harder to impress. She snapped a diaper, then folded fast. "Sounds to me like he's working up a con for the parole board."

"Can't you hear the new and better man? It's an open man able to confront his deepest feelings, a man not afraid to show his feminine side. How could he fake that?" There was a trace of peevishness in Candide's voice, partly because he realized Delilah might be right. Pangloss could be faking it all.

Seeing her mate's unhappy face, Delilah softened. "Ernie," she said gently, "sometimes I forget you're Plunderian. It's as natural for you to be optimistic as for me to be pessimistic. You may be right about the general. You know him better than I do."

Candide wasn't dumb. She was humoring him. And of course she was right about Pangloss. Was it really credible that in a few short weeks the bloodthirsty martinet had meditated his way to sainthood? Sadly, the old war dog was far too set in his ways to ever learn tricks that new. Pangloss was just trying to con him into testifying at some future parole hearing. Feeling older and wiser, Ernie ambled into the living room. He was drawn to a window. A light snow filtered down from a gray sky beginning to darken. As he watched the snow, he was haunted by images from his wars—gruesome visuals echoing with Pangloss's high-pitched screams. Such flashbacks tended to come when he was feeling down.

The doorbell rang, interrupting his funk. Ernie used the peephole to see who it was. He recognized Corky and opened. She held a rolled-up blueprint. "Better take a look at this, Ern." On the dining table they unrolled the print and pinned it down with coffee mugs. "Found out our building was once a fancy bordello. This suite here," Corky pointed to a third-story flat, "is your unit." Her finger moved to a small rectangle. "Here's my concern. I'm thinking this might be a trapdoor to the attic."

Candide leaned back and looked around the ceiling. "Where is it?"

"Well," said Corky, sliding her finger, "it's twenty-two feet from the front wall, and six feet inside the outer wall." She looked over her shoulder and pointed. "Try that closet." Ernie opened the closet and turned on the light. He unhooked a rolled umbrella hanging among bagged clothes and used it to push up on the closet ceiling. Sure enough, the ceiling rose on one side, revealing a trapdoor, totally unsecured. Pigeons could be heard flapping.

"I'll take care of this," said Candide. "What do you think, nails or screws?"

"Screws," said Corky. She pulled a paper from her pocket. "I've figured out nineteen other ways to breach the security of your unit. When you have time, take a look and then we can talk."

"Appreciate you watching our backs."

"There's another security issue…well, sort of," Corky said, looking bashful. "It's got me stumped. Can't decide what to do."

"Shoot."

She took a deep breath. "The sprinklers in this building were installed on the cheap thirty years ago. Now the whole system's full of rust. If we have a fire in more than two units I expect a general breakdown. And since this building is wood…"

"A deathtrap without sprinklers."

"Found out a couple years back. Following company policy, I filed complaints all the way up the ladder to our president and—guess what?—every stinking one of them says new sprinklers aren't feasible costwise. Sometimes I think they *want* the place to burn down so's they can collect on insurance or somethin'. You know how things work these days."

"Afraid I do."

"Ernie, I've toed the line all my life. I've followed orders to the last period and I've never rocked the boat. But I can't help noticing that for the most part my loyalty has got me screwed—me and people like me. Take this sprinkler thing. What if I shut up and then folks die? How am I gonna live with myself?"

"You're right."

"If I blow the whistle to the fire department, I figure they'll make management fix things. But then what?"

"You could lose your job."

"Sure could."

"Corky, that's a tough one."

She shrugged. "I know. It *is* my decision. And I've already made it, haven't I? I'm just an old scaredy-cat. Thanks for listening, Ern."

"Don't thank me. You're the one sticking your neck out." Candide was grinning, happy for his friend, who'd never stood taller in

OPERATION SUPERGOOSE

his eyes. He walked Corky to the door with his hand on her shoulder. "Keep me filled in."

After dinner, Candide secured the trapdoor. He was driving the last screw with his power drill when Delilah appeared in the closet doorway. "Ernie, didn't you want to watch the president's speech?"

He hurried to turn on the TV. The moment he saw Twofer's corrugated forehead he knew the leader of the free world was already knee deep in his strategic doo-doo. And so it was: "That's why I'm putting North Korealand's cocky little Elvis on public notice. In your rush to build nukaler bombs you are flirting with silent but deadly danger. Same for you Persians, who seem to have your holy headgear wrapped too tight or something. Think our Peeping Toms up in the sky can't see every move you make? Stop playing with fire or we'll give you free that big bang you seem to want so bad. Heh heh heh."

"Punk warmonger!" Candide yelled at the TV. "Draft-dodging, lip-flapping chicken hawk! Blustering Texas titmouse!"

Corky's shouts drifted up from the floor below. "Shameless candyass! Phony two-bit buckaroo! Peewad!"

Twofer, smirking in full appreciation of his own robust frankness, moved to the next villain on his hit list. "That brings me to Chinaland, a country we've treated as our friend, but who is now acting in fragrant disregard for international law and common decency. Think we don't know you unconchable sneaks are migrating your coastline to try and swallow up brave little Tywawa? Every hour on the hour our high-roving supersnoops measure to the nearest micropeter the position of your creeping beaches and tiptoeing cliffs. To thwarp your slow-speed attack, I have commandeered seven carrier task groups instantly to the Black China Sea. Even now our hearty naval shipmates are forming a protective iron daisy chain around plucky Tywawa, blocking her chaste harbors from rogue penetration.

"Lastly but not leastly, I must deliver a stinging rebate to Cubaland's bearded scorpion—"

The president's "stinging rebate," surely worth hearing, was cut short as the screen filled with snow and roared like Niagara Falls.

Candide picked up the remote and ran through the channels but all were the same: snow and roaring. Had the cable connection come loose? As he rose from the couch to check, the picture cleared and Moolah al-Razir, dressed in the robe of an ancient Moslem prophet, appeared on camera with a rocky hillside behind him. Moolah's beard was grayer than before, but he looked healthy. The staff upon which he leaned was a sleek, state-of-the-art Rooskie missile launcher.

In a resonant voice he began. "I speak tonight not to my friends, but to mine enemies—you Plunderians with your big bombs and lackey supporters. I speak to your chief buffoon and to all the Plunderian people. Hear my message and tremble—for I come to tell how you will perish."

Candide realized this harangue was the one he'd foreseen in his trance. Delilah joined him on the couch, looking worried, as the terrorist leader continued. "Following our attack on your flag factory, you invaded our homelands in Ragistan and Qroc, just as we prayed you would. Stupidly, you brought only a few allies with you. Now you have grabbed Qroc's oil and, like the monkey holding the prize inside the jar, you are trapped because you can't let go. Pay attention greedy monkey. Here is where your wars are leading. We will kidnap and behead your allies and anyone who helps you. We will assassinate your puppets and terrorize the international aid workers until they all leave. One day it will be just you and us in the bloody sand of the Middle East, eye to eye, fighting to the death. We are millions and we are ready. We have waited centuries for this satisfaction. Even if it takes another century, we will feed all of you to our desert worms. This I promise.

"Blind with arrogance, you Plunderians think you can tell us how to live. You believe your way is the only way, so it must be our way. But we despise your way—your sick decadence, your obscene and wasteful greed, your two-faced insistence you have the right to kill us in any number but we don't have the right to kill even one of you. You have behaved as the infidels you are and must be punished for your sins. God has chosen us as the instruments of your humiliation. We are not peace-loving Buddhist rice farmers. We are desert warriors and in our wrath you will suffer your apocalypse. Allah's will be done, on earth as it is in heaven."

As suddenly as he'd come, Moolah vanished and roaring snow filled the screen. Chaff Gentry appeared, seated behind his news desk in New York, seething with anger and defiance. "Based on information now coming in, it appears all Plunderian media broadcasts were jammed simultaneously to clear the way for Moolah's preposterous threats. Such widespread interference is a technical feat of almost superhuman complexity. We can be certain, therefore, that Moolah and his desert ruffians didn't pull it off by themselves. Some major world power must have provided technical assistance. I shudder to think who we may be forced to bomb next. Perhaps one of our most trusted allies."

Candide, angry, snapped off the set. "Hell, why not bomb all our allies and be done with it! What a load of crap!"

"When people become so unreasonable," said Delilah, "you know things have to get worse before they can get better."

"If things get much worse we're going to have World War III."

"Maybe we will."

At that less-than-happy moment Yonita flew into the room, executed a triple somersault over the TV, and fluttered down gently onto her father's lap. Ernie's arms closed around her in a hug and she giggled. One of her pigtails had come undone. Looking at it, Ernie felt a pang. He thought about the world his daughter would likely inherit—a world (if it survived) of lethal disorder stirred by perpetual war. A world almost certain to exploit and pervert Yonita's miraculous gifts. Could he watch that happen without lifting a finger?

Nathan Rader used politics to work for a more human-safe world, and Candide knew political activity was one way to accomplish such things. Maybe he should run for governor of Nebraska as Rader proposed. Ernie for sure had name recognition, though not all positive. And if he got into office his talent for seeing into the future couldn't hurt. Deep in his heart, though, he knew a political career wasn't really his wish. What he wanted was to live his life based on what he believed was right—just that, no more and no less. He was reminded of Corky in this regard. Doing the right thing would likely cost her a job, but she was going to accomplish something important. Wasn't Corky actually the kind of person who, on a day-to-day basis, most often changed things for the better?

Candide's book project now seemed less significant to him. Even if he got the thing published, and even if thousands of people read it, he knew it wouldn't likely change the world. Individual humans working for themselves and for their families would do that, if anyone did. Ordinary folks just hoeing their own gardens. Ernie still planned to finish the book, but now he was looking beyond. One of Rader's ideas had stuck in his mind like a cocklebur. Having given it a lot of thought, he sounded out Delilah. "Should we move away from here?"

"To be safer?"

"I know we can't be completely safe as long as people want our daughter. But wouldn't we be better off in a town not run by Buzz Twofer and his boys?"

"Where do you have in mind?"

"A place where strangers in hundred-dollar crew cuts and fancy sunglasses would really stand out."

EPILOGUE

AN endless patchwork of different shades of brown. Dead wheat fields, dead alfalfa fields, dead cornfields and dead grazing land stretched on all sides to the horizon, sweltering in the summer sun. Amidst this sea of brown floated a small island of humanity—call it a hamlet, call it the boondocks or the sticks. On the outskirts rushed a muddy creek swollen with recent rain, almost ironic so late in the growing season. Along one bank of the creek stood tents, teepees and all manner of shacks with clotheslines strung between. Several campfires raised columns of smoke into a blue sky.

Half a mile away, radiating heat, lay a potholed two-lane highway devoid of traffic. Where the highway met the creek an old steel girder bridge had collapsed into the current and was packed with debris. Beyond the bridge the highway continued into town, becoming its main street. Here stood all the local businesses, four blocks of them. Half the stores had dark or painted-over windows. Nearly all the storefronts needed paint. A rusty pickup turned onto the main drag, backfired, and rolled slowly through the dying business district.

A few blocks south of "downtown" in a neighborhood of modest homes and large trees a man in a blue suit bicycled a shady avenue. He passed under the bole of an oak and was briefly lost to view, then reappeared. The man's suit hung loose upon him and his cheeks were gaunt. He coasted to the curb and stopped. Next to his shoe an address was stenciled in white paint. He took out a handkerchief, dabbed perspiration from his face and neck, then dismounted and dropped the kickstand. He started across a lawn of buffalo grass behind a yellow stucco house shaded by walnut trees.

A blue baseball cap was moving among tomato plants in the garden and the bicyclist walked toward it. As he approached, the cap rose slowly and turned his way, accompanied by snapping sounds. Beneath the cap stood a well-built blond man in cutoff jeans and a white T-shirt, stooping slightly and leaning on a hoe. He offered his hand, twisted and gnarled. "Ernest Candide," said the former superhero, now in his thirties.

"Harvey Pickett."

"Quotidian Daily Bugle, you said."

"Right."

"Don't get many requests for interviews nowadays, Mr. Pickett. How'd you find me?"

"Oh, one of the wire services did a where-are-they-now piece a couple of days back. Learned you were living here in Quotidian, so I looked you up in the phone book. Heck, next to the Baroness and Jellyroll, you're the most famous local we've ever had. Figured there was a story in it."

"Don't know about that," said Ernie, smiling. Laugh lines radiated from his eyes. His features had matured into a face some might call handsome, though in his own view he was far too average to ever fit that description.

The reporter gestured to Candide's gnarled hand. "War injury?"

"Wore out my joints playing superhero. I call it superarthritis."

"Ouch. Collect disability?"

"Don't qualify, or for veteran's medical. The army says I injured my joints while engaged in treason."

Pickett smiled wryly. "Must make you angry."

"I'm okay with it. Few countries have ever treated their veterans well. If you're dumb enough to let yourself get talked into the military, better accept what comes with the package."

"According to the wire story, you're employed as a tightrope walker. How do you manage that with the arthritis?"

"Heck, when those hotshots call, no telling what I'll say."

"Maybe I don't deserve the truth either."

"So far you do. If I've got you figured, Mr. Pickett, you're looking for a real interview—not four sentences suggesting that without fame I don't have a life."

The journalist chuckled. "I'm here for an interview all right." He reached into his pocket. "Mind if I tape?"

"Not at all."

"If you don't walk a high wire, what do you do?"

"You're standing in it."

Pickett looked around at the tomatoes, corn stalks, carrot tops and other evidence of small-scale agricultural activity. "You garden?"

"Exactly."

"That's all?"

"We garden, aiming for sustainability. What with these vegetables, our fruit trees out front, our walnut and chestnut trees, our vineyard and our root cellar, we now raise enough food on our property to feed us year 'round. If we don't grow it, we trade for it." Candide held up a pan of tomato hornworms—fat, green and ugly. They were squirming. Each had a big green horn on its butt. "We use virtually everything."

"What are those for?"

"Roasted and sprinkled with cayenne pepper, they make a snack you can't put down."

"Hmmm," said Pickett, raising his eyebrows. "Maybe you could explain sustainability a bit more."

"For three years now our family's been living a fully self-supporting lifestyle. We provide for all our needs with zero damage to the environment and zero use of nonrenewable resources."

"Must not be easy. What's the point?"

"Well, if we can do it, other families can too. Besides it's a good way to live, Mr. Pickett—fewer needs, less reason to fight over things."

"No nonrenewable fuels?"

"The Native Plunderians lived like that. Why can't we?"

"What do you do for power?"

"We refine ethanol from our corn byproducts, a small amount. Mainly we use electricity generated on the property." He pointed. "Notice the roof."

"Solar panels."

"Right, but see those ten hatches along the roof peak?"

"Yes."

"Under each is a windbugger with its own generator. When the wind blows, we pop up the buggers and juice batteries. Inside the house we ride exercycles to charge more batteries."

"Exercycles? How much electricity can you generate with one of those?"

"Me, about enough to light a sixty-watt bulb. Yonita, enough to keep Omaha warm and bright on a winter evening. She's already sold enough juice to pay for her college."

"A real money spinner is she?"

"Sure. But that goes into her trust fund, so as not to contaminate our sustainability experiment."

Harvey Pickett began walking toward the house, squinting. "I can't figure out what the heck your walls are made of. Concrete blocks?"

"Those blocks are pressed from nontoxic refuse—shredded car tires and old newsprint—bound together with an adhesive fire retardant. That way the construction material doubles as insulation, at rock-bottom cost. Our rope-operated windows allow us to ventilate with great efficiency. And I'm working on a duct system that uses the temperature difference between cellar and attic to help cool us in summer and warm us in winter."

A tall man in overalls ambled past. "Hey, Ernie," he said. "Back for more batteries." He held up a pail full of eggs.

Candide gave a thumbs-up. The rustic continued on into the house.

"Ted used to manage our local drugstore, as you may recall, Mr. Pickett. When the store went out of business, he began cutting firewood with a battery-operated chainsaw. Ever hear a quiet chainsaw?"

"Don't believe I have," said the reporter.

"Purrs like a kitten."

Ted exited the house carrying three gunmetal cubes. "Thanks, buddy."

Ernie tipped his cap then turned back to the journalist. "All our irrigation is drip. We collect and store rainwater. And I'm thinking of digging a fishpond because more animal protein in our di—"

The halt in Candide's lecture coincided with the arrival of a stupendous vehicle: the private coach of the Baroness and Jellyroll, lit up like a Vegas casino. One by one the banks of running lights shut down. The deep rumbling of the twin 1600-horsepower engines ceased. Soon Plunderland's premier songwriter hustled around the front bumper to receive Baroness Cunegoody, descending from shotgun position on a flight of red-carpeted stairs.

Ernie, smiling warmly, hobbled across the yard and engaged Jellyroll in an elaborate male greeting ritual. They touched knuckles at various angles, rotated their shoulders and jived their hips. Jellyroll turned to the journalist. "Harv, my man." He and Pickett pressed the flesh as Ernie and Solange exchanged a hug.

"What's up, kids?" Candide asked the musicians. Jellyroll looked shy, unusual for him. He poked a thumb at the coach. "We need an estimate on a conversion job."

"Sure. What kind?"

Jellyroll shrugged. "You know. Make it over into a low-gas buggy. That thing you people do."

Candide's eyes explored the motel on wheels. What a chance to save energy! His mind reeled with possibilities.

"I know we should dump the damn thing," Jellyroll continued, contrite, "but when we're on the road—"

"—We did *not* come here to dump it," said the baroness with certainty. "What we want is to reduce energy use. Many of our fans need a clear message that the days of wasteful gas consumption are over. They still don't get it."

Candide smiled. "We can cut your fuel bills eighty percent—more if I can find a hydrogen engine big enough to pull this baby. What about the lights? You need all the lights?"

Jellyroll glanced at the baroness, who looked embarrassed. "We thought we needed them when we were clawing our way up. Now they seem a bit much." She waved her hand. "They can go."

"Your savings are really going to surprise you," said Candide.

As the singers were departing, Harvey Pickett inquired whether Candide converted blunderbuses, too.

"That's our specialty."

"Can you cut fuel costs by eighty percent in one of those?"

"If it's gasoline powered, you bet. Fifteen-dollar-a-gallon gas has made new, nonpolluting technologies much more cost effective."

"Maybe you could take a look at my Land Raper one of these days, give me an estimate?"

"Sure. But before you decide on a fuel conversion, you might consider a realty conversion."

"Realty?"

"For under two thousand dollars we can turn your blunderbus into a free-standing rental unit with a foundation and city hook-ups."

"It's just sitting in the garage now, taking up space, so it's not like I need it. But who would rent?"

"One of the working homeless families in our community. There are several hundred now, more all the time. I've got some brochures inside if you want to see what we do."

Half an hour later Candide and Harvey Pickett were seated at a table under a skylight nursing glasses of iced mint tea. With no warning whatsoever a blue streak flew in the open door and passed over the ducking heads of the two men. The streak sped into the exercise center and struck the heavy bag with a tremendous *ka-whump!*, almost tearing the steel anchors from floor and ceiling. Clinging to the swaying leather cylinder was a nine-year-old girl clad in dark blue shorts and a light blue T-shirt, her blonde hair an absolute fright.

Ernie rose from the table, perturbed. "Where did you learn the Balinese flying squirrel?!" he demanded of his daughter.

Corky Cochran entered.

Candide turned to glare at her. "I thought we had an understanding. I thought you weren't going to teach her any more lethal blows."

Yonita slid off the bag and pulled down her T-shirt. "The flying squirrel isn't a lethal blow!" she asserted.

Ernie looked back and forth between the two, then spoke to Corky. "The squirrel *is* a lethal blow, and I thought we had a deal."

Corky's chin went up. "According to the Army Ranger Combat Manual, the squirrel is an incapacitating blow, not a killing blow."

Candide, still fuming, realized his friend would never take a stand she was even slightly unsure of. Maybe the squirrel wasn't a killing blow, but hell's bells, was it something his kid needed to know? Even as he was mulling that, another area of parental concern surfaced in his mind. "How did the piano lesson go?" he asked.

"Same as last time," said Corky.

Candide was incredulous. "She's been assigned 'Chopsticks' *again*?"

"I got nothing different to tell you from all the other times. Yonita plays 'Chopsticks' louder than it's ever been played, but the teacher says she still needs work on her rhythm and phrasing before she can move on to harder stuff."

"Lord Almighty," exclaimed Ernie. "We've got 'Chopsticks' tattooed on our brains. It's probably why our cat committed suicide."

"Did not!" shouted Yonita. "Her boyfriend dropped her and she died of a broken heart."

Candide raised his hands and appealed to the ceiling. "Why after six months of lessons can't she get off square one? That's all I want to know."

"Maybe her heart isn't in it," said Corky quietly.

That stopped Candide. He wasn't sure what to say.

"I want to study martial arts!" whined Yonita, pouting. "Why can't I?"

"Because there's no point," said her father. "Because you are *not* going to be a soldier. Get that idea out of your head!"

"Being a soldier for World Congress is different. I can use my special powers to fight for peace!"

"Fight for peace??!!" Candide snorted. His lower lip was trembling. "Do you have any idea how ridiculous you sound?"

"It's my life!" yelled Yonita.

"Why throw it away?!" He held up his hand with its crooked fingers pointing nearly everywhere. "You want to be a cripple? You want nightmares playing in your head day and night? That what you want?"

"You're only saying the bad part," Yonita countered. "What about the good part?"

Candide looked disgusted. "What good part?"

"You met Mommy and she had me!" stated his daughter. She ran to Corky, hugged her around the waist and began to cry. Corky smoothed Yonita's hair as the child spoke with her face buried. The words were barely audible through sobs, sniffles, and Corky's shirt. "You're always saying how Mommy and the war taught you how to think. That's more important than your funny fingers."

Candide stood stunned. He felt tears on his eyelashes. Somehow, once again, his kid's words had hit him where he lived.

The door took this opportunity to open dramatically as Delilah entered with a suitcase, looking tired. She glanced from face to face. "Oy. Who died?"

"Daddy's being bossy," said the reluctant pianist.

"Ernie?" asked his wife.

"I lost it," said Ernie, ashamed. "I'm sorry, Yonita. I *was* bossy." His daughter walked to him, wiping tears. Ernie rested his hands on her shoulders and squatted painfully down to her level. "You do your best in school," he said. "And if you still want to be a soldier when you grow up, I'll back you. Deal?"

Yonita nodded, holding out her hand. She helped her father to his feet.

"You'll probably get drafted anyway," said Ernie sadly. "Our troops are stretched so thin by these wars, I see no way around a draft."

"If *they* draft me, I won't go. I'll never fight for oil."

Candide and Delilah glanced at one another with pride.

"Daddy," said Yonita, capitalizing on the moment, "If I can be a soldier, why can't I study martial arts?"

Ernie started to oppose, then realized her argument was almost unassailable. He shrugged. "I suppose you can."

Yonita hugged him around the waist. Ernie looked at Harvey Pickett. "Welcome to our family, Mr. Pickett. Got a little sidetracked."

"Something more important came up," said the reporter, touched by the exercise of Plunderian family values he'd been privileged to witness.

"Harvey, this is Delilah." Ernie held out his arm as his wife came to him, joining the familial hug. "She's doing a residency in pediatrics in Omaha, so we have her home only on weekends."

"A pleasure, Dr. Candide."

"Can you stay for dinner?" Delilah asked.

"I've been smelling the most delicious something," remarked the reporter.

"Two chickens are stewing in our solar cooker," said Ernie. "Along with garden veggies. Please join us."

"Love to. Tell you the truth, I wasn't going to eat tonight."

"You don't look like you need to diet," said Candide, noticing again that Pickett seemed a bit lost inside his suit.

"Call it the necessity diet. About a year back the newspaper began filling its pages mostly with wire stories and since then I'm just a stringer. If I don't sell at least one piece a week, I pretty much don't eat."

"Married?" asked Delilah.

"I am, but my wife and our two sons moved back to Chicago to live with her Dad. He can support them."

"What does he do?" Corky asked.

"Salesman for a defense contractor. He's the only guy I know with a good-paying job."

"People feel lucky these days to have any work at all," sighed Corky.

"And even if they work, they often don't have benefits," said Delilah. "Can you believe the nurses at our hospital have to buy their own medical coverage? If they can afford it."

"Years ago they called this kind of thing a depression," said Corky. "But I see in the paper near every day that times are good. What the heck's going on?"

"Times *are* good for the big corporations," said Harvey, "and since they presently own all the newspapers and other media, who's going to tell you different?"

"Guess our interview won't make it in," said Candide with a knowing smile.

"Actually, it's what sells papers that gets in," said the reporter.

"And a lot of people are looking for ways to make it in these tough times. Why not your way, Ernie? Wouldn't be surprised if a wire service picks this up."

Later, in the long afterglow of a Nebraska summer day, a Plunderian family and their guest were seated around a hand-carved oak dining table. Chicken and stewed vegetables steamed on plates. Delilah, now wearing her working-mom hat, brought a loaf of just baked bread to the table. In a heaped bowl, hornworms loomed temptingly, roasted to a golden green. Ernie, having dispensed a bottle of his finest in-house chardonnay, returned to the head of the table and lifted his glass in a toast: "To a good life today—and a better tomorrow."

"Hear, hear!" said Corky.

"To decent jobs for all Plunderians who need work," said Harvey Pickett, raising his glass.

"To guaranteed healthcare for everyone," offered Delilah.

Yonita held up her Popeye mug full of apple juice and piped with feeling, "To my daddy, the best daddy there is!"

Thus it was that Ernest Lafitte Candide, our defrocked superhero, wiped another tear from his cheek that day. What's wrong with me? he wondered. I haven't blubbered like this since I was seven and my pet lizard ran away…

◦ ◦ ◦

DEAR reader, after a long and I hope enjoyable ascent, we have at last crested the climax of this classically structured narrative, the ideal point at which to leave Ernie and our other friends as they dine in peace and good fellowship.

Much in their story remains unresolved, I know. But only the passing of time can bring to full harvest this family's experiment in good living. As for Buzz Twofer and his CWAP puppeteers, their story lines have been left hanging, as it were, in flagrante delicto. Such loose ends are easily woven into the narrative fabric, however.

Secretary of Defense Clayton Minefield, a bit of a worrywart, was troubled late in the Twofer administration. The war in Ragistan, declared a victory many times, inexplicably seemed to keep

OPERATION SUPERGOOSE

getting worse. More Plunderian soldiers died there every year and opium production was at the highest level ever—85% of the world total. Worst of all, Petroking was about to abandon the pipeline project because the great steel tubes were being blown up faster than they could be laid and Petroking workers were dying almost daily. Finally Minefield had had it "up to here." Madder than a thwarted dung beetle, he jetted into Ragistan in the middle of the night on a trio of secret missions—to buck up the troops, to demand more spine in the puppet government, and to give those whining ninnies at Petroking a verbal goosing they'd never forget.

Unfortunately, the secret was not secret enough. On the highway from the airport into Kabul, Minefield's motorcade was ambushed, his bodyguards slaughtered, and the secretary of state kidnapped. Princeton's fiercest middleweight wrestler of all time was last seen being whisked away over the rocky badlands by three truckloads of Bedouin warriors. Then nothing for a month. Just as media speculation was beginning to wither for lack of new sensations, Moolah al-Razir commandeered television sets worldwide for a bit of live circus. The leader of ASP appeared with someone draped head to foot in a peaked black shroud. The victim's arms were outstretched to the sides and a thick wire was wrapped around each thumb. The camera pulled back slowly to reveal the high gauge wires leading across sand to an electric turbine. Behind the turbine, powering it, was a Hummingbird engine (sans Hummingbird). Atop the gigantic motor was mounted a seat, and there sat—to be perfectly accurate—a camel jockey.

Moolah lifted his palm slowly and the shroud rose to reveal Clayton Minefield, naked except for a big white diaper. He looked thinner and his rock-like face had shriveled into that of a frightened monkey. The poor chicken hawk was so intimidated he probably didn't realize he was on camera. Moolah snapped his fingers and the eager jockey stamped his accelerator. The massive engine roared, shaking the picture as the turbine built to a penetrating whine. The wires began spitting sparks as Minefield's salt-and-pepper hair stood straight up and he emitted a high-pitched screech strangely at odds with the persona he'd nurtured over a lifetime. "Does it hurt?!" he screamed. "Yes it hurts! Please stop! Oh please please please! I'll tell you anything! *Anything!*"

"Today," said Moolah calmly, "I want to know about the effects of depleted uranium on humans."

"Yes, yes! What do you want to know? Effects on enemy combatants? On civilians through collateral damage? On Plunderian troops?" Minefield turned his face down. He seemed to be examining himself.

"First, tell about the effects on your troops. And look at me when you speak. If something burned off—don't worry, you won't need it."

The turbine grinder tapped his accelerator, the engine growled and Minefield quickly launched into the findings of a highly classified Department of Defense study. It concluded that inhaled or ingested radioactive dust from exploded DU munitions had killed more than 11,000 Plunderian veterans of the 1991 Gulf War, and had put another 325,000 on permanent disability. These men and women were dying like flies, often of cancer.

"Radioactivity can interfere with reproduction," said Moolah. "What about the children of these cancerous soldiers? Birth defects?"

Minefield clammed up, thrusting forward what remained of his iron jaw—until another electric stimulus was sent his way. After his eerie screams died down he blew a smoke ring and spoke. "Are children affected? Oh, maybe they are, but war is messy, you know. Stuff happens."

Thus began the first installment in a long series of Minefield's shocking admissions. On that initial broadcast a spellbound audience learned that all earth's inhabitants for the next few thousand years would be getting sick and dying of airborne DU dust, as winds carried the fine particles around and around the globe. On subsequent broadcasts, Minefield's computer-like brain was tapped for startling facts on a wide variety of subjects. Persons interested in the extended outpourings of the turbine-powered songbird can order the boxed set of DVDs from ASP Studios. The 20-disc collection—

OPERATION SUPERGOOSE

"War Criminal: the Confessions of Clayton Minefield"—has already gone platinum. To the best of our knowledge, the former defense secretary is still cutting new tracks, probably somewhere in the mountains along the Ragistan-Pockistan border.

Parson Rupert Weed did not anticipate the repercussions of Minefield's disclosures on one of the goodly reverend's most starstruck devotees. Ma Parker, a 48-year-old Oklahoma housewife previously best known for her Yuletide peppernuts and her collection of European military weapons, deduced from Minefield's first broadcast what had happened to her son Arlen. Arlen came home from the 1991 Gulf War with two Congressional Medals of Honor and urine that set off Geiger counters fifty miles away in Tulsa every time he took a whiz. He died in 2001 with cancer in every cell of his body, even his hair—leaving behind three young children with hideous birth defects. Ma exhausted her life savings on Prayers by Weed in vain attempts to grow organs of sensation in her grandchildren. Then she learned Parson Weed was on the board of Raidax Corporation, suppliers of depleted uranium to the Plunderian military. Ma employed a 1952 French Monde de Merde bazooka to blow off the parson's door and a 1941 Krupp .50-caliber machine gun to fatally perforate the holy man in his classy sauna.

When the parson regained consciousness, he found himself in a spacious, lushly furnished office. He knew instantly where he was—in God's own workplace, just as he'd imagined it since childhood. He'd been right all along! Heaven wasn't a namby-pamby salon with clouds to sit on and harps being plucked, as fools supposed. Heaven, like the church itself, was a big rich business, and God was King of the CEOs. Heaven even smelled right to Weed, earthy rather than perfumed, robust with promise. The one false note he detected was the heat building in his body. It was like he was inside a microwave, getting baked. He felt heat even between his perspiring toes.

Behind the sleek marble desk, a luxurious chair with its back facing the reverend until this moment now swung suddenly 180 degrees to reveal the impressive figure seated in it. More than seven feet tall, the thing had the head of a goat and the body of a man. It wore a white silk suit. Glowing red eyes cast ruby light over the furry, quite expressive face—which happened to be grinning. "Disappointed?" asked a deep voice smooth as old rum.

Parson Weed was indeed disappointed in his post-mortal destination, surprised too, but knew instantly he needed to make the best of a bad show. "How can I be of service, my master?"

"How can you be of *further* service, you mean. The two of us have been working hand in glove for many years. Warmonger, of all earthly callings, is surely the most evil."

"My only wish is to be called upon again, my liege."

"How does Director of Public Relations sound?"

"An honor beyond my humble expectations. An enormous responsibility—given the scope of your operations." He spread his hands.

"Joe Goebbels has been doing a bang-up job for many years, but I think we need new blood in there. Someone with your skill in duplicity is rare. Very rare."

"You flatter me, my excellency."

His excellency frowned. "Cut the sucking up, Rupie. We're very blunt down here. And fairly informal."

"What should I call you?"

"Earlier, you called me master. That works." He winked a glowing eye.

Vice President Chain Dickey, throughout the Twofer reign, gave much thought to providing adequate energy for the greediest society in human history. The veep's fingers on the control knob may help explain the series of brownouts and blackouts that afflicted the nation's power grid in the years leading up to 2010. That year was significant for the occurrence of the first superblackout, which took down the entire grid east of the Rockies for five days. During this catastrophe the backup generator supplying current to Dickey's life-suspension vault burnt out a rotor and switched off. Juice was cut to the bunker, knocking out the elevator and the phones. By the time the breakdown was discovered, Chain Dickey was rotting. The doctors feared pumping life into him, and Dickey's own family

OPERATION SUPERGOOSE

felt further resurrection might damage the patriot's legacy. A closed-casket funeral was held instead.

The Chainman awoke in the same plush office Parson Weed had passed through not long before. And Dickey felt the same intense heat between his toes. The VP, though, was not disappointed when he learned where he was. Dickey had predicted his destination and was planning to outwit the guy in charge. The Chainman, two full jumps ahead of the Devil from the moment they met, smiled out of the side of his mouth, cracked heat jokes, and otherwise charmed the old goat until he'd wangled an appointment as Director of Black Ops. Next he negotiated a corner office overlooking the Gloog Rapeworks. From day one Dickey fit right in. He and the man he replaced, Vlad the Impaler, downed a few beers together on the afternoon Vlad cleaned out his desk. No hard feelings even there.

It was Dickey's key to the executive handball courts that led indirectly to his downfall. He and Parson Weed met there daily for a little male bonding. This gave them ample time to chat, which in the case of such high-octane individuals really meant time to plot. Weed had discovered that brimstone burns for a century without energy input. And through his PR duties the holy man was acquainted with several forms of commerce between their deep realm and earth. Dickey snooped out the techniques of brimstone production. Gloogs, he learned, formed the rocks in molds from a mixture of lava, white phosphorous and unholy oil. Armed with this information, the two masterminds put their heads together and cooked up a scheme for marketing brimstone to surface dwellers over the Internet. They hoped to make trillions, maybe enough to buy their ascension to a higher existence. Only one question remained. Should they cut the old goat in—or cut him out?

It didn't occur to either plotter that the old goat might have bugged their thoughts. Or that eternity is a long, long while. Weed and Dickey were summarily fired from their executive posts and reassigned to the Gloog Rapeworks—to serve there as surrogate mothers until the end of time. Stationed side by side, they loyally birth little Gloogs somewhat as chickens do eggs—one a day, rain or shine. No need to go into the reproductive mechanisms involved, dismaying to all but Gloogs. What's important is that Weed and Dickey have at last found worthwhile uses for their talents. And if suffering makes men better, both are destined for sainthood.

Lastly but not leastly, Buzz Twofer, in the year after he left office, was clearing brush on his ranch near Crawdad when he fell in a hole containing a nest of 200 copperheads. The political cowpoke was bitten so severely all about his corpus that when the dying flesh was cleared away with scalpels and saws, what remained was his living head alone. A miracle of modern medicine to be sure. Such a setback might have embittered a man of lesser inner resources than Buzz, but once he was back up on his, well, up on his neck, he soon became his irascible old self. Why not let him tell it though, since he wants to and is able?

"It's not so bad bein' just a head. Heck, I got my two good eyeballs and my ears and my nose. And I got my mouth as you can hear." Twofer smirked happily. "Guess what? I took up smokin' again, because I don't have no lungs, so how can they catch cancer? Heh, heh, heh. Bet you never thought of that." The former president rolled his eyes 360 degrees, tongue in cheek. "I also got this here beautiful box I'm a restin' in, made of thirty-two-karat gold and studded with zircons. Yep, that cushion under my head is genuine red velvet, which provides a heap of dignity. And it's nice and soft when I need a nap.

"Lots of folks they ask me, 'Are you mo-bile?' They seem to think a head can't go nowhere. And of course I am mo-bile, cause I can go anywheres somebody carries me. I even go on the road now and then, to give speeches to my supporters. I get paid for it too—one hundred bucks a pop. May not sound like much, but it seems I don't have too many supporters these days, and what of 'em there is, well, they're kind of lukewarm, or worse. Heck, I plumb gotta be careful where I go. Back when I was commander in chief I spoke to a lot of military folks, but since that stuff come out about the depetered uradium, me talkin' to military folks has got plain scary. Last VFW post I lectured tried to tar and feather me. Would have done it too if me and my secret service hadn't shot our way out. Listen, you can't afford to let yourself get tarred and feathered if you happen to be a head because that could be fatalistic.

"Course, bein' mo-bile isn't purely a plus. A month back here I went out on a toot with my twin girls Missy and Prissy, and they got so plasterated they walked off and left me high and dry in the ladies pisser at the Bull & Chips in Austin, Texas. On account of my helpless state, I panicked and rolled off my nice safe shelf into a wastebasket. I would have got throwed out with the trash if I hadn't hollered my head off, which lured some ladies to me. Too bad they turned out to be a wild band of eco-feminists, who kidnapped me and held me captive in their lesbian love nest. They tortured me for days by injecting me with their views on everything from the Arctic Wildlife Refuse to abortion rights. Thank God for the Patriot Act, which allowed a crack team of my boys to storm that den of pinkos, shoot 'em all, and free me up to spend more time with my family."

A rapid clicking noise was heard: click click click click click. Alarm gripped Twofer's face as his eyes rolled to the side. The clicking was followed by the muffled padding of four feet on carpet. Then, up onto the chair supporting the gold box containing the presidential cabeza leapt Barfy, former first pooch. Barfy placed his paws on the lip of the box, raised himself and looked inside. Twofer, terrified, attempted to glower. "I see what you're thinkin'. Better not even *think* about it!" Barfy dropped his front paws back to the chair and yawned a big one. He lifted his hind leg up over the box. "No, Barfy, no. By all the powers invested in me as your master, I hereby command you to hold your water! Help! Where is ever'body? *Help!*"

In narrative literature the most basic conflict, and the noblest, is that of man against nature. Even so, as author I feel duty bound to pull back from the crisis now unfolding between Buzz Twofer and his disobedient pet. Otherwise we soon will witness a great dishonor being visited upon a handsome and undeserving red velvet cushion. Each of us, I am sure, can use imagination to conjure the appropriate liquid comeuppance.

And while we're at it—imagining that is—why don't we imagine something more constructive? Let's imagine what it would be like if there really were a Plunderland, a mighty nation turned against mankind and our mother earth by arrogant and deluded leaders. Imagine what it would take to put that country right again. And imagine how a thinking citizen might pitch in.

Just imagine.